DANCING

WITH THE

DEAD

CHARLES FREEDOM LONG

A Silver Star Book

Copyright © 2015 by Charles Freedom Long
First Edition

Published by Silver Star Press

ISBN-10: 151519325X
ISBN-13: 978-1515193258

This book is a work of fiction. Incidents, names, characters, and places are products of the author's imagination and used fictitiously. Resemblances to actual locales or events or persons living or dead, is coincidental.

Printed in the United States of America

to Barbara,
my ålska kön

Words and phrases that might not be familiar to Terran readers will be found in the GLOSSARY at the end of the book.

Universal translator implants are available in the Antal Pavilion at the Terran Trade Center, One TTC Plaza, New Manhattan. Requests for Nord universal translator implants should be made directly to the Nord Embassy, also at the Terran Trade Center. Military personnel requests for Krieg UT's must be made through commanding officers.

CONTENTS

NEXUS

What is truth?
Pontius Pilate

Fahd Abdul al-Sharfa had fooled them.

He was on Luna. Where he would do what he had sworn to do, lived to do, worked and struggled for twelve long, hard years to do.

Kill them all.

And die doing it.

Fahd's neck and shoulders pulsed with pain. He rolled his small shoulders and stretched his hands back to massage his neck. His whole body ached from nervous tension. It had been a close run thing. He had nearly blown it at the last minute. He wanted to sleep, to rest. To regain his composure before he made another false step that might mess up the whole scheme, and, he shivered, bring down the wrath of Ahmar Saif on his family.

The clan had taken Ahmar Saif's gold and guns in exchange for the precociously brilliant boy, Fahd. He'd been bought, educated and trained for one murderous, suicidal task, and he was well aware that Ahmar Saif, the Red Sword of vengeance, was a ruthless organization that did not forgive those who took its gold and then failed to deliver.

As he rubbed the pain out of his shoulders, Fahd was acutely aware that he must die if he wanted his clan to live.

He stared up at the light grey lunar concrete ceiling in his Luna City bachelor's quarters and permitted himself a long sigh.

He was on the moon. At last. What matter that he was in a utilitarian concrete room like a monk's cell: he wouldn't be there very long. Neither would the room. Nor Luna City.

But as he lay back on the small bed he neglected to adjust to the moon's one-sixth gravity, and literally flew backward, his head bouncing on the softly cushioned mattress that doubled as a day-couch.

As his bouncing head slowly sank back into the cushion he reflected, *Thank Allah I didn't hit the wall. It's a good omen. But I must be more alert. The hardest part is yet to come. I must not, I cannot fail.*

He let his fingers slide slowly along the grey lunar concrete wall, practicing the low-gravity manual dexterity skills he would need to construct the devices that would destroy all this. The scratchy, waterless lunar concrete, made with phosphates and anorthite from lunar highland regolith, stronger than steel on earth in the moon's gravity, felt rough to the touch of his small, dark, almost delicate fingers. *Stronger than steel*, he thought disdainfully, *well, it'll all come apart easily enough when the time comes.*

When the time comes. When the order to strike comes. His deep brown eyes darkened. Frowning, Fahd grimly reminded himself he had a challenging task ahead of him and should not waste any time. The call to action could come at any moment. He must be ready.

Ready.

Ready to die, ran through his mind. He took a long, deep breath. The super-purified, reconstituted air was cool and dry. It took him back to childhood mornings in the harsh high desert of the Mahrat Mountains before the hot sun roasts everything and only death

2

awaits the foolish, the weak, the unprepared.

I will never see the desert again, he reflected sadly. *I will die here on the moon.* Then with a grimace, he bucked up his courage. *I have a debt of honor to repay and I shall not falter. Luna City will die with me.*

Was it strange, he wondered, running a manicured fingernail silently along the black silicate side table next to the bed-couch, to be thinking of springtime and home, childhood and the smell of flowers as the desert sun rose when he was about to die? No. It was right-eous! He was about to become s*hahid*, a martyr for truth and enter into an after-death world of eternal springtime.

The unfamiliar whirring of the ceiling vent cycling on drew his eyes apprehensively upward. When he realized what the sound was, he inhaled more deeply and thought he noticed a faint scent of jasmine in the reconstituted air, again, like his childhood desert home in Yemen in springtime.

The life support system pumping that air into his compart-ment was one of his targets. It ensured the integrity of Luna City's atmosphere. It would be destroyed. He reached carefully into the small kit bag he had placed on the side table, removed and delicately held the key to the weakness of the double redundant system in his hand: a small, seemingly innocent vid-game.

Yes, he nodded solemnly. *We will all die.* The world will watch helplessly as the two space stations and Luna City implode under their own weight. His father would be proud. More importantly, his family, his clan would remain prosperous, and alive.

He laid the vid-game carefully aside and permitted himself to remove the half-bottle of Chateaux Margaux his mentor had insisted on giving him, despite the astronomically high cost of transporting such a weighty item to the lunar surface.

Fahd had thought it was a brilliant diversion: adding to the image of an affluent westernized disbeliever they had so earnestly

3

developed.

He, Fahd Abdul al-Sharfa, was the culmination of twelve years of planning by Red Sword. Twelve years of harmless vid games being brought to, and left on the moon by Ahmar Saif's agents. And now the one man who could put it all together into the explosive devices that would destroy everything, including himself, was about to complete the strike group. He clutched the vid-game to his heart and silently repeated the words he had been made to repeat so often: I am Fahd of the al-Sharfa clan of the Mahrat tribe. I have been chosen to unleash Allah's Truth on the works of Satan. I will not fail.

He knew he would do what he must do.

It would be difficult, but he had gotten this far.

He had been uneasy when they took him from the desert to the home of Asim al-Yasir. Uneasy when al-Yasir took him to the clerk's office, registered him as his second cousin's child, under his protection, obtained a great mass of papers, documents that would facilitate Fahd's entry into the modern world. He was distinctly nervous when they brought him to the English school dressed in a constricting, tight western suit and a school tie that felt like a noose around his neck.

But al-Yasir became a second father to him and the brilliant Fahd soon began to enjoy western-style living. He excelled in school and was generously, opulently rewarded. And as he matured and took on the appearance of total westernization was taught how to live a lie for truth.

In the lead-shielded basement of al-Yasir's luxurious home, where Fahd received all his covert training, hard men dressed in black dishdashi who came secretly through a dark, dank tunnel that ran from a house in the village, under the compound into the basement of the main house, trained him in explosives, sabotage, intelligence, kidnapping, hostage taking and guerilla theory. In no uncertain terms

4

they reminded Fahd constantly who he was, what he was doing, why he was doing it, and what the results of failure would be.

Twelve years of study, a PhD in aerospace engineering. Success in the tough schoolwork and tougher covert training had been offset by al-Yasir's lavish gifts: clothes, wine, a BMW, parties, and easy western girlfriends.

After graduation, he applied to Lumina Corporation's subsidiary, Moondust, the company that ran the magnetic mass mover where Fahd was headed and entered the next gauntlet of trials, the incredibly strict Lumina vetting. The Lumina gauntlet washed out anyone with the slightest physical issue, anyone who might display the smallest inclination to mental illness, anyone prone to corruption, inducement, enticement.

The medicals were a snap. He was in great health. Al-Yasir had seen to that. As al-Yasir had seen to the rest. When Moondust processed Fahd's detailed background checks, complete runs of photos, DNA samples, cross-matched against all police and secret service records, they turned up nothing. A second cousin's child from a war-torn land, adopted by a successful Riyadh businessman, a brilliant young man who had repaid his protector by excelling at everything he attempted.

Next came the Lumina Corporation psychological screenings, not one, but four, any deviations from the norm noted and analyzed to ferret out any lies he might be telling, any truths he might be hiding.

But in al-Yasir's basement, more hard men had come and put him through the Lumina psych tests over and over again. They questioned, interviewed, cross-examined, interrogated, terrified, threatened, even beat him — until there was no doubt he would pass the screenings.

Fahd had been ready.

5

Finally, the testing focused on the greatest threat to Lumina Corporation security: individuals ready to die to destroy it.

Men like Fahd.

He was packed off to the Luna Approach Course, a ninety-day intensive program, where lunar candidates were removed to the isolated Lumina Training Center in Brazil for hard physical training, Luna accommodation bookwork, underwater training in spacesuits, claustrophobia and boredom education, and intensive screening.

Where sensors recorded everything.

Everything.

Two thousand cameras recorded every action, fed it into computers programmed to detect any unusual act and then passed that disc on to a human observer.

When the young man who roomed with Fahd had moved just oddly enough in the shower so a sensor lost sight of one small part of his body, a body search team had appeared immediately. Fahd never saw him again. He watched silently the next day when the young man's personal belongings were removed from the room by a blue-suited security man.

Retina and fingerprint scans were required at every doorway. Full visuals of everyone entering or leaving any section of the Training Center were made. If anyone tried to get into a room or area where he or she was not officially cleared to enter, the system would prevent access and silently report the incident. A security team would follow up. And that person would be gone.

All communication between the candidates and their homes, every person who called or was called, any electronic communication method used, was intercepted and recorded. Any material entering or leaving the LTC was opened and recorded, checked by experts, scanned by another set of computers to break any code, or detect hidden, invisible, inaudible messages. All contacts were surveilled.

During the ninety days of designed high stress, Fahd, like all candidates underwent weekly physiological and psychological tests.

But Fahd knew the price of failure. Fahd had passed them all with flying colors. He had fooled them, successfully concealing the greatest lie of all: behind his western style of dress, the BMW, the cigars, whiskey and western women, he was *takfir*. He had adopted every custom of the west to pass as a disbeliever, an apostate, in order to accomplish one terrible task.

When Fahd graduated from the LTC, been accepted into the Space Service, and given a three-day pass to go home and make his farewells, al-Yasir had thrown an extravagant party in his honor for his last night in that home, on the terrace, so the surveillance satellites they assumed would be watching would have final, conclusive proof of Fahd's total westernization.

The terrace was filled with diplomats, bankers, westerners, and modern Arabs in expensively tailored suits. Forbidden behavior was flaunted. Dom Perignon and hors d'oevres gave way to Montrachet and lobsters, and in turn, to Chateau Margaux and thick steaks. An extravagantly profligate ice swan sculpture steadily dripping into nothingness in the desert evening heat decorated a table of chilled cream pies, fruit tarts and outrageously expensive Sauternes. On a second patio, vintage Port and Cohibas awaited, where some of the women mixing freely with the men even smoked the smaller Cohibas Asim al-Yasir had set out for them.

Fahd recalled how al-Yasir winked to him, raised his eyes to where he assumed the spy satellite would be and delicately put a manicured forefinger into his glass of port, withdrew it, flicked a drop of expensive wine into a fern, and announced with a deprecating chuckle, "The Qur'an says thou shalt not let a drop of wine touch your lips. There! That's the drop! I'm afraid I'm not a very good Sharian." Raising his crystal glass, al-Yasir declared, "But why would Allah create

7

such wonders if we were not to sample them?"

His guests laughed politely. It was an old, comfortable joke.

Fahd had luxuriated that night, just a day ago, in the approbation showered upon him. He ate, drank, sang, danced with abandon and made a point of having a blond western girlfriend stay the night so the roving surveillance cameras would record her leaving in the morning, just before the mag-lev taxi came to take him to the Riyadh Spaceport where he boarded a mini-shuttle for Brazil.

Now, in his grey cubicle in Luna City, which he had sworn on his life, his honor, his family, to destroy, Fahd sighed apprehensively, hoping that his one stupid mis-step along the way would not be the death of all he held dear.

At first, the journey from earth had gone well. He'd slipped right past the metal, chemical and biological detectors, cameras, and security teams that screened each Lumina aspirant on departure from Earth into the Antal-built starlifter to the low orbit station.

Right through the gauntlet of drug, hazmat and explosive-sniffing dogs, on earth and the low orbit station (LOS). Through the dark tunnel-like, CHEM-CATCH 600 Cat Scan Tomographers and SENSE-ALL 5000's that could detect less than a millionth of a gram of explosive or the residue of an explosive device under someone's fingernail. And finally, the intense, embarrassing strip-down visual, tactile inspection by humans.

Though it was on the "approved" list, the vid-game had been taken from his luggage, scanned several times, and finally replaced next to the bottle of wine that had drawn more than its own share of attention.

On arrival at the low orbit station, Fahd and the other new Lumina employees were herded into a secure restricted area until the Antal-built lunar shuttle was scanned by a LOS security team. Fahd had stared nervously around the room, trying to surreptitiously pick out the imbedded plainclothes ID teams his trainers had warned him about. He did his best to look appropriately, but not too anxious, to perfectly play the role of the scientist eager to go to his new adventure.

Then the shuttle with the silver wings on its side took them and the imbedded ID teams on the four hour journey through the heavens to Luna City.

And now he fidgeted nervously on his bed as he went over the details of what might have been a fatal slip.

When the ceiling slid back and revealed a huge ceralloy overhead viewing panel as they approached the moon, Fahd had been awestruck by the sight. He watched enthralled as the large round silver-grey and white lunar orb came closer and closer, surrounded by the utter blackness of space, swelled to overfill the screen until Luna City's immense round ceralloy dome dazzlingly reflected golden sunshine like a shining jewel. Nothing could have prepared him for that breathtaking sight.

The shuttle swept downward and west on its approach, until it flew right over the magnetic mass mover. It was launching a projectile destined for the low earth orbit space station. The twin half cylinders and two-mile-long launch tube of the mass mover glistened silver and gold in reflected sunshine like a colossal gun barrel. Fahd gasped. As a dazzling green light coiled around the end of the mass mover's mile-long launch tube, Fahd became totally transfixed. His eyes were riveted to the tube as he watched the light move slowly and purposefully, then faster, further and further along the length of the barrel, moving more and more rapidly, until the gold and silver tube glowed an eerie, lethal green and the magnetic energy created hurled a silver projectile into the blackness of space.

The virtual reality simulations he had gone through over and over again in his training suddenly seemed to have come alive in the

9

here and now! He lost control of his mental rigidity. Swept away by the emotions of the moment, he almost blew the whole twelve years in a few brief instants. *There's my weapon launcher! The gun I will use to blow the two space stations out of the sky!*

In his mind's eye, Fahd saw the low earth orbit station explode in a golden shower as the first of two projectiles struck the hub of the small torus, the four spokes connecting the hub to the outer ring disintegrated into flotsam and sections of the outer ring tore themselves loose and spun off into space until nothing but blackness and softly tumbling shiny fragments remained.

His breath came in short, static bursts and he began to pant.

He saw, as if it were really happening, just as it had when he had successfully completed the VR simuls, how the two ten-mile long O'Neil cylinders of the high orbit station (HOS), would begin to spin out of control, twisting like worms on a hook, spewing skyscraper size buildings outward into the freezing non-atmosphere of space, until both cylinders imploded, leaving only another massive pile of debris.

Fahd had shockingly returned to reality with a jolt. His palms were sweating, his hands tapping on the armrests. He shifted nervously in his padded flight chair, terrified that there might be a sensor hidden in the flight chair arms or that the imbedded ID teams might have noticed just how agitated he had become. *Oh No! You fool! Not when you're so close!*

Fortunately, just then, the shuttle turned hard east and swooped silently down, pressing all the passengers back into their recliner seats and contorting their faces with g-forces as it made straight for the Luna Space Port's runways and landing pads.

A few of the new Lumina employees groaned from the g-forces. Fahd made a point of looking straight ahead and controlling his breathing, praying that his tenseness would be mistaken for the excitement of seeing the lunar surface and the magnetic mass mover where he would work close up for the first time. He concentrated on controlling his breathing until the shuttle came to a full stop.

Along with a number of other passengers, he expelled a great gush of air. He waited, edgily.

A cold wave of fear swept over him along with a sick, sinking feeling in his stomach as the landing pad and shuttle suddenly dropped beneath the lunar surface and a blinding set of lights made him turn his face away and close his eyes.

Then the plastalloy seat restraints lifted ceiling-ward.

He was herded out of the shuttle, through one more full body scan. Fahd felt himself sweating again. He tried not to fidget every time a security officer approached.

The group was transferred from the spaceport to a Luna Welcome Lounge, where they were seated. Once the shuffling of feet ceased, a side door panel near the front of the room slid open.

An audible sharp intake of breath from several of the newbies awkwardly hissed through the room. They'd all been briefed of course, that the first time one encounters a living, breathing Coryllim can be unnerving.

The being just stood there patiently for a few moments that seemed like an eternity, raising and lowering the two long drooping auricles on the side of its bark-covered, pecan-shaped head, to pinpoint the embarrassed by the sound. Then it slowly lifted one stemmy chestnut brown leg and planted the first of four black hooves firmly inside the room. Pivoting its stiff, pear-shaped body slightly from side to side, it entered, tolerantly scanning them all in its single oblong green eye, fixing faces with names in its mind. Clip-clopping up to the podium, it reached out with two half-webbed hands to grasp the shiny black plastalloy sides, as it opened its two other arms wide in greeting.

"Salva Terrans," it began, its small pink lips pulled back from beaming white incisors just below its reddish brown snout, "I am Ardine, Corporeal Assets Director for Lumina Corporation. I welcome you in abyt, the language of my people, to Luna and to Lumina. Luna City and the two magnificent space stations, Redemption, which you all passed through on your way here, and Starfarer, which some of you will get to visit, are the result of Lumina's partnership with Antal and Coryllim companies. Lumina is a multi-species organization where you will have the opportunity to make many new acquaintances. You will meet both Antal and Coryllim workers here. We hope you will make the effort to learn a bit of each of our languages."

Ardine paused, scanned the group with her oblong green eye once more. Her ears and snout turned rosy brown as she gave them her most fetching smile. "We hope your stay here will be a pleasant and profitable one. We have a short orientation vid we hope you might watch. Thank you."

She turned, folded all four arms against her trunk, and walked slowly toward the door from which she had entered. Another gasp, more contained and hushed this time, emanated from a few Terrans who were noted by Ardine's other elongated green eye, the one in the back of her bark-covered head.

The lights dimmed to the sound of her hoofed feet on the carpeted floor as she left the room. The door whooshed shut behind her.

Then the vid came on and rudely jarred Fahd back to the reality of why he was here. The scientist in him had become entranced with the newness of this creature. But he was not here to make friends, to meet aliens. He was here to kill them, all of them. And he wasn't safely aboard yet.

After the orientation video the new arrivals were treated to a planetarium show of real stars while the fifth search and scan of their luggage was completed.

In the darkness, a grim-faced large man marched right up to him, looked sternly into Fahd's eyes, wheeled, and snapped smartly into a military ready standing posture next to his chair. Fahd looked fearfully at the man's sharply polished boots, stun wand and the blaster on his hip. He had no way out, nowhere he could run. They had him if they wanted him.

Then the star show ended and the room lights flashed on, making Fahd blink once more.

"Thank you for your attention," a computer voice announced. "You will now each be escorted to your personal quarters."

The big man looked down his large nose at Fahd and Fahd rose, marched tensely out of the room, guided by the hulking, unsmiling man in the dark blue uniform holding Fahd's right arm in one large hand. First left, then right, without a word from the big man, just a gentle tug that bore no deviation. Into an elevator, up, out, then down dimly lit, unfamiliar hallways Fahd expecting to be unceremoniously seized and hurled through a door into an interrogation room.

He prepared himself; made himself remember his training. *They're trying to make me nervous.*

The walk seemed endless, with the big man's boots ominously tapping out a death march.

When a door to his left suddenly hissed open, Fahd jumped back into the chest of the big man but to his relief, the security agent merely snorted, said, "These are your quarters Doctor al-Sharfa," and ushered him inside.

Fahd unpacked nervously in the presence of the security man who bid him "a good lunar experience," and took his officially-issued corporation luggage away.

He was safe—for the moment. Whatever they had seen had not been enough to take him into custody. Yet.

Fahd held himself together. He couldn't show any untoward signs of relief. He wanted to scream. *Damn! You fool! How could you lose concentration so close to the goal!*

Fahd forced himself to stand still and breathe until he felt he could move without shaking.

He swore to himself never to let his guard down again.

He needed a shower, but first, he needed a drink. He went into the living room. With shaky hands, he successfully if somewhat jerkily, twisted the vacu-seal off the bottle of wine. Carefully controlling his movements, he poured a dollop into one of the clear plastic glasses on the silicate side table his employer Moondust Corporation provided.

Taking care not to move too swiftly, he raised the plastic cup to his lips and let the scent fill the low humidity cabin air near his face. He appreciatively sipped the wine that cost a thousand credits a bottle on earth, and at least that much to transport to Luna.

Since they gained their independence, the open-minded Lunies did not allow recording devices in personal quarters. Looking up at the juncture of the ceiling and walls, he could see the small holes where a cable must have connected to a camera in the years that Luna had been a Lumina Corporation-owned colony.

But he'd been told by his trainers to maintain his *takfir* persona, assume that wherever he went he would be observed, and in order to succeed must successfully deceive everyone. Fahd poured a second drink, raised his plastic glass in a silent toast to his mentor, Asim al-Yasir, who had taught him how to live a lie.

He had done it.

Lived a lie for truth.

The wine went down nicely. Too nicely. Fahd sat on his bunk in Luna City's bachelor's quarters, poured a somewhat smaller amount of wine into the plastic glass.

14

He hadn't eaten since breakfast, and he felt the wine warming him. But as he savored the feeling and realized how much he had needed the alcohol he also wondered after twelve years of playing the role just how much of the *takfir* disbeliever image remained a charade. Unlike everything else, that had been too easy. He swallowed hard.

He tenuously congratulated himself. He had fooled them all. And now he was here.

On Luna.

Where he would do what he had sworn to do, lived to do, worked and struggled for twelve years to do.

Die. And kill them all.

"To truth!" he said out loud, and exuberantly raised the plastic glass once more.

Still unaccustomed to the one-sixth lunar gravity, his hand moved too quickly. Two hundred and fifty credits of wine sloshed upward in a great arc, and Fahd watched aghast as it cascaded downward in a slow motion, blood-red river. He moved his hand quickly, too quickly again, then backward and successfully caught most of the terribly expensive liquid before it dashed itself against the lunar concrete floor.

He sucked his breath in sharply. *Was this a portent?*

Fahd caught himself. *What?! I might have been born a superstitious desert tribesman, but now I'm an ultramodern astrophysicist and I do not believe in omens.*

At that very moment, a chime rang. Fahd nearly jumped out of his skin, barely managing to keep the red liquid in the glass.

Then he heard a computer voice announce, "There is someone at the door."

DANCER

Behold indeed, the gallows fifty cubits high
. . . Hang him on it!
Book of Esther 7:9

The Krieg battle cruiser hovered invisibly like a great black bat in high orbit near Luna, its cloaking device the best in two galaxies. On the battle deck, a Krieg warrior in black battle armor paced slowly, deep in thought, wide shoulders back, long brown furry chin high, when the *klinngklong* of the alert chime rang.

He looked up at the bank of opaque red overhead screens. His yellow eyes noted the flashing yellow light turn to green recognition. A satisfied smile spread the commander's black lips wide across an intimidating set of gleaming white fangs. He barked a wolfish laugh and snorted through the large black nostrils on the tip of his muzzle.

The endless drills he had ordered to keep his crew sharp throughout this tedious Terran watch-dog assignment had paid off. He had been noticed! Grand Marshal Pardek had chosen his vessel for a clandestine meeting with Vice Marshal Natil. He was honored!

He knew only something extremely important had brought Pardek so urgently and secretly to his ship. He knew Natil's Eagle Legion must be involved.

16

He ached to know more.

There had been rumors of yet another Terran plot. This primitive sub-species never tired of murdering each other, it seemed. And it might be that this time, it had gotten out of hand and the fleet arm would need to be involved in putting an end to whatever it was. With any luck he would now have his chance to cover himself in glory, perhaps be promoted to wingmaster. His right hand tensed into an angry fist. *Why don't we just incinerate this troublesome lot as so many said we should have and be done with it!*

His yellow eyes caught the sharply flashing signal transmission from Vice Marshal Natil's cloaked battle shuttle alerting him to its imminent arrival. He growled an order to come about on a course ordained to minimize the decloaking time to dock the incoming vessel. He grinned once more, puffed out his chest against the gleaming black plasteel armor and clapped his helmsman on the back with a *whap*! His crew was the best in the fleet at this exercise: for the precisely .32 Terran seconds they were visible, they would release a cloud of neutron gas to camouflage their position. No one would see the shuttle decloak and arrive, just as no one had seen Marshal Pardek's personal starlifter *The Sharpened Blade*, decloak and glide into the bay a few Terran minutes ago.

Then the commander stopped cold in his tracks. The dark brown fur on the nape of his neck bristled. His wolfish snout dropped open. The entire command crew stared in stunned silence.

A pale Terran female with long, flaming red hair suddenly materialized on the battle deck to the piercing *waaaooog* of blaring intruder alarms.

Aidan Ray Good, the human in charge of integrating the dead into human society, stood quietly in a flowing white robe, with her hands folded before her in the Vita-Kor Sisterhood fashion.

The commander's breath caught in his furry throat. *The Terran witch who dances with the dead!*

Some living Terrans could see the dead, some could hear them; Aidan could see, feel, hear, and talk with them, all of them, all the time. Many said she danced with the dead. Some sneeringly called her **witch**.

The commander was one of those. Krieg warriors loved blasters, steel, hand-to-hand combat, and held themselves above all other things to honor in *Kuldok*, the way of the warrior. They distrusted the Vita-Kor Sisterhood and their witchy mind-warping ways. It was not honorable. He had heard tales of the red-haired Terran witch, but to have her abruptly appear on the battle deck of a fully-armed, cloaked Krieg warbird was impossible, incomprehensible. "What? How?" he stuttered.

He took a stumbling step backward, bared his fangs in a snarl. At the sight of that, in one swift motion, the cruiser's security chief drew his blaster, aimed at the intruder and squeezed the trigger.

She just stood there, looking coolly up to meet the widening yellow eyes of the startled commander. He felt her dark green eyes piercing his shell of cocky overconfidence, peeling back the layers to perceive the ambitious, conniving creature at the core of his being.

In a nano-second, the fierce wolf-being with the blaster in one furry hand aimed at the intruder's heart stopped immobile. Other members of the battle deck crew reached for weapons. They too, froze in mid-motion. She gestured toward the battle deck doors and a howling, whirling wind arose that slid them shut with a *whoosh* against the armed security troops arriving on the run.

The commander's eyes opened wider still. It was the only part of him that could move. They burned with fury. *Puk! The Vita-Kor witch shames us! Strike a blow! Kill us! Do not reduce us to impotent shells! Have you no sense of honor, Terran bitch?* He raged against his invisible bonds, wanting nothing more than to strike out, to kill at least this one Vita-Kor witch or die trying.

But the surprises were just beginning. A dazzlingly brilliant blue light form eight feet tall swiftly recalibrated its atomic form right next to the Terran female. A head, necklessly attached to the body and crowned with shimmering blue light waves that spread out three feet to all sides appeared first. Right in the middle of the head, where a face should be, a three inch wide, dark red eye appeared, joined by a concentric bright red band that jutted out another inch, a thin dark violet ring around that, an orange circle spread out another inch from that, and a bright yellow fifth glimmering halo eye to complete the multicolored spherical, five-tiered Nord eye. Five penetrating lights, focused on him like a huge multicolored headlamp on a runaway train.

The commander's mouth opened wider but only a rasping croaking "aaak" came out. *The witch brought the dead with her! The Nord dead! A Va-Tor master! Vitok the Nord!*

The female Terran spoke. "Forgive us for the unannounced entrance commander, but time is of the essence. Marshal Pardek awaits us. And as for honor, it was not I, but the Va-Tor master who put a stop to your crew's rash attempt to use their weapons. Although it was I who commanded the Terran passed-beyond who accompanied me to shut the bridge doors."

The commander's eyes were raging slits of xanthic anger. *The witch dares insult me further? She brings Terran dead with her who fail to show themselves, but instead slam my bridge doors shut! Puk! Even the dead on this semi-sentient planet are sub-species barbarians without honor!* He now became certain the Terran dead must be involved in this crisis. Why else would the witch and the deceased Va-Tor master be here to meet with Pardek?

Though he was unable to move, internally, he shuddered. He had no idea how they had seen his cloaked vessel, even less compre-

19

hension of how they had both gone through his supposedly impenetrable shields. And knew Pardek was aboard!

His mind raced along an agonizing, terrified path. Many things, he knew, were possible for the Nord deceased sorcerers, but the sudden, unannounced appearance of the legendary red-haired Terran witch who used invisible dead to slam shut doors that could withstand the fiercest warrior's strength, *on my battle deck! Insufferable! These Terrans are inferior, primitive, savage beings! A primitive who holds such power is intolerably dangerous! Those who call for the incineration of this planet speak wisely!*

The witch cast her emerald green eyes his way. He felt himself sinking deeper and deeper into them, and them into him. A cold chill ran up and down his spine.

Many Terrans and off-worlders were acutely uncomfortable in Aidan Good's presence. Everyone had secrets, and if one thought them too loudly around a gifted psionic like Aidan, the telepath "heard" them. People would abruptly end a conversation as they realized she was reading them faster than they were speaking, seeing the emotions and desires behind their words, hearing the secrets they wished to hide, looking into their souls.

The commander was no exception. *What could she see?*

He began to work very hard to keep his thoughts under the level at which she might read them. Like more than a few Krieg warriors, he had been prejudiced by a growing radical wing of *Kulgarka*, Krieg dead warriors, against the Terrans. He was deeply suspicious of the Terran officer core in Natil's Eagle Legion, longed for it to fail and be replaced by Krieg warriors. He hoped to be one of those who covered himself with glory after that happened.

She said nothing, but her eyes burned like green flames. The commander felt his body return to him. He was now relieved to not be invited to the meeting. This Terran witch was unnerving, *intolerable!*

He shook out his furry hands to regain his composure. Grand Marshal Pardek awaited Vice Marshal Natil, and he had no reason to doubt, Vitok, and this Terran witch. He had his orders and he would obey them.

He shot an inky look at his visitors.

The blue Nord raised a filmy limb that mimicked an arm, formed fingers which flayed the air: the frozen security chief's dark brown furry hand half-squeezing the trigger unwound from the blaster, which remained suspended in the air. The trigger slid forward. The safety locked with a resounding click. The weapon rose slowly into the air and floated silently back into its holster. The snarling Krieg officer found himself once more in command of his body. He came to embarrassed attention, his eyes wide yellow on yellow. Veins bulged out black and angry on his furry neck. Spittle dropped from bared fangs.

"My sincere apologies, lieutenant," Aidan declared in her most soothing voice, turning toward the fuming spacer. "But it appeared necessary, as you had begun to pull the trigger, and unlike my discarnate Nord friend here, the energy bolt would not have passed through me harmlessly." She turned toward the commander. "The Vita-Kor Sisterhood is not wont to grant powers such as I have to dangerous savages. Believe me when I say I adhere strictly to the *Jintu Kor* rules of behavior. I am here on a matter of great urgency and importance to both our worlds. Please *Kulvak*, take me and Vitok *Maks Tak* to Marshal Pardek." She added, "As for my invisible guardians, I assure you, they are now on their way back to Earth."

The bridge doors opened to reveal several dazed Krieg security troopers.

The commander slowly shook his head. This brazen Terran witch dared to call him "comrade" in his own language and command him to bring them "right now" to Marshal Pardek! He was

21

right to distrust the Vita-Kor. Powers such as this properly should not be in the hands of sub-species Terrans. Then he resignedly stared off at nothing and spoke only in mono-syllables. "Come."

Saying and thinking as little as possible, the commander led the two unwelcome visitors off the battle bridge to the war room.

If he had been relieved not to be invited to the meeting once the Terran witch arrived, when he saw the dark, forbidding glower in Marshal Pardek's yellow eyes as Aidan and Vitok entered the room, he became completely content to avoid it. Whatever the meeting was about, he was certain it would not be pleasant for those attending.

Two tones announced the arrival of Vice Marshal Natil's shuttle, and the commander trotted in bipedal wolfish style down to the landing dock just as two semi-circular outer doors shut like a great eyelid behind the gliding battle shuttle. It sailed past the other moored vessels and settled into the closest available mooring to the main landing dock. A floating air-lev pier uncoiled itself like a tongue from the main dock, ran out to the midpoint of the shuttlecraft, rolled to the right and locked itself onto the main hatch with a sucking sound.

Natil strode purposefully down the pier with two more Terrans, both in Natil's Eagle Legion uniforms. One was a big brown human as tall as a Krieg warrior. The second a slim, darker brown, surprisingly small human who even more surprisingly, had the seven point wingmaster star adorning his cape clasp. *Outranked! By a Terran!* The shocked battle cruiser commander saluted fist against chest, sullenly escorted them to the War Room and withdrew, heading for the bridge, growling quietly to himself. He'd had enough unpleasant surprises for one Terran day.

He would have been even more surprised to see who really ran the meeting once it began.

ALARUM!

If you're going to walk on thin ice, you may as well dance.
Anonymous

The commander had set out his best Krieg homeworld delicacies for Grand Marshal Pardek's private meeting. In the belly of the great black bat the group of six gathered around a sleek panel of black plasteel suspended three feet from the polished black deck. A plastalloy container of crystal clear Terran water and six plastalloy glasses stood like soldiers on review in the center of the floating tabletop. Two concessions to the otherwise austere setting were a tray of Kot rabbit tenders on crispy rye-tack and a flagon of Kumla.

Aidan looked past the frown that darkened Grand Marshal Pardek's bronze forehead and carved sepia furrows in his shell-like fore skull and read Pardek's thought forms. To Aidan, Adept of the Vita-Kor, thoughts were visual: blazingly obvious patterns, shapes and colors, discernibly shallow or complex, distinctly casual or intense. The Krieg field marshal was troubled. He was not used to being summoned to a meeting by a Terran, even less so summoned telepathically while on a dreadnaught from a being on the planet it orbited!

Aidan noticed he was wearing a large, seven pointed gold star on the breast of his grey dress cape: the Consular Medal of Honor, the highest Krieg military award, most often given posthumously.

The triple red ribbon hanging below it indicated that it was the third such Medal of Honor earned by his family: an astounding feat. *He would not feel the need to display that unless he were deeply concerned about appearing less than fully in charge before his vice marshal. I must go carefully, tactfully, reveal only as much as necessary of what he and I discussed earlier, let him take the lead and appear to run the meeting as much as possible.*

Without moving her eyes from Pardek, Aidan used her Vita-Kor training to assess the fierce-looking female Vice Marshal Natil, who stood stiffly at attention along with the two Terrans in the Eagle Legion uniforms, all waiting for Pardek to give them the signal to stand at ease. Natil's furry brown prognathic jaw thrust forward sharply, black nostrils slowly puffing in and out proudly, black lips curled tightly over her fangs. But her yellow wolf eyes blazed with envy and awe at the sight of the medal Pardek displayed.

Aidan gauged the thought forms: she could see Natil's customary decisive, disciplined, analytical aspects, shot through with habitual haughty green flashes and *oh, my,* she could tell by the blazing red color of the high vortexes, *Natil's unusually volatile tonight! That's not good.*

And then Aidan saw the black-edged thought raging through the wolf-warrior's aura: w*hat is **she** doing here?* Aidan bristled. **She** was here because **she** had received a distinctly disturbing vision from the dead with a message that bore no waiting. Evil was afoot, the moon was concerned and the dead of both planets were involved. ***You***, *you haughty bitch,* she thought despite her best effort to control herself, *are here because this new plot, whatever it is, involves the living and your Eagle Legion must deal with them, even as I must deal with the dead!*

She saw her own thought forms shot through with flashing red fury and forced herself to take three deep breaths in the Vita-Kor way and calm herself. She could not control Natil's thoughts, but she could control her own. There was too much at risk to afford antagonism.

When she contacted him, Pardek had told her he thought the dead from his planet, Kot, were also implicated and somberly inferred that the plot had deeper, far-reaching repercussions.

At this, Aidan recommended they meet with Natil and Vitok as soon as possible. Pardek suggested the battle cruiser and relayed the hour he expected Natil would get there.

Aidan knew that each of the Seven Worlds had integrated their dead into their society. They believed this was an absolute requirement for a civilized society and that not doing this was one of the reasons the Terrans had remained so ecologically destructive and socially barbaric. Because Aidan uniquely could naturally share both thoughts and feelings with the living and the dead, her task, with Vitok's assistance, was to bring the earth's dead into active participation in the social transformation process imposed by the Seven Worlds as the price of Earth's still tenuous reprieve from destruction: a reprieve that remained at the end of a trigger held by the battle cruisers of the Krieg war fleet, like the one she was on, in orbit around the planet.

And from what the cruiser commander had so palpably revealed to her, a significant portion of the Krieg war fleet was all too ready to pull the trigger. If Pardek was correct, this reprieve was now hanging by the most gossamer of threads. The plot against Luna City and the space stations involved the living and the dead on two worlds, and endangered both those worlds.

No wonder Pardek looks so ill-tempered. Natil? Well, Natil might not like my being here, but Natil will obey orders, and I can count on Pardek issuing orders. I'm just not sure what they will be.

She felt terribly thirsty, reached out a hand to grasp the water pitcher, poured out a cool, clear glass of water and slowly began to sip. *Pardek has long been a friend of earth. We'll have to see if he remains one.*

Pardek moved his vulpine head slowly around the room,

called the soldiers to ease, and reached for the flagon of Kumla. "Aidan and Vitok can see the thoughts of the living and the dead," he growled. "We others need Kumla to see more clearly. Here," he ordered, handing each of the three others a full glass of the blue liquid and taking one himself. "Drink! Eat! Let the Kumla do its work. Then we will talk."

Aidan reached for a Kot rabbit tender on the hard-tack the Krieg liked so much. The succulent Kot rabbit was perfect with the crunchy, dry crisp-bread that was a staple on all the warbirds in the Krieg space fleet. She looked across the floating tabletop to Natil, chewing petulantly on the Krieg delicacy. *Well, warrior-woman, you and I will undoubtedly have to work together on this, like it or not, and I'll try not to step on those big wolf feet of yours.*

Aidan had done her job well. But as Aidan knew all too well, earth's dead still had much to learn about integrating into a society. Not everyone was reconciled to the new order. She had quickly realized that a separate police force was required to deal with malicious, reactionary discarnates and formed the PBM, the Passed-Beyond Monitors, as they called themselves. Sometimes the PBM intervened gently, and sometimes called upon those with extraordinary powers to remove certain players from the game by whatever means necessary.

And that was where the rub with Natil had grown sore. Natil's all-Terran Eagle Legion was supposed to be the planetary uber-police force, and on several occasions, when the PBM intervened where Natil felt her Eagle Legion could have taken care of things, Natil took it personally.

As she did today. A half-blind-non-psychic could read the irritation in Natil's grim gaze, the way her razor-sharp black claws tapped on the tabletop as she lifted another Kot rabbit tender on hard-tack to her black lips and crunched her way through it.

And it appeared that both of them now had another problem to confront. She could feel Pardek's anxiety, could see that Pardek wanted the Kumla to take effect before he went into the "repercussions" added by the involvement of disgruntled Terran and Krieg dead! Aidan watched Pardek pour himself and Natil another glass of Kumla, tap his glass to hers, and down it in one gulp, just as Natil did.

She slowly ran the fingers of one white hand as nonchalantly as she could through her long red hair while her dark green eyes darted here and there as if by sheer force of will, she could pierce the mystery. *Something concerning the moon, the space stations, and a young martyr. And the dead of two worlds.*

It was time to begin. She could tell from the thought forms that everyone's mental activity was enhanced and each of them was now able to pretty much read the emotions and hidden thoughts of everyone else. She placed her hands together in the way she'd been taught by the Nord Vita-Kor Sisterhood and recited aloud the first of the nine Jintu-Kor suggestions as a prayerful way to begin the meeting. 'Let us distinguish the true reality from that which we desire it to be."

"So be it," Pardek growled, spread his dusky brown hands, extending the sharp black claws. "Interworld diplomatic discussion: recording devices off," he commanded.

His eyes turned cold and a new darkness spread black rivulets across the formidable shell-like frontal pate. "Now that we all can see the truth of what is being said, Aidan has had a vision in which she has seen into the near future. Aidan, relate what you have seen for the group."

She swallowed hard. In relating this, she would re-experience the distress it had visited upon her, not as fiercely, but, still, agonizingly painful.

27

"I was looking up at the moon when I felt an overwhelming sense of evil and danger. I felt it touching me, my family, my friends, with an icy cold finger like a dagger stabbing into my heart. I called out to my guides in the dead, 'What is this menace? Why does it come to me?' and they brought me a vision. Sand was blowing with a bitter, unearthly fury. A quick jitter of edgy, spiky telltale evil made my skin crawl. It came and went, repulsively malevolent, in a whirling wall of sand. I squeezed my eyes shut, blinked. Now the image cleared and I saw an enormous, round golden jewel shining on the moon, an immense silver and gold gun barrel, brittle images of space stations, seemingly coming apart, a huge snake attempting to devour the earth, Krieg warbirds blasting each other out of the sky, and a young man in the white robe of a martyr . . . Then it was gone. There was a sickly sweet smell of rotting frangipane in the night air. I could not take my eyes off the moon. From deep within me a voice said, 'Act now. Two worlds are threatened. You must act immediately to avoid a catastrophe.'" Face pale, hands shaking, she turned to Pardek.

In a voice so deep and strong that he had no need to raise it above conversational tone, at which it seemed to echo off the walls, Pardek then rattled off the facts in typical Krieg directness. "Terran living are the main actors. But Terran dead and our own dead are involved. One reactionary splinter group of our Kulgarka has shared secrets of power with a Terran dead group that calls itself the Red Serpent Brotherhood. Our Kulgarka group is agitating within the officer class claiming that Terrans of the Eagle Legion, *Khlyvak Wokulen*, 'subspecies mercenaries' they call them, will soon replace them. These semi-sentient beings who have devoted most of their history to ruthlessly murdering each other will turn on their benefactors and overthrow the Empire."

Preposterous! Natil's mind shot back as she rejected that idea but dared not interrupt her superior officer.

Seeing the thought pattern, Aidan audaciously interjected, "Marshal Pardek, is it not true that a small, but not insignificant portion of your people would still incinerate or occupy Terra."

The fur rose on the back of Natil's neck. Her aura flashed red with anger at Aidan's interruption. *This Terran witch was even worse than her Vita-Kor sisters! At least they knew enough not to interrupt a grand marshal!*

Pardek, thanks to the Kumla, had seen the thoughts. *It appears the dislike of the Vita-Kor runs more deeply through my officer corps than I would like.* "A wise commander uses all the forces available for the task at hand," he growled.

Natil's face turned a deeper brown. She struggled to not let the anger she felt at being reprimanded by her commander in front of this Terran sorceress and her own Terran subordinates rise to the level anyone could perceive.

Even less used to being interrupted than to being summoned to a meeting by a Terran, Pardek raised one black-clawed hand to the side of his face, sighing and brought everyone back on point. "Yes. It is true." He turned to his vice marshal. "Natil, you and I know that we could easily defeat any Terran threat. But this group's argument is emotional, not rational: they enflame our concern about the emergence of another warrior society with *Gor Thab*, the fire of fear. They still hold sway over those Krieg who believe violence is part of the Terran genetic, and that, once given the opportunity to attack, they will. They say in the most recent five thousand years Terra has had forty-eight hundred years of recorded war, that these semi-sentient aliens have demonstrated a willingness to use any weapon to slaughter their own kind, so why would they hesitate to slaughter us?"

Natil nodded and barked out, "Understood!"

Aidan seized the opportunity to continue. "Apparently, Krieg Intelligence has been aware of a long-term plot on Terra to destroy

29

the space stations and Luna City. If Terran forces, which include the Eagle Legion, fail to stop it, there will be calls to destroy or occupy the planet."

Pardek now inserted, "This could possibly thrust Kot into a civil war. Aidan has given us the indication that this threat is imminent. We must stop it. Time is running out."

Aidan moved toward Natil in a flowing motion that was more light and energy than the assembly expected from even a Sister of the Vita-Kor, to meet the gaze of that particularly fierce Krieg warrior whose piercing yellow eyes glared at her. "The clock is ticking. Both our homeworlds are in jeopardy. Some fool on Luna is playing dice with the fate of two planets. Whoever these plotters are, one of them is going to make a mistake, take an unnecessary risk, speak out of turn to someone, go through a door he shouldn't somewhere. And one of us will find out. Marshal Pardek will work on Kot, but God help us, we will have to work together here somehow on this, because then your Eagle Legion and my PBM have to stop them."

Natil's strong right hand rose up, black claws extended. A single acidic tear fell from one blazing yellow eye. She pounded her fist against her chest, exclaiming, *"Ravkul! Kulrav! Ravkut!"* the Krieg military oath of Duty! Honor! Homeworld! It was as clear a sign as she could give that she understood.

But when push came to shove, Aidan knew if Natil had to choose, she would choose her homeworld's good over Terra's even as she would choose Terra's over Kot. She decided it was time to mobilize the PBM and telepathized a strong mental message into the ethers.

After the meeting, Aidan rode down from the space station in Natil's battle shuttle. There was no need to make herself a quantum bit again, bend space, and ride a quantum wave down to the planet. And it gave her a chance to share some thoughts with Natil and the two Eagle Legion officers. Whoever these conspirators were, they were just chess pieces on the board of a bigger player, and she had a strong intuitive sense of who that was.

As the shuttle swooped toward Terra, Aidan broke the uneasy silence between her and Natil. "I think I know who is behind this plot, Natil."

Natil's head shot up, her yellow eyes blazed. "Then why did you not say so, Terran," she barked.

"It is only an impression, an intuition, and I'm well aware of your opinion of intuitives," Aidan snapped back.

They looked deep into each other's eyes. No one was giving an inch. Finally, Natil snorted, rolled her yellow eyes and emitted a wolfish sigh.

Aidan continued. "When my spirit guides brought me the vision, I was struck by an edgy, spiky telltale feeling of evil that made my skin crawl and I saw a huge snake attempting to devour the earth."

Natil looked away at the battle shuttle's controls.

"That exact same edgy, spiky, evil feeling came to me each time I met the Russian billionaire on the World Com Board, Vladimir Koscientzi, who's constantly trying to take over. Behind his back, his countrymen call him, *zmeya,* the snake! Natil, that snake, Koscientzi, is involved in this."

At the mention of the Russian's name, Natil's sharp yellow-eyes glared, her nostrils flared and the brown fur rose on the back of her neck. On Kot, Krieg justice, exacted in pools of cerulean blood, was renowned for its swiftness. On Kot, Natil's rank gave her the power of judge, jury and executioner. Her quick-tempered decisiveness was legendary.

With a predator's grim reserve, Natil leaned forward on her wolfish haunches. Taut furry hands stroked the elbow patches on her

grey issue turtleneck and the flat, spade-shaped Kuldai knives concealed within it under the dress cape. "I could rid us of this viper
with one motion," she snarled.

Pardek had given Natil carte blanche to act, but Aidan wanted to put an end to both this threat and the people behind it. She
wanted Natil to be looking beyond the immediate problem. Chess
pieces could be replaced. Aidan wanted the chess master behind
them.

"I have no proof, Natil, only a deep suspicion," Aidan declared.

Natil snorted. "*Wom Puk!*" she growled back ominously. "I
could smell the evil on that man."

"We will need more than my intuition and your outstanding
ability to scent, Natil."

The wolf-warrior snorted again, turned toward her two Eagle
Legion commanders and barked, "Alert your spies. And double our
off-planet drills, beginning this afternoon."

The smaller of the two men popped to attention. The larger
merely nodded.

Natil looked hard at the smaller Terran, Wingmaster Shafat
Bajar, commandant of the Eagle Legion. A toothy grin spread across
her dusky brown face. "We will seek out these plotters," she stated
decisively. "When we find them, we will kill them."

The five-foot-six man nodded. He would carry out the order.
The diminutive Pakistani was the model of military efficiency and,
Aidan could see, when he needed to be, a cold-blooded killer. *Uh oh.*
Natil may just slaughter everyone who could lead us to the men behind this, and
the next plot.

Aidan watched Natil turn her gaze to the other man and
slowly shake her head. Bill Peebles, the Reverend Doctor Peebles, a
highly intelligent man who preferred to follow common sense and

intuition rather than regulations and accepted practice had his lips pressed tightly shut and was clenching his large brown hands into fists by his side. *He can't say what he wants to say, but Bill has gotten the message loud and clear!*

The commander of the First Terran Para Rescue Detachment, 1PRD, called "One Perd" by troopers who would follow Peebles into hell armed only with water pistols, was also Aidan and Michael Good's best friend, and the protégé of the most powerful Terran on the planet, Robert Walker.

Peebles had tried Natil's patience on too many occasions though. That time he swept down with his para rescue team against orders, to save an Eagle Legion platoon trapped in a steaming Kuldorian swamp almost got him discharged. Only the direct intervention of Marshal Pardek kept his command and his skin, intact. Natil would likely have executed a Krieg officer with her own hand for the same offense. One of her staff officers had a nasty scar on his left cheek Natil's slashing claws had given him when he dared question an order.

Unlike the unconventional, irreverent Peebles, Bajar had never tempted Natil to slash his throat with her razor-sharp black claws.

"We need information more than we need dead bodies, Natil," Aidan interjected.

Natil glowered.

"I have alerted my agents in the PBM and I will share anything we find with you Natil."

The wolf-warrior turned her face away. "*Zadank,*" Natil curtly responded in Urtok, merely saying, Thank you. She was doing her best to shield her mind but Aidan could see Natil did not intend to reciprocate. Aidan, trained by the Vita-Kor to respect the privacy of all beings, would not probe the mind of an individual without that person's consent. But the agitated Natil's thought forms were so vivid it was impossible not to clearly see what was on the vice marshal's mind.

"Natil, you don't have to like me."

Natil snorted. "That is correct."

"But we must work together."

The wolf-warrior let a long, rumbling outbreath groan through her throat. "Yes. Unfortunately."

The rest of the journey was singularly uneventful and devoid of conversation.

When the battle shuttle set down in the private aviation area of the New Manhattan Spaceport, Robert Walker's sleek Bodil aircar was parked right next to Natil's well-armed Krieg-built Kul military aircar. Walker's *Silver Arrow* was one of only twelve Antal aircars on the planet. And the only one with supersonic capability. Yes, it made Aidan's alpha female status clear.

Aidan stepped lightly across the tarmac and into the open passenger door, turned, and waved brightly to Natil. *Just in case you need a reminder of who is backing me and my PBM team in this endeavor, vice marshal.*

The door whooshed closed behind the red-haired psionic who danced with the dead. The aircar lifted up almost noiselessly and true to its name, once it had reached cruising altitude disappeared in a flash. Aidan was on her way to Walker's Connecticut estate.

QUENBY

Fate never comes in the shape men look for.
And no man can outrun the destined end, from the day he is born.
Mary Renault

Fahd struggled to steady his hands. *Would they announce themselves if they were coming for him?* He apprehensively called the view screen on.

A face, dazzlingly white, ethereal and captivating appeared on the small rectangular visi-screen over the portal. Silver grey eyes coyly drew him toward them. He switched the visi-screen to full view and found himself taking a step toward the image, stumbling, nearly spilling the wine again.

Fahd had been specifically advised about the Antal. He remembered the session vividly. The Lumina trainer had paused, drawn a deep breath, "And then, there are the Antal: refined, reserved, financiers, scientists and engineers, polite and reasonable in the extreme," paused again, raised the forefingers of each hand, "except, during the biannual kön, when these tall, cat-like bipeds toss their normal side away and engage in omnigamous mating driven by the females. Just as the first time a Terran meets a Coryllim face to face can be disconcerting, even startling, the first time a Terran male encounters an Antal female in full kön, when a pink nimbus surrounds her, can be stupefying."

"Consensual sex between adults is accepted as a fact on Lu-

35

na," he was advised in formal tones, "and inter-species sex is not excluded. Officially, it is neither encouraged nor discouraged, though Lumina Corporation cautions you it can be problematic." But the returning earthman delivering the training had another version: "Antal females in full kön are irresistible. And if you are fortunate enough to be chosen," he wistfully, longingly related, "and make no mistake, she will choose, not you, the sex will be legendary."

Yes, Fahd had been advised.

And now there was one at his door.

In a floor length white body robe that clung provocatively to every nuance of the intoxicatingly sensual seven foot tall female. She was stunningly attractive. Set against the hazy pink cloud that swirled around her, the satiny whiteness of her hair was overmatched by the beguiling alabaster luster of the face he could not tear his eyes away from.

Fahd realized he had stopped breathing. *Breathtaking! Everything they said about the Antal is true. I don't believe I've ever seen such an alluring creature before. But why is she here?*

The wraithlike vision made more ethereal by the hazy pink cloud surrounding her, spread her silver lips wide in an enticing smile that made her snow white cheeks glow like a layer of translucent ice above a white hot inferno. With a sing-song musical lilt, she declared in husky, Antal-accented English, "I am Doctor Quenby, your co-worker from the magnetic mass mover."

Fahd stared mouth open, enthralled, watching Quenby's sensuously glowing silver lips carefully enunciating each word, while her silver eyelashes fluttered provocatively over the dazzling, silver-grey cat's eyes that burned with arousal from the fire of the kön.

Fahd felt a hot searing sensation rush along his spine into his pelvis. He shivered. *Those eyes!* They burned right across the vidscreen into his mind. Like beacons drawing him toward them. *That*

36

voice! That sing-song voice danced along every nerve in his body wanting to ignite a flame that would consume him. His mouth was suddenly terribly dry. He swallowed hard, struggled to curb the desire rising in his body. He was a man of the world. He'd had his share of women. They were a distraction he could not afford now. *Get control of yourself. You don't know for certain why she's here. For all you know this is another investigation. You can't let yourself get unfocused again like you did in the shuttle. You could slip up. You have a job to do.*

With great effort, he pushed the vision of the magnetic mass mover into the forefront of his mind. Held on tight to it. Still, he felt her siren song dancing, penetrating. *That voice!*

"P-p-please enter," he said uncertainly.

The doors opened with a swisssh, and Fahd stared, spellbound when five feet of shimmering, satiny white hair cascaded tantalizingly toward him then sailed outward and around to ripple along her shoulders and back as Doctor Quenby bent over to step through the portal and then raised herself to her full seven feet. She smiled again and Fahd found himself smiling back infectiously.

As she strode gracefully into the room toward him, silky white waves of hair floated delicately back from her high forehead, flowing all the way down her back and below her invitingly swaying hips.

His heart pounded in his chest. She was mesmerizing. Here, in his quarters, with her so close, he felt overwhelmed by the translucent pink aura of sexual energy that radiated all around her, flaunting the curves of her slender, pearlescent white body and making those silver nuances glow.

Once again, he forced his mind back to business, to the mass mover, to the job he had to do. He struggled to keep his mind taut.

She tilted her head slightly to one side and looked him straight in the eye. She was almost a foot and a half taller than him and he found himself gazing upward into a face that shone like a pearl, once again enraptured by those blazing grey cat's eyes. The pink halo surrounding her seemed to give off the scent of springtime jasmine. He found her intoxicatingly beautiful.

Had he ever seen so strikingly white a being before? So tall, so slim, so beyond white, beyond the whitest Terran woman he had ever seen! *Legendary* thundered in Fahd's mind. Erased the mass mover. He fought to regain control.

"H-hello, Doctor Quenby," he managed to breathe, realized he was holding a glass of wine, turned, found a second plastic glass, filled it with the precious Chateau Margaux and held it up to her. "Please, Doctor Quenby, allow me to offer you one of Terra's greatest treasures."

She took the glass in a long white hand, flared her nostrils and inhaled deeply. Spreading her silver lips wide in a smile that bared her ivory teeth, she locked her eyes enchantingly on his, raised the red liquid elegantly to her lower lip and let it slide slowly down her long, lithe, white throat. She swallowed appreciatively, hedonistically closing her eyes and then daringly flashed them down at Fahd.

He reached out to shake her hand. "It is a pleasure to meet you Dr. Quenby."

She slid her elegantly long white fingers gracefully into his hand, all the while demurely fluttering her silver eyelashes. "The pleasure is mine, Dr. al-Sharfa."

They stood there, holding hands entirely too long.

He remembered the briefing: "Do not be shocked if you touch an Antal and feel a chill. Antal body temperature is normally 75 degrees, except during the high kön when it rises to 95." Her long, sensuous fingers were noticeably warm, he might even say hot.

"How was your trip from Terra," she crooned, still not releasing his hand.

"Not bad, Dr. Quenby, though all those security searches became wearisome."

He watched those silver lips deliciously annunciate, "Ah, you poor dear," as she slid her long white fingers along the inside of his hand and then delicately stretched them out to touch his arm. *What is she doing? What am I doing!*

Then he watched her silver cat's eyes look at her empty wine glass, the bottle on the black silicate table, and back into his own eyes. *I really shouldn't do this,* he told himself, but he reached for the wine and poured each of them another glassful. "To your time on Luna," she said, "may it be very pleasant."

They drank slowly.

Her hand continued to stroke his arm delicately, moving the jump suit sleeve upward then gliding back to stroke the exposed wrist, slowly sliding her fingers along his skin in a way that made him tremble.

Those fingers! What is she doing to me?

Her eyes never left his.

She set her glass down and returning his overlong handhold, twirled one long, silver-clawed hand over and around his small brown one.

Then, emboldened by the wine and her beguiling pearlescent eyes, daring to take that long, silver-tipped hand into his dark brown fingers, and caressing it more than he should, Fahd raised it to his dark red-brown lips to kiss, while staring into those entrancing eyes.

Now he saw the silver grey eyes locking on him like a cat on a fluttering bird. He felt long silver claws extend from her fingers and grip his hand. And for the first time in his life, he felt sexual arousal and fear mixing together in his loins.

"Mmm," he heard her hum throatily.

The pink haze deepened, thickened and began to surround

both of them palpably, running sensually up and down his body, rubbing, embracing, coaxing his body to respond.

The silver claws retracted. Fahd felt Quenby's long fingers begin to stroke oh so softly along his lips, teasing, tantalizing, tempting in a way no earth woman had ever tempted him. When Quenby leaned back, sensuously moved her slender shoulders and stretched her legs to display her body then let her long silver tongue luxuriously moisten her silver lips, every nerve in Fahd's body cried out to touch her, to join with her.

His mind swam.

Legendary . . .

He shook his head. *I can't, I have a job to do. Have to keep my focus on that.*

Legendary . . .

But she's an alien! His eyes swept downward, stopped abruptly at her furry white four-toed paws peeking out from under the white robe. He watched long, silver, razor-sharp claws extend from them, as her toe-pads moved sensuously up and down and a low, purring growl rumbled through the room.

Oh God she's hot. But she's an alien. And I can't let this happen. In near panic, Fahd watched his obvious hesitation and more obvious desire light up the silver in Quenby's eyes.

She began to purr and scratch a circular mark with one very sharp claw into his pink palm.

Legendary . . . And if you are fortunate enough to be chosen . . .

The little brown, almost pretty man with the piercing eyes that exuded schoolboy innocence and enthusiasm looked helplessly into her blazing silver eyes. He felt the pink nimbus encircling him, embracing, holding him tighter. Felt his vacillation falling away as she carried him higher and higher into irresistible sexual craving.

Quenby took his glass from his hand and set it beside hers,

then stretched out the three long white fingers and thumb of her right hand to softly stroke his curly black hair.

Fahd felt an overwhelming rush of desire. It was as if those long white seductive fingers were stroking the resistance right out of his mind. Her fingers were drawing him to her. "Ohhhh," he moaned softly as those fingers slid in and out and through his hair, over his eyes and ears and face, stimulating, enticing. And he began to not care about anything but this overpoweringly alluring being.

She caressed his neck ever so gently, then looking deeply into his eyes, pulled his face toward hers and locked her silver lips on his dark red-brown ones.

They were soft and lush, warm and ripe. He tasted the wine and a voluptuous silvery promise of the best sex he would ever have.

She dug the silver nails on her right hand into his neck. Fahd's eyes opened wide with shock. He gasped. And when he did, felt her seize the opportunity to spread his lips further apart and thrust a long silver tongue deeply into his mouth, twirling, probing, searching.

That did it. Fahd let go of all resistance. Gave himself up. He crushed his lips against hers, fiercely returning the kiss, searching with his own tongue to dance with hers.

An Antal! In the kön! He told himself, *What the hell, I'm going to die soon enough. Why not enjoy a tumble with her? She wants it sure enough. And I may never have another chance like this.*

Quenby freed her left hand to pinch the shoulder clasp of the long white robe she wore. Several layers of translucent fabric fell to the floor and she stood before him, glowing like a silver white pearl.

Fahd stared unabashedly at her inviting upturned breasts and the silver nipples that glowed vibrantly, pulsing like brilliant lights on alabaster white skin. He reached out to embrace her breasts, like silky cream, floating in his caressing hands, so soft, so smooth, so nearly human.

Her blazing eyes never left his as her hands seized the one-piece Lumina-issue flight suit by the shoulders. She extended her claws and ripped the clothing off his body with one terrifyingly swift motion. She eyed his dark black pubic patch and the erection standing up and out toward her, then reached out to touch it, gently running a long set of silver claws along its length.

Fahd groaned as she squeezed with one hand, stroked his face with the other then ran her fingers through the curly black hair on both sides of his body with her silver nails sending shivers up and down his spine until he shook.

Gone was the man-about-town who took the women he wanted when he wanted them. Gone was the man who was always in command. Fahd raised his eyes, clouded over with the uncontrollable desire of a dark little Terran for this white and silver being and told Quenby *Yes, Yes, Yes,* with his gaze.

She growled. Began to gently bite his neck. Made him groan again in ecstasy. Then she drew back, pointedly aimed his face downward in the direction of her silver pubic hair which now glowed intensely pink.

Fahd fell to his knees, half from the unexpected strength of her hand pushing him downward and half out of the most intense desire he'd ever experienced. With his hands, he stroked the long white hair that covered her lower legs like a silken carpet. She began a deep basso female moan as his hands moved up and down, pressing, clasping, squeezing. Her long straight hair cascaded over and around the head of the kneeling man.

Fahd dreamily ran his hands along her white creamy thighs, devoid of hair, so like a Terran woman's. Quenby seized his head with silver claws and pulled him closer. He flicked out his tongue and began to lick up her thigh, from where the hair stopped toward that glowing pink, luminous "v". He reached his destination and she threw her head back and growled from deep in her throat. The pink glow was now intense crimson, dazzling and hot to the touch. Fahd lifted his head to watch her eyes glaze over and begin to shine like silver spotlights as she shook her head violently from side to side, sensuously whipping his face with her long white hair, moaning uncontrollably.

Then Fahd rose, reached out and up, running his hands appreciatively along her slender, supple ribcage, caressing, seeking folds of luminescent white skin to roll between his dark brown fingers, panting with pleasure until he reached her long thin arms. She was mewling in ecstasy.

He lifted her in the air, in his excitement and the one-sixth gravity, banging her head against the compartment ceiling, then covered her silver mouth with burning kisses as he carried her through the portal in bounding leaps that were meant to be careful steps, to the bedroom, and half-dove onto the bed with Quenby writhing in his arms.

He penetrated her immediately, and she groaned with delight and whipped him with her hair as she flailed from side to side like a Terran wildcat. He began to move in and out as he had done so often on earth.

Then something astounding happened: she wound her arms and legs tightly around him, and he found he could not move an inch. The Antal female held him in a grip of iron while her internal organs pulsed and pulled, strained and relaxed, beginning a rhythm that matched the growling whine coming from her silver lips.

Oh God! He'd never felt anything like this! He was shocked and excited beyond measure by the exquisite sensations she produced in him.

Then she terrified him. She began to levitate their bodies together off the bed, rising, twisting, sinking, dancing in the air, while her legs and arms took on an elastic quality and wound themselves around and around his body until he felt like he had been encoiled by a python. *What was she doing?* Waves of fear and the most intense coitus of his life alternately washed over him.

The rhythm built slowly, then faster and more aggressive, Quenby spinning, turning, whirling them, winding and unwinding her arms and legs around his small dark body. In one terrifyingly wild spiral, Fahd gave himself up to it, moaned, let his own arms and legs flail wildly, cried out, sunk his teeth into her shoulder, groaned until he screamed in passion and blasted his seed into her. Quenby barked out four ear piercing yelps and another deep growling moan.

Fahd came back to Luna. Quivering. Terrified. They were still a foot off the bed in the air. But Quenby slowly lowered them to the mattress, kissing and licking his face all the while with that long silver tongue.

On the bed, she stretched out luxuriously, letting her long white hair cascade over the sides of the space pillow. Fahd watched her eyes go from bright silver to grey and the pink cloud begin to fade.

She drew her head back, looked piercingly into his eyes and tenderly kissed his lips.

"You are different from other Terrans I have known." She nibbled on one ear with her sharp teeth, making Fahd squirm with pain-pleasure. "There is something pure and sweet about you," she whispered, "something I have not encountered before."

"Pure and sweet? I have never thought of myself that way," Fahd sighed. He reached out to run his hand languorously along one of her smooth white thighs and up along her firm flank, felt the silky marble skin cooling, her temperature dropping, looked up to see the pink cloud fading away. Still he couldn't stop caressing, fondling, touching.

"I like you little Terran," she whispered huskily, running four long finger claws gently along his dark back. "If you like, we will do this more, while the kön is still strong within me."

Fahd wriggled sensuously, moving his back against her hand. Luxuriating in her touch, enjoying the hand moving down his back, along his buttocks, now pressing, squeezing, making him want her more than he'd ever wanted another woman. *If I like?* he marveled, still panting. This was beyond anything he could have conceived. *By God*, he thought, this was the best sex he'd ever had. For Fahd, sex had always been just sex. A woman was just a woman. But this was more than the best sex he'd ever had. This was not just sex. And this was not just a woman. "If I like? Oh yes I like!" he breathed.

Westernized or not, his Arab upbringing made him believe that the man should be in charge. But she was different, this beautiful creature. He could feel it. Something about this woman, (*did I just call her a woman?*), something about her made him want to let her take control the way she did. *I may be about to die, but I sure am going to have some fun with this she-cat before I do.*

Then he realized he had let go. Relaxed. Surrendered. Given up the firm control he so prided himself on. He sucked in a sharp breath, mentally slapped himself. *What just happened?* He had let go of his mission, for sex. With an alien.

Ah but what sex!

And she said she wanted more. *Well why not? We're all going to die anyway.* "Kiss me again, beautiful woman," Fahd pleaded. "I want to feel your lovely lips on mine."

Quenby purred, stretched out languorously, teasingly displaying her body for him, then swept over against him with startling Antal speed and agility, took him in her long arms and kissed him long and lovingly.

"Yes," he said simply, when they untwined. "I want you again, and again, and again."

She laughed throatily and swirled her long white hair around and around, gently sweeping it over his naked body.

He looked deeply into her grey cat's eyes and knew that he never wanted to leave this woman's side —-yes, dammit—-he knew she was not a woman, she was an alien, a being from another planet, but he didn't care. Something had happened to him in her arms. Something wonderful. A feeling he'd never had before swept over him. He wanted her forever. For the first time, he wanted forever.

He stretched out his hand to run his fingers along her pale white ribs, across her flat white belly, to gently caress one sliver-tipped breast. He began to kiss her all over. He couldn't stop.

"Yesss," she hissed, teasingly, "again and again and soon."

Then he noticed the vid game on the black silicate side table. The vid game that he would use to kill them all. *Soon?* Something else would happen soon, Fahd knew. *Forever? Forever will be a few days, a few weeks. And then I will have to kill her! You fool! You stupid, stupid fool! You're going to kill her!* When he fired the weapon, Luna City would implode under its own weight, and she would die, choking on her own breath. The thought made him shudder in revulsion.

For the first time in years, doubts that had been trained, drummed, beaten out of him besieged him. For the first time in years, he wondered, *how can I do this?*

Fahd reached out for Quenby. Stroked her silky white hair, ran his fingers along her silver lips. Laid his head against her pale white breasts. Heard and felt her living heart beating, her soft breasts rising and falling with each breath.

He realized it was quite one thing to imagine killing faceless, nameless beings you'd objectified as Satan's minions, to push a button in a simulation. Quite another to kill this beautiful person lying next to you. He closed his eyes against the ache welling up inside him.

He looked at the vid game again. Cold and black and menacing. *No. I won't, I won't think about that.*

He looked at the bottle of Chateaux Margaux. Paid for with Ahmar Saif's gold. The gold the clan had taken for twelve years. The gold that paid for Fahd's schooling and his privileged, luxury-laden life. *If I do not do this thing I have sworn to do, then I condemn my father, my mother, my clan, all of them to death. I dishonor myself and the al-Sharfa clan forever.*

He felt his rational, compartmentalized mind control unravelling. Fought against the sensation. *No. I must die. She must die.*

Quenby raised her head from the space pillow and a concerned look changed her eyes from glowing to querulous. "Sweet Terran man," she hissed in sing-song, "what is it?" Then more solemnly, "Tell me, what is wrong?"

Fahd looked fretfully from the vid game to the wine bottle and back again. He felt trapped. She knew something was wrong, but he could not speak of it. He could not tell her that he had been trained for twelve years to come up to Luna and kill everyone. Including her. He turned his face away, tried desperately to hide his anguish from her, fearful she might read it in his eyes.

Quenby raised herself up halfway from the bed. "What are you trying to hide," she whispered, reaching out with her unexpectedly powerful hands to grasp his face, and turning it toward her despite his resistance.

Fahd said nothing.

"What are you trying to hide from me?" she demanded. Her silver cat's eyes bored into his.

How could he tell her? He had to kill her. How could he kill her? How could he not? He looked down at the floor.

47

Quenby glared at him. *I thought he was different.* She looked away, up at the lunar concrete ceiling and sighed moodily. Then, she let go of his head, sat up, brought both her hands to her mouth, sighed once more, reached out with one hand to gently stroke Fahd's face, uncurled her long legs and stretched them out over the side of the bed.

Her voice became businesslike, and she continued the introduction she had begun when she came in, several minutes ago as if nothing had happened, as if there had been no wine, no kisses, no love-making, as if they were not here in bed naked.

Talking all the while in that enchanting Antal sing-song English, she rose from the bed. "I came here," she took the first step away from him, "to take you on the tour of Lumina assets specific to our work together," she purred, striding on her long legs toward the portal, aware that his eyes were as good as glued on her assets, stepped sensuously into the living room and put her robe back on, "particularly the mass mover."

She wanted to take her robe off again. To lie beside him. She was certain she could raise the kön heat again, but, they had things to do now. There would be plenty of time for that. She stood graceful, reserved and apart. Her voice had become polite, refined, reasonable. "It would please me to call you Fahd, Doctor al-Sharfa. May I do that?"

He nodded.

Rubbing the top of her head, and faking a laugh she said, "You must learn to move properly in one-sixth gravity. You must learn what we call the lunar shuffle. And you must fly in the great center mall someday. All the Terrans love to do that. But now we will go directly to the mass mover and I will show you the way we work here."

He was still naked on the bed.

She stood in the doorway, gave him an icy stare and flipped

the fingers of her left hand commanding him to dress and join her.

The look she gave him broached no argument. He broodily scurried into a new Lumina jump suit and they made their way out into the hallway and marched silently together to the elevator, where he reached out one hand to touch hers. She curled one long white hand around his, releasing it when the door swooshed open at the blue transportation level.

She led him out onto a cement platform to a waiting mag-lev train and sat next to him, close enough to draw smirks from the three Lunies already in the tram as it took them to the transfer station where they walked across the subway platform to the smaller carriage that would take them to the magnetic mass mover, twenty five miles away on the plains of Mare Nubium.

Quenby was used to Terran males fawning over her, hoping that she'd choose to have sex just once with them, and after sex being totally entranced by her. She could see several humans in light blue Lumina jumpsuits in the carriage fidgeting, shuffling their feet, looking her way. They had all they could do to keep from drooling on their jackets at the sight of her sitting next to Fahd in the clinging white body robe. *Oh these straitlaced Terrans, making so much of a little sex.*

But every time she glanced his way, she kept noticing the undeviating dark mood that remained hanging over Fahd's features. She saw desire in his dark brown eyes, but also something sinister and foreboding. He looked like a doomed man climbing the steps of the gallows.

Had he gotten drunk? On so little alcohol?

Well, she would find out what he was hiding from her. She would make him tell her. No Terran could resist an Antal female in anything for very long. And there would be plenty of time.

MALEVOLENCE

They sleep not, except they have done mischief;
And their sleep is taken away, unless they cause some to fall.
For they eat of the bread of wickedness,
And drink the wine of violence.
Proverbs 4:16-17

"Time is running out for all of them," the man whose two thousand credit, hand-tailored blue suit icily set off the arctic coldness in his pale blue eyes, sneered under his breath.

As the meeting was called to order, he looked around the room at the rest of the planetary governing board, World Com. They had just been granted permission by the powers who held earth's fate in their alien hands to create a mining operation and permanent settlement on Mars, but not the way he wanted it to go, *damn them*!

Koscientzi took a sip of the clear, cold water produced from waste products on the high orbit space station and looked venomously past the board members out the ceralloy window at the full moon hovering like a large round jewel, a jewel he once had securely in his hand, but now . . . Vladimir Koscientzi's glacial eyes narrowed tightly over his pockmarked, pallid cheeks.

He slapped the glass noisily down on the Brazilian tiger-wood table top brought at tremendous expense two hundred thousand miles from earth and scowled. "I move we dispense with the reading of the minutes and all other business and proceed directly to the

50

question of Mars Base," he growled.

No one objected.

Instead, they all turned to look out through the same ceralloy window where a large battle cruiser of the Krieg war fleet had just decloaked. It hovered in orbit like a great black bat with wings three thousand feet across, protruding blood-red eyes that glowered menacingly and in its swollen black belly weaponry able to send the planet the aliens called Terra back to the biologic period where slime would be the highest form of life.

This final meeting on the high orbit space station, Starfarer, and the presence of the Seven Worlds' dignitaries in the adjoining reception room signified a milestone had been made along the path of Terran reformation dictated by the Seven Worlds and enforced by the Krieg.

But Terra was still very much on probation. Still only a trigger pull away from incineration. The battle cruiser was an unsubtle Krieg technique to make that point absolutely clear.

Ever since the day the Krieg war fleet decloaked overhead and the Seven Worlds' non-negotiable submission terms were revealed to the planet's leaders, Terran politics had become a minefield the World Com Board had to guide the planet's steps safely through. But Koscientzi persisted in trying to make World Com dance to his tune. He wanted what he wanted and appeared not to care how perilous the game was.

The cold-blooded Russian billionaire was not called **zmeya**, the snake, to his pockmarked face. But even Russian mafia bosses trembled when that frosty snake eye locked them in its sight. Koscientzi was one of the concessions to malevolent earthly power that had been made to save the planet from incineration. The stakes were simply too high and the time too short. A seat on the World Com Board had been the price of his cooperation, and he took every opportunity to enrich himself.

Now he scowled at the battle cruiser. Its belly disgorged a flashing battle shuttle toward the space station. *Marshal Pardek*, he thought, *coming to show us who is truly in charge. Da! Fear! The Krieg know how to rule.* Those aliens would want someone who could control these people. He was that man. They would appreciate him.

"You see!" he shouted. "Force! Power! Rapid reaction! You understand that." He pointed one manicured finger at the glaring red eyes of the battle cruiser and the war shuttle already docked at the station. "**That** is how we should rule Mars Base from the beginning!"

He thumped the finger on the table to draw the board members' eyes to him and cast that cold snake eye on each of them. "It is too important to be left to its own devices so soon," he stated in the challenging, half-whisper tone that he used when truly agitated. "You know how difficult it was to resolve the Lumina insurrection on Luna."

The Board Chair, Robert Walker, slowly shook his head and replied in his own quietly commanding way, "We finally had to recognize Luna's right to be free and independent, did we not, Vladimir? They are going to want independence sooner or later. Why not start them on that path from the beginning, so the transition will be peaceful and friendly this time?"

Koscientzi blanched white with fury. That fool, Walker wanted to begin the planned colonization of other worlds by setting up a free and independent Mars Colony. Motivated by the diminished ability to manipulate the decision-making processes of an independent Mars and the diminished personal profits, the Russian billionaire had been vociferously opposed. The showdown had come. Three other World Com Board members were not certain an independent Mars Colony would be in their cartel's best interests. He only needed one more vote.

Knowing that the board members needed to keep their cartel's profits high to hold onto their own power, the greying Russian fired back with the accusation he would later point like a smoking gun at Walker if he lost this battle of words, "Because we did not resort to force, as **I suggested**, and **you refused** to do, we lost billions of credits in revenue!"

"And we gained an ally as opposed to a rebellious, vengeful colony where we would need to maintain a large force. Short term loss, long term gain," Walker retorted angrily.

Koscientzi pounded a fist on the table for emphasis. "A weak ally, with little means of defending itself against the reactionary elements we all know are still alive and well here on earth, contrasted to the kind of security force I **had in place** from the beginning, but you were too liberal-minded to leave in place. A force that could have put down that rebellion before it began!"

He cast an ice blue gaze around the room, again meeting the eyes of each board member in turn, challenging them to refute him, hoping to turn just one more vote his way. "And saved us all billions!"

Now he played the trump card. He raised one finger and pointed it at Walker. "Letting the Martians and the Lunies run their own show leaves too many security loopholes, and you know it."

But in the end, as his spies had informed him they would likely do, Koscientzi's allies on the board abstained, and he cast the only negative vote.

He looked disdainfully at the rest of the World Com Board. "Gutless bastards!" he muttered, hoping some of them would hear. "Afraid to rock the boat, afraid to make a move without a guarantee."

But he wasn't. No. He was a man!

Koscientzi's last angry, sullen words on the subject were,

53

"Something will yet go wrong on Luna, Robert, mark my words. A disaster will occur. And you will be the one to blame with your liberal attitudes. Mark my words!"

And thanks to his gold, the little astrophysicist was on the moon and the disaster was well on its way.

His thin, pale lips silently formed the phrase, *da svi'daniya*, good bye, and for the first time, a wicked smile briefly crossed his face. *Da svi'daniya Luna City. Your feeble security will melt like the snow before the sun. After you explode into nothingness, I, Vladimir Koscientzi will take my rightful place as Chairman of World Com and run both Mars and Luna the way I see fit.*

He smugly, silently congratulated himself. It was twelve years in the making, this brilliant master move. Oh, he'd used those fanatical fools in Ahmar Saif before to rid himself of some unwanted competition. When they first approached him for funding, though, he'd been reticent. *Train a scientist to destroy scientific marvels? Crazy!* But after al-Wahab had explained the strategy to use a dirt-poor, ignorant desert boy, educate him, turn him into the perfect weapon, almost above suspicion, and hold his entire clan hostage against him turning away from a suicide mission, Koscientzi decided it was crazy like a Siberian fox! He calculated the odds of success against the possible monetary gain and decided to fund the project as a back up to his other plans to oust Robert Walker and take over World Com.

Twelve years was a long time, he knew. If he took over World Com beforehand and no longer needed Ahmar Saif's boy on the moon, he could always leak the info to the right sources and make himself a hero by so doing.

But now the die was cast. Now, twelve years on, he saw the way clear to rid himself of all his enemies, all of them, at one fell swoop. A disaster of this magnitude would give the Krieg homeworld senators he had been secretly working with the excuse they wanted to disband the all-Terran Eagle Legion, remove that pain-in-the-ass she-wolf, Natil, take firm control of the earth, and justify his own takeover and military clamp down on Luna. *Walker will look like the liberal fool he is. I'll denounce him and take my rightful place as Chair of World Com and then make them dance!*

He'd give World Com its profits all right. Let them gorge themselves. He would see that Luna City and Mars base would yield untold earnings. He ruled Russia. Soon he would add Luna and Mars Base. And then . . .

As he entered the reception room, Koscientzi moved crossly and stood alone, apart from the crowd, and though it was an open cocktail event, few people ventured near the man. His perpetual scowl was one reason. His insistence on bringing a skulking bodyguard even to the high orbit station another. And when he was drinking, as he was tonight, his foul temper and abusive manner made most people avoid him. Tonight, angry as he was about losing the board battle over Mars Base, he was absolutely certain that time was on his side, *and,* he mused sourly, *it's about time!*

The Russian billionaire irritably ran the manicured fingers of one hand over his dramatically receding hairline. He could taste the millions he had lost because of Walker sticking in his throat like a burning canker.

He angrily swilled down a glass of champagne and took a second from the Coryllim waiter hovering nearby, ready to meet every need of the crowd of dignitaries in the reception room. He would get it all back, and more, more.

This was a good night to get drunk, he decided. He had already finished the flask of vodka he always carried with him. He cast a meaningful glance over to his bodyguard, who stepped quickly to his side, relieved him of the empty and handed him a second, elaborately engraved with the initials VK. Koscientzi took a hard pull, slid the silver flask into a silk-lined inside jacket pocket specifically tailored to hold it and chased it down with a long swig of champagne. He hardly needed to hold the empty glass up before another Coryllim waiter replaced it with a full one.

Mars Base had been the last straw. Those wimps on the World Com Board had slunk away from him like the cowards they were. Well, he'd get them too.

He knew they'd run like rabbits. He had set a trap for that rich American bastard Walker, and when he made his move, those spineless rabbits would all piss themselves and scatter and he'd have control again soon. *Da!* He took another long pull of vodka and polished off the new glass of champagne.

And then he saw Marshal Pardek and Vice Marshal Natil, looking their fearsome best in black battle armor. And Aidan Ray Good standing next to a very large, brown Eagle Legion officer, watching him from the other side of the room. *Go ahead you red-headed bitch!! Watch me! Report it all back to your pimp Walker! I'll fix you too when it all comes crashing down.*

Koscientzi reached out a grasping hand, took a smoked Antal salmon strip on a narrow piece of crunchy Antal hardtack from one of four silver trays another circulating Coryllim waiter delicately balanced in his four hands. He popped it whole into his mouth, crushed it with his teeth and downed it in three sharp, short bites. He froze the waiter with an icy glare, enjoying making the alien wait while he dangled his hand over the tray, finally selecting another salmon snack, then signaled him sullenly with an imperious nod of his head to move on and slowly masticated this one, relishing the feeling of the flesh coming apart. *Just like I'll tear you apart with my own teeth, you little bitch. I'll make you squirm and squeal and beg for mercy. And then I'll . . .*

A flash from his communications implant interrupted his vodka-laced thoughts. *Da.* He had a message on the scrambler. He shifted his eyes right, then left, suspiciously checking to see who was watching him, then blinked twice to open the line. *The asset is in place.* He blinked twice to shut the line, then once more to erase the message.

He became quietly furious. He reached for the flask, brazenly tilted it upward and drained it. *Of course, the asset was in place! Did that imbecile al-Wahab not think I had my own sources within Ahmar Saif? Why did that self-righteous fool have to call me here, on a trans-planetary scrambled line? To show off? I have millions invested in this operation, and that fanatic al-Wahab wants to boast. Well, he and that fat bastard al-Yasir had better have done their jobs right! After all I spent on payoffs, training, booze and women, their boy from the wadi had better succeed or I'll kill every man, woman, child and goddamn goat in the wadi as a lesson!*

Koscientzi's cold eyes flickered. *He wants to brag? Okay! When it does happen and the Krieg wolves are hunting the perpetrators down like dogs, then, I'll gladly let al-Wahab take the credit. And then I'll see that his bragging mouth is shut forever.*

SHADOWS

There is no calamity greater than lavish desires.
There is no greater guilt than discontentment.
And there is no greater disaster than greed.
Lao-Tzu

Faisal Hashim al-Wahab, ultimate holder of the bloody red sword of Ahmar Saif, touched the OFF button on his trans-planetary phone and slid it into the pocket of the loose fitting black trousers he wore under his dishdasha.

At six the hot desert day had turned to dusk and the air temperature had begun to drop with alarming speed. At seven it was completely black and the chill set in. It was now nearly eight pm.

The time he had longed for was drawing close. He looked up into the night sky. Stars were beginning to show themselves. The full moon had risen above the hills. Soon, Fahd al-Sharfa, the boy he had taken from the Mahra in this wadi in the middle of nowhere, would do what he had been trained to do. Soon, *Inshallah*, the moon would be freed of that cancer, Luna City, and those metallic monstrosities would be gone from Allah's heavens. The stars and the moon would shine as Allah intended them. And he, Faisal al-Wahab would have his vengeance.

Al-Wahab barked an arid, scornful laugh into the chilling desert wind. He had dealt with that devil the unbelieving Russian for over twelve years. And trusted him as much as a hungry cobra. But

58

Koscientzi's gold was good for many things: bribes, weapons, hi-tech computers, heavy equipment to build terrorist training camps. It was a good joke, using one of Satan's minions to destroy their depraved works corrupting the heavens.

He pulled the night-black dishdasha closed against the rising wind that brought stinging sand with it and curled his lips in a disdainful sneer. No, that infidel Koscientzi was no ally. He was truly a snake to be watched vigilantly, even charmed, and someday, crushed. Al-Wahab turned again, twisting his sandal viciously, trampling the ground hard under it. When the time came. . .

He turned his back to the wind and spit violently into the sand. For twelve years he had delivered gold and weapons to the boy al-Sharfa's clan, and siphoned off enough of Koscientzi's largesse to provide advanced weaponry to the Russian's enemies, the Chechnyan insurgents, true believers, ready to die for Allah. Koscientzi was not the first infidel who thought he was a fool, a tool to be used. But because their god was money, greed blinded them all. Allah's time was on the side of true believers.

Yes, he mused, *twelve years*. Soon al-Sharfa would die for Allah and take the Great Satan's works with him. Tonight, it was time to conclude his business in Wadi Shiban. He could see the wadi elders in the glow of the campfire that made the date palms between them and him stand like wary black sentinels. He knew the elders were armed. They were not fools.

No non-local has ever been safe in the high desert of the harsh Mahrat Mountains where the fiercely independent, predatory Mahra live in ancient caves dug into the lower slopes of the red mountainsides. Al-Wahab trusted the Mahra just slightly more than he trusted Koscientzi.

Moving behind the flap door of his tent so none could see what he was doing, he adjusted the Makarov pistol against the small

59

of his back inside his waistband so it would not be visible.

He stepped out from behind the tent flap into the cold desert night and silently signaled one of his black-robed bodyguards to pick up the black box inside the tent with the gold he would deliver tonight, the final payment. Unless, Allah forbid it, the boy Fahd quailed in his duty, dishonored his oath. Then the final payment would be death, for the boy, his father, his mother, his brothers, and his clan. The other Mahra clans would understand. He would distribute the dead men's weapons amongst them. And a gold death payment.

Al-Wahab sniffed deeply. The wind carried the gamey odor of spit-roasted goat, the bleating of a hundred camels, the pungent smoke from palm wood fires, and the sweet, syrupy, caramel scent of ripe dates to him.

Life in the high desert is severe and uncompromising, but each year, in Wadi Shiban where he stood, deep within it, a grove of over a thousand date palms in a long, twisted string of struggling green patches filled the air with the sweet, honeyed odor of its harvest of succulent medjool dates. Tents, mule trains and camel caravans filled the wadi as owners of palm trees from tribes living east and west of the wadi returned. No one with any sense missed the harvest and everyone who wasn't actively picking dates was armed. If a tree was left unpicked too long, the Mahra claimed it, often at gunpoint. How long is too long has been the cause of more than one death. Compromise is as foreign to the Mahra as it is to the region.

Each year, during the date harvest, when an armed caravan could cross into Wadi Shiban unnoticed, al-Wahab's men had brought gifts of gold and guns to the Mahra.

This year, the end of the abundance was near at hand. Al-Wahab himself traversed the hundred mile long howling wilderness of the great sand sea, vast salt marshes and mountainous *jebels* from Al Ghaydah on the Gulf of Aden, to the Wadi Shiban with more guns, a very large box of gold—the death payment for Fahd, who would soon become a martyr—and a video on an electronic tablet al-Yasir had insisted he show the elders.

Al-Yasir, plump al-Yasir, the man who knew the high desert and the hard mountain people who scratched out an existence there, his partner in this enterprise: *takfir, perhaps too takfir, too ready to enjoy the temptations of the West, but necessary. For the time being.*

The lean man in the black dishdasha dedicated to one idea, vengeance on the Great Satan, turned a hard, solemn stare toward the tablet lying on the small table inside his tent. He recalled al-Yasir's strong admonition. "I know them. They are ignorant, superstitious, mistrustful and dangerous. And honor is everything to them. They will not hesitate to kill you, even if it means their own death if they feel you have sullied their honor. But when they see and hear the boy, they will know you have acted honorably. They will see he is well and from his words know he is ready to die for truth. And when you tell them where he is, and he repeats what you said, they will know your power and fear you even more."

Al-Wahab had heard the tales of Mahra ruthlessness, knew that murder was nothing new to them. He grunted, reached for the tablet he had carried all the way across the great sand sea with the message he had resisted producing but had finally succumbed to al-Yasir's judgment. He would show it to the elders then destroy it and all copies of the message that could foil twelve years of effort if the wrong people got their hands on it before he could strike.

The moon was now fully above the hills, high in the night sky. With the tablet safely inside his black dishdasha, he tapped his left hand against the pistol butt to assure himself. He would take six bodyguards to the campfire tonight. The rest had by now positioned themselves strategically in the red sandstone hills above the wadi.

He nodded to the phalanx of black-clad bodyguards and

moved silently through the sand to take his place at the campfire where the grim-faced Mahra elders sat, rifles in their laps or at their sides.

Twelve years. And still the threat of instant death hung heavy in the air.

When al-Wahab first came to Wadi Shiban twelve years ago, the three Imams he had sent ahead of him and the fifty black-garbed mujahedin he brought with him had ensured a place at the fire for him. His sinister reputation as a ruthless terrorist leader, and his gifts, a box of gold coins and a camel load of the latest Kalashnikov rifles ensured the attention of the notoriously trigger-happy Mahra.

Ahmar Saif wanted young Fahd Abdul, the brilliant young boy whose astonishing mathematical ability had been reported through the Imam grapevine to them, he had explained, to be trained to deal a terrible blow to the Great Satan and his devils, and were prepared to pay the Mahra handsomely.

With pictures of yellow eyed, wolfish Krieg warriors, four-legged Coryllim, and ghostly white, silver-eyed Antal to show the Mahra the Great Satan's new allies and their new enemies were devils from other worlds, he told them how he had sworn to destroy these monsters. When the Mahra tribesmen saw al-Wahab's images and heard his tales, they were glad for his gift of weapons and more than willing to discuss collaboration with him, even while they kept their own weapons securely in their hands.

As they did tonight. And no less than twelve years ago, death hung in the balance. A false word, an affront to Mahra honor, those rifles would be raised and the night would end in a blaze of gunfire.

When he was close enough to the campfire to make out the glint of gunmetal in the elders' eyes al-Wahab stopped, raised both hands to his forehead, then cascaded them down to his lips and heart and spoke. "*As-salaamu alaikum.*"

"*Wailakum assalam*," the desert tribesmen replied with one voice. And peace be unto you. But they kept their hands on their AK-58's.

"*Allahu akbar*," al-Wahab responded. God is great. "*Wa barakatu.*" May He bless you.

"*Wa rahmatullahi.*" May he show you mercy, the black-robed Imman seated next to the clan leader replied, keeping the edge sharp.

Taking this reminder that he might yet need Allah's mercy, al-Wahab turned his head slowly, so the Mahra tribesmen did not mistake the motion for aggression, and with a nod, waved his bodyguards back three paces. He turned slowly and carefully back to face the elders. He had no need to die here, and he knew, bodyguards or no, one wrong move and his life blood might yet stain the desert sand. He lowered himself to sit on the ground and took the place which had been set for him in the circle around the campfire.

A wooden platter with fresh, roasted and dried dates had been laid on the sand awaiting him. Al-Wahab reached out his right hand, took a ripe, brown medjool date and popped it into his mouth. The plump, soft fruit filled his mouth with honeyed syrupy sweetness that was all the sweeter against the contrast of the harsh desert, the unforgiving Mahra, and the smell of automatic weapons.

At the very moment he bit into the fruit, a desert fox barked from a short distance away in the date palms to terrify prey into death-dealing flight. The men heard the sound of rats abandoning the fallen fruit they'd been devouring and scurrying across the sand in panic. One very large brown rat ran terrified across the foot of a black-clad mujahedin bodyguard.

The man swore and swung his rifle butt at the rat. Uneasy Mahra hands tightened on weather beaten AK-58's. Al-Wahab turned his head sharply, anger burning in his pitiless eyes. *The fool! Anything could incite these mistrustful tribesmen!*

And then al-Wahab watched in awe as the bright white light of the full desert moon reflected sharp and silver against the scaly skin of a cobra that struck out from a nearby date palm to sink its fangs into the rat.

Two of al-Wahab's bodyguards reflexively swung their guns toward the snake. Mahra fingers shifted toward triggers. The dark eyes of four more hard-faced bodyguards standing mutely near al-Wahab darted this way and that. Backs against date palms tensed. Left hands all around the campfire slid along trigger guards toward triggers.

Then, to everyone's shock, a horned desert owl swooped down from the treetops overhead, pounced viciously on the skimmering snake as it devoured the rat, then swiveled its horned head to look fearlessly at the bodyguards and the elders in the circle with its predatory yellow eyes, spread its dusky brown wings and took off, flying directly over al-Wahab's head with the wildly writhing cobra spraying snake blood on the man's hands, face and clothing.

Al-Wahab stared blankly through the snake blood on his face at his bloody hands.

The Mahra began to look anxiously at their leader and the Imam. This was an ill omen of great portent. Al-Wahab's bodyguards began to twitch. Two Mahra elders raised their automatic rifles and al-Wahab looked straight into the face of death. *The superstitious fools are going to kill me!*

He did what he had to do. He was not here to die. No trigger-happy, ignorant Mahra tribesman was going to undo what he had labored for so long. He wordlessly called in his second pack of more malicious, unearthly bodyguards.

The Red Serpent Brotherhood had been protecting al-Wahab for twelve years, keeping him safe when all else failed, influencing him to change seats just before an assassin's bullets tore a wall apart or move just hours before a drone strike blew a house into hell. Hovering in the air rising from the campfire, an unseen nimbus made a soundless wave of his ghostly hands. The ethers stirred and the Red Serpent Brotherhood announced their participation in al-Wahab's mission with a show of force.

Against a sudden gust, the palm fronds rattled with a malevolent cackle echoing from the ethers. A menacing blackness high above the trees gathered strength. With a baleful, ghostly, unholy moan, it dropped suddenly to the ground and whirled tightly around the small group of men gathered around the flickering campfire. The Mahra tribesmen felt the presence of evil surround them, shivered and stared hard at each other through sand-clouded eyes.

An even stronger gust of chilling night wind sprayed stinging sand into the men's eyes and ears and chattered against the palm trees like a burst of gunfire. The fire sputtered. A chilling darkness reached out with icy fingers to enshroud the wadi. The elders around the fire felt a stark chill hand choke the air out of their lungs.

Constricting his brow into a blood-covered frown, al-Wahab shielded his face from the predatory vortex that choked the very breath out of the night. He, like everyone else, struggled for a gulp of air.

The baleful moan grew louder, the wind stronger. Darkness dropped in a thick, smothering cloak around the wadi. Sinister black shadows slithered along the sand like hungry wraiths reaching out for prey. Date palms groaned and swayed. A scrawny brown dog shivered and whimpered.

A dozen Mahra dead who had been silently, invisibly watching over the men around the campfire were seized by a phalanx of malevolent, equally invisible Red Serpent thugs. Mentally pummeled into semi-conscious, shriveled up grey matter, they were thrust headlong into the dark ethers of the Terran limbo, where they would remain indefinitely trapped. "So much for those who oppose the dark powers," one of the thugs snarled as the swirling miasma swallowed the men up. The Mahra dead shrieked, struggled in the murky gloom as they withered helplessly, unable to interfere with what came next. Only a piercingly woeful wail carried on the rising wind.

The wrathful Red Serpent Brotherhood had decided it was time to put the fear of malignant forces from beyond the grave into these ignorant Mahra, so they knew with whom they were dealing. And to make certain any tribesmen who were not sufficiently fearful of al-Wahab's mujahedin and might want to brag about the gold and guns they had extracted from Ahmar Saif for a mere boy, would know the Red Serpent's violent forces from beyond the grave were more than equally able to extract vengeance on the foolhardy.

Dogs who had cowered close to the legs of their masters trembled and howled as some of the gasping Mahra in the circle shifted apprehensively this way and that.

This amused the deceased Imam El Sawy, who led the small band who had come to this meeting. When these works of the Great Satan were destroyed, the old ways would be restored. The Brotherhood would see to it. He signaled his mob. The daemonic gust departed leaving a silence like the tomb hanging forebodingly in the cold night air.

Al-Wahab was now not the only man there with blood on his face. Men stood or sat, stunned, rubbing sand out of their eyes, cleaning faces where the sand had driven hard enough against them to cause rivulets of blood to run.

A log tumbled with a jarring whumph! The fire flash cast a malevolent orange blaze on the spare, hawk-nosed faces of the Mahra tribesmen in the circle and al-Wahab's black-clad bodyguards lurking in the shadows. And a spark burst exposed al-Wahab's eyes – dark as a viper's lair and as treacherous as desert quicksand.

The Red Serpent Brotherhood had demonstrated its power. *Al hamdolillah!* Thanks be to God. *So be it.* The Mahra now truly feared him and respected his power. It was time to conclude his business in Wadi Shiban.

He reached for a black box held out by an unsmiling body-guard and somberly handed it to the Mahra elder leader. "I do not think we have need of further demonstrations. Do you?" he sneered chillingly and watched the old man slowly shake his head from side to side. "Good. So let us conclude our business as honorable men. With the grateful thanks of all true believers, please accept this small gift."

Fahd's father nervously muttered appropriate words of thanks to God and his guest. With shaky olive brown hands leathery from years of sun and sand, he opened the box to display its wealth of gold coins to his sand-covered tribesmen and immediately gave the tenth part to the black-robed Imam sitting rigidly upright next to him on his right.

Now al-Wahab opened his dishdasha moving just as slowly and carefully as he had before. Withdrawing the small tablet, he spoke in a reedy voice that underscored the spareness of his body. "Hamood al-Sharfa, I thank you in the name of the Most High for sending your son Fahd Abdul into our care these twelve years." He raised his malevolent, pitiless eyes and lifted one hand slowly toward the moon above them. "Even as we speak, your son is on that very moon above our heads, preparing, *Inshallah*, to deliver a crushing blow to the Great Satan."

Two of the Mahra elders shifted slightly, murmured shakily, "Fahd? On the Moon?" Another two licked the sand off their lips, looked anxiously at the black-robed Imam sitting next to Hamood al-Sharfa, whispered, "Was this all deviltry? And the black-garbed man's doing?"

One of al-Wahab's black-clad bodyguards began to nervously

finger his weapon. His eyes flickered from wind-furrowed hand to hand, seeking out the slightest indication of movement. If the fools insisted on dying tonight, well. . .

But the now unsmiling al-Wahab pressed the green ON button, turned the screen toward the Mahra and froze the tribesmen into awed silence. "Behold the blessed son of the al-Sharfa clan," he announced, "who has left a martyr's farewell message for you all on this electronic tablet."

The older man took it in his desert-weathered hands. A radiant Fahd Abdul al-Sharfa, the boy gone from the wadi twelve years, now a man, dressed in white dishdasha and the red-flecked keffiyeh of a gulf Arab, with a heavenly glow to his tanned face and a clear purpose in his eyes, filled the screen. From the speaker on the tablet, Fahd spoke with a man's assured voice.

"Greetings, revered father, my brothers, my own blood. May Allah's blessings be with you always. As Allah wills it to be so, I will leave shortly for Luna City on the moon," he said proudly. "*Inshallah*," Fahd solemnly intoned, "I will obliterate the Great Satan's two space stations and then I shall annihilate Luna City itself, restore the wondrous moon to the way Allah created it and enter paradise. Praise Allah. *Allahu-Akhbar!*"

The young man's voice showed absolute determination for what he was about to do, what he had studied and worked and aimed for single-mindedly for twelve years. He would soon be *shahid*, a martyr for truth.

Al-Wahab looked up at the full moon, hanging low above the date palms like a prize, so tantalizingly close. An arid, cheerless smile creased his face. *Fahd al-Sharfa will die magnificently*, the darkly ominous terrorist leader smugly concluded. *Or not. If he hesitates at the last moment to kill himself, Massoud Rashid will kill him, take the weapon from his dead hands and push the button. Either way, I will annihilate Luna City and the space stations and the whole world will witness the vengeance of al-Wahab's Ah-mar Saif!*

The screen went black.

FAHD

Beloved seeker of truth, it is not what we do not know that hurts us,
it is what we know for certain that is false.
Kirsan Tabiyat

At first, there was a blinding flash of pain. I felt a thousand needles pierce my body. I heard screams. And then the blackest night I had ever seen swallowed me whole. I found myself floating in a dark passage, tumbling head over heels again and again, then drifting, rolling through a dark tunnel. I was dead. But I was alive, aware. I caught a glimpse of a golden light and I knew I had to move toward it and away from the darkness. As I thought this, I felt myself being sucked upward faster and faster on an obsidian channel of air. I could not see anything around me but the tunnel. I felt heavy ropes falling away from me as I willed myself upward toward the light at the other end. It was as though the ties that bound me to the world I knew had been severed with the explosion that killed me and now I felt myself becoming lighter and lighter and moving faster and faster. I looked up. As I changed, the light at the end of the tunnel changed, became clear, brighter, radiant, intense. And then I was there!

I was met by a group of sun-bronzed Mahrat elders, men who were glowing from the inside like bright golden lanterns. They greeted me as a man of great worth. *"Salaam marhabat, ahlana wa sa laam*," Hello. Welcome. Welcome home, rang in my ears. Brilliant light came from everywhere. Yet it was as delightfully cool as morning shade in the wadi.

When I beheld my body I could see no signs of the explosion that had torn me apart. I was whole. Dressed in the purest white raiment. The delicate scent of frangipane rode foremost on a gentle breeze, surrounded by the countless fragrances of a garden brimming over with fragrant flowers, where running waters gurgled down channels of the purest gold.

My grandfathers appeared and embraced me with tears of joy, kissed me on both cheeks. "Young man," they told me, "You have become *shahid*, a martyr."

A wave of cold fear slashed through my consciousness. "A martyr?" I demanded of them. "Does this mean Luna City and the two space stations have been destroyed?"

"Calm down, young Fahd," they responded. "You have become a martyr for truth."

"Truth? What is truth!? And Quenby! What of Quenby? How do I find out what has happened!" I tried to shout.

I say "they spoke" and "I spoke" but it was not like that. I found no words coming from my lips. Yet the grandfathers clearly understood me. We did not speak. We thought at each other and our thoughts were like words, but with full meaning and emotion such as words cannot express.

"All will be revealed in due time child," they told me.

"Then am I in hell? Is this an exquisite torture to remind me of what I could have had? What I could have been?"

One of the grandfathers passed a soothing hand over my brow. "Patience. Watch. Listen. Learn."

What have I done?

Then fatigue overcame me. I do not know from where the

71

sleepiness came, but I was overwhelmed. I slept for what may have been days, or weeks, I cannot say.

When I awoke, I found myself in the presence of two Imams. When they drew closer and I saw beyond their black dishdashi, I recognized them as great Yemeni holy men from the past, but wonder of wonders, not old, as the pictures I had seen of them on earth, but young again, with faces devoid of wrinkles, save for the serious demeanor with which they regarded me.

Where am I? In a mosque? Am I to be judged? Found wanting, guilty? Condemned to eternal hell?

At that precise moment, a small red spirit in baggy white trousers and a large blousy white sleeved djabella appeared seated on a golden cushion behind the Imams. *My judge!* Though his bright, pebbly-grained red skin and the huge glowing mass of curly silver hair that stuck out from his head was oddly familiar, and I knew I had seen this type of creature before, it made me wonder if he was an angel or devil. Still, I was somewhat comforted to see him in such garb. I could tell he was of the desert.

At least I shall be judged fairly. By one who knows the ways of the desert and the value of honor.

He drew closer. I could see a cascade of skin folds bridged his hooked nose like waves of crimson sand, spreading upward and outward in a triangle rising right up through his forehead like the root of a bush firmly planted within his skull from which a wooly shrub of silver hair grew. His dark eyes were profoundly mysterious, an abyss as endless as the deepest cave in the Mahrat mountainside.

And then it struck me: I had seen a being similar to him on Luna, yes, it was Luna. I became certain of that. Though the details of the incarnate life I had lived wavered in and out of my consciousness, the diminutive, crimson-skinned bipeds with silver mops of lightning-bolt hair were entirely too unique to be forgotten once encountered. *Yes! He was of the Jabar.*

The Imams bowed reverently toward him, and addressed me. "*Salaam Marhabat.* All honor to Allah, the One, the Perfection. May our song bring joy to His ears." Then their faces became as solemn as their words. "Fahd Abdul al-Sharfa, it is a great honor to the Mahrat that Imam Kirsan Tabiyat of the Jabar has come to judge your worthiness, to bring you further into Allah's truth. Listen well to his words. Take them to heart. As you studied on earth, study well here!" They threw their arms around me and kissed me on both cheeks. "You have been called. If you prove worthy, you shall be chosen to unleash Allah's truth on the works of Satan." They turned and bowed once more to the little red man, then disappeared in the flick of a goat's tail.

Kun namla wa takul sukr

fluttered in golden letters before my eyes, dancing in the air then slowly dissipated into the ether. Their parting guidance for me, the ancient proverb, Work like an ant and you'll eat sugar.

My jaw dropped in wonder. I gasped. I felt the radiant inner light from the crimson Imam sweep over me. I felt dizzy, caught in a thrall. I had died. I was alive. But I was on trial. *And no one seemed willing to answer my questions. Why?* I bowed low, then slowly lifted my head to turn my gaze to the holy man who would be my judge, determined to seek the truth.

The angel-Imam's dark eyes blazed as I thought these things. Kirsan Tabiyat touched his bright red seven-fingered hands to his forehead and extended them together, palm upward. The soft white sleeves slid back revealing the rubbery skin of his hairless red arms.

A silver Qur'an and a pomegranate appeared beside me.

"Fahd Abdul, it is good you seek truth."

He could perceive my most secret thoughts!

"By the grace of God I bring a gift for you, a personal copy

73

of the holy text from El Adem, the Kitab-al-kashaf."

I took the holy book in trembling hands and opened it. The words were in delicately lettered Arabic. *The book is from another world, yet in Arabic? How can this be? And is it truth?*

Again, he responded to my innermost thoughts. "This book is truth, written in Kabir, my language. It appears to you in the language you know as it would to another who knows yet a third or a fourth language."

With his long fingers, he dissected the pomegranate and offered me its fruit, red and juicy. He spoke soothingly and I felt cool breezes sweep across my brow like the sweet morning breezes of Wadi Shiban when the dates are ripe. "You have been called, Fahd Abdul, seeker of truth, to take on a task, as I have been chosen to assess and assist you if you prove worthy."

I felt the bittersweet pomegranate fruit seeping into my very soul when he spoke these words. *A task? Was there yet more to do even beyond the grave? Grave? What grave? A thousand questions began to swirl in my mind like a desert sandstorm. A flash of memory made me shake like a date palm in the howling wind. Luna! The space stations! Quenby! What has become of Quenby?*

He passed a red-rippled, rubbery hand over my brow and the scent of sweet bougainvillea now filled the air as he spoke. I could almost see the thoughts forming in his mind, and I began to feel myself calming and to sense the importance he placed upon this choice.

"But why are there great blind spots in my recollection? Why can't I remember what happened?"

"You have suffered a great trauma. On this side of the veil, one does not just remember, one relives the experience. All shall be revealed in due time. But we have little time and much to do."

"Time? Much to do? What do you mean? Why am I here? Why are you here?"

"In a very short while, a unique opportunity to serve truth will be presented to you. A task as bittersweet as the fruit you eat. But you will need to choose which fork of the road before you to take. You may choose the sweet without the bitter if you wish. Because the time is so short, and the opportunity, once gone, will never come again, I am here to help you prepare."

He offered more sweet-sour pomegranate seeds to me in long, slender fingers as red as the fruit. "Let us begin where we must. You know that you have died."

"Yes, Imam," I replied, "Some time ago, in an explosion on Luna. I felt myself leave my body. Then I passed through a dark tunnel and arrived in a place of light."

He folded his seven-fingered hands together in silent prayer, then uncurled his seven-toed red feet from underneath him, before he answered: "It is a good sign that you recognize you have died to the physical plane. Some people never truly realize they have died. They go on imagining their old world and so create a new one: different, but similar, with new people, new but somehow familiar places. They are somewhat aware that they are no longer who and where they were, but they're indifferent to that, and they go on, almost as before. Others realize they have died but yet are alive. They have no faith in an afterlife and become confused. Still others, believing they have gone to heaven, live in what they imagine that heaven is. As you have recently done."

"Imam, I am told I have become *shahid*, a martyr for truth. But if you know my inner thoughts, you know I must ask how can that be?"

Kirsan Tabiyat unfolded his hands and held one long red finger upright. "We shall get to that in due time."

I felt crushed, shamed. *What was it I had done that was so terrible he would not speak of it?* I felt a cold black chill sweep over me. Blackness and despair beckoned.

And then I felt Kirsan Tabiyat's soothing hand reach into my mind, bringing me back from the hell-world I had descended into.

"Take care, young man," he gently chided. "You have let your imagination run away with you. Once you have died, imagination becomes more important than anything else. Whatever you imagine becomes real. Without the physical limitations of a body, your thoughts are free to create your world. It takes some getting used to," he added with a shrug. "Awareness is the key to progress. Whatever mental discipline you developed, to the degree you developed it, becomes your safety net in this new world. Without discipline, you drift, remain stuck in the same place, or fall into lower states."

His silver-hair glowed.

He paused. "Are you ready to hear the truth? Allah's truth about the greater jihad?"

His dark eyes burned into my soul and I became fearful as he had read my mind once again. But he waved his hand gently over my head and all fear dissipated. Then he spoke.

"I ask again, do you seek truth, Fahd Abdul al-Sharfa?"

I nodded mutely.

"You wonder if you are *shahid*, an Islamic martyr."

It was a question in the form of a statement. I nodded again. He went on. "There is no martyrdom without struggle in the cause of truth."

His long-fingered crimson hand held out the last bits of pomegranate seeds to me. "So let us seek truth, Fahd Abdul. The bitter with the sweet. The full aim of jihad is to establish and uphold the truth. Recognize, declare it, and be ready to die for its sake and thus become the model for seekers of the truth."

Yes. I knew this. And I felt, deep in my heart, that I had failed.

He stood up, walked in a circle, sat down again in one swift, easy motion, looked straight into my eyes and announced, "*Shahid* means model, true guide. The men whom Faisal al-Wahab brought you to were not true guides. They misled you in many ways. You began to perceive this when you were confronted by the Imam Sai'd bin Jubair on Luna, when you attended his lectures."

What! I could not believe my ears. *How could he know all this? How could he become aware of my innermost feelings on Luna?*

"Your mind was led astray by false guides on earth. But your soul is pure. You are a genuine seeker of truth. That is why you have been given this unique opportunity to learn so quickly after passing over to the afterlife and if you choose, to take on a special task. That is why I am here."

What special task? I've been fooled once, why should I believe even this being that seems to be able to read my mind? "Do you say that you are a true guide, then?" I queried.

Kirsan Tabiyat waved one hand in a circle about his silvery head. "I claim nothing. A model attracts and leads people to the truth. He does not force or mislead them. The prophets are called *shahid* because they are the super models of the way of peace and truth. Follow my words, regard my thoughts, observe my actions and judge for yourself. Seek the truth, not a simple set of rules to follow, black and white declarations of right and wrong. Redemption must be earned and deserved. Not everyone who says Lord, Lord shall enter paradise, but he who does the will of Allah."

"Earned?" I shouted. "How can I have earned redemption after what I have done?"

Now he leaned forward, and his dark eyes bored into my soul. "Those men who came secretly through dark, dank tunnels into the basement of al-Yasir's house, who trained, terrified, threatened, and beat you until there was no doubt you would pass the Lumina screenings, hounded you relentlessly, reminding you what the price of failure would be, forced you, misled you like a rat in a devilish maze . . . and you realized that on Luna in the presence of Quenby of Alvar and Sai'd bin Jubair. But like the rat in the maze, you were trapped!"

He drew back and his eyes swept mine with the kindest, most loving feelings, as I felt my mind swirl and spin with the realization that he knew the darkest secret of my training, and the depths of my despair on Luna.

"What is truth?" I moaned.

A carpet of great intricacy appeared beneath us. The Sage rose and circumambulated the medallion in its center, softly murmuring *Alláhu, Alláhu, Alláhu, Haqq*. Then his blazing eyes seized me.

"Yes, we seek *Haqq*. Truth. And we have little time before the crucial choices you have will disappear and you will lose your greatest opportunity. On Earth, you learned both obedience to the will of God and the scientific method, which is to question, to doubt, to demand proof before believing. I can see the scientific method becoming stronger in your mind. So let us move forward. Doubt everything I say, but suspend that doubt momentarily and ask yourself, 'Could it possibly be true?' Ponder what you hear and see. Draw your own conclusions."

Now, he sat with the medallion between us.

"You were told by al-Wahab that you would have seventy-two virgins—*abkarun*—for wives as reward for your martyrdom, were you not?"

"Yes!" It now occurred to me. "Yes! I was!"

"So where were they?" he asked with a sweeping motion of his billowy white sleeves.

I had no reply.

"This is not *Haqq*," he said shaking his head sadly and sighed. "The accurate translation of the word, *abkarun*, is angels, not virgins.

Did you not see angels when you awoke on this side of the veil called death?"

Yes, I did, but he asked me to doubt, and so I queried back, "Are there no doe-eyed *houris?*"

"Remember what I said about imagination. There is what you want." And then with a candid grin, "And for some, there are dark-eyed angels of whatever choosing they have, and there is nothing wrong with that." He paused, looking deeply into my unbelieving eyes. "God is great. God has promised the believers, goodly dwellings in a garden of perpetual bliss. Is sexuality something to be feared, repressed and a work of the devil? Do you believe that? Tell me! Whose truth is that?"

In truth, I had wondered about that even as I was being trained in the path of *shahid*, as my pro-western *takfir* persona was being created, and my scientific education perfected. Though at the time, I dismissed these thoughts as unworthy, temptations of the great Satan, as I had been taught.

I thought for a long while, weighing what he and they had said, and in my heart knew he spoke truly.

I sat, confused, ashamed to respond.

"You have been told the prophet said, 'The smallest reward for the people of paradise is an abode where there are eighty thousand servants and seventy-two wives, over which stands a dome decorated with pearls, aquamarine and ruby as wide as the distance from Damascus to Sana'a.' But how can this be? From whence come the servants and wives?"

A billowing wave of frangipane swept over me, bringing a sense of ecstasy, when he continued, in honeyed, loving tones, "The important word here is, 'smallest'; this is available to those who wish it, but it is the least of the elements of paradise, and for the least of its inhabitants, not the greatest. So for the least of Allah's beloved, the smallest reward must come from the imagination."

I started. This man's words rang true. Could it possibly be so?

As if he read my mind once more, Kirsan Tabiyat held one long red finger upright to re-emphasize the point: "I told you that whatever the dead imagine becomes real. Is this not possible?"

I nodded.

"Many Imams look upon the seventy-two virgins story in the same way that many Christian theologians look upon the idea of spending eternity in heaven sitting on a cloud playing a harp with the angels."

The little man stopped, cocked his silver curled mop to one side as if listening to a far-away conversation. "I will," he said to the air.

Then he turned to me. "These false guides misled you about the seventy-two virgins because they misunderstood the Qur'an. They read into it to find what they wanted to find, rather than reading it for the truth within it. They misunderstood the truth. Perhaps they deceived themselves. But they definitely deceived you."

I was stirred by these words as if a sword cut through my soul. Kirsan Tabiyat had penetrated to my deepest doubts. What had appeared as truth to the young boy from the wadi had faded into questionable assertions to the young man. But the supposed wise men surrounding me had taught me otherwise. I had failed to trust my own instincts, relying on their words. *Were they true practitioners of salama?* In my heart, I knew the answer. Yet I had the duty to save my clan from their murderous hands.

I felt waves of guilt and sadness sweep over me and I thought I would be lost. *What had I done? Sacrificed truth on the altar of false honor?* My failures dragged me down like a millstone around my neck.

Kirsan Tabiyat's hand and voice reached out of the gloom to pull me like a drowning man out of a sea of misery. "Take heart,

Fahd. Though you feel great pain, in your struggle on Luna to pierce the veils of ignorance that blinded you, you succeeded far more than you realize. And now, continue your search for truth. I invite you to come with me."

Then Kirsan Tabiyat lifted his hands and the carpet took wing. We flew along the wind into the desert, until we came to an immense garden of sand, rock, and brown, red and yellow thorny plants. Paths of raked white gravel led toward a jebel and we flew upon the carpet through spiny rows of barbed trees and succulents along the garden paths, until we came to a baked clay entranceway, went into the hillside along a corridor of thick clay walls and came to a well-lit central room, with a dome refracting the sun's light and heat and filling the chamber with a golden warmth.

In the center of the room a feast was set out before us. Cool green mint tea, a tray of dates and another of succulents sliced and laid decoratively around a thick circular white rope of dip with a small pool of olive oil and lemon in its center.

A warm breeze wafted gently through the chamber.

"I knew you would appreciate some of your own home's cooking. We Jabar are not easy travelers. We prefer our home planet, much as the Nord do, and even when we no longer have a body, we like to make life as similar to home as possible, to remind us of El Adem."

I dipped a folded slice of flatbread into some exquisitely scented hummus and brought it to my mouth. Best of all though was a bowl of steaming hot Yemeni *Salta*, broth, eggs, ground meat, onions, lentils, tomatoes and *hilba*, fenugreek and grated leeks.

How I had yearned for that on Luna! I dipped my flatbread eagerly into the stew and marveled at how much it tasted like my mother's *Salta*.

My mind whirled once more. *Home? Luna? How long ago was*

that? How long have I been dead? How long did I sleep? And what is this task he keeps speaking of?

The small man looked deeply into my eyes for a moment, then drew slightly back and appeared to focus nowhere in particular, as if he were talking to someone not present. He nodded.

"Just as you were trained in the earth life, so it is in the after-life. I am here to teach you, Fahd Abdul al-Sharfa, for your soul is good. Your knowledge is incomplete, as is your awareness of reality. I am here to help guide you to the true reality. There is no worse lie than a truth misunderstood by those who hear it," the small red Imam told me. "As Ibn ben Thala has told us, truth is beautiful. But so are lies. Terrans seem to believe that faith and reason need to be at war. Either one defines oneself through the tenets of faith or makes a religion of reason. Either approach leads to error."

He gently patted the holy book he had given to me, which had appeared on the carpet beside him.

"The Kitab al-kashaf describes the interaction of faith and reason. We Jabar have no problem reconciling philosophy and religion. Our philosophy is the constant search for wisdom. A longstanding tradition we have is the compatibility between reason and faith when both are properly understood. Terrans seem to have missed this approach entirely. So let us continue your search for truth together, Fahd Abdul, for truly, we progress at the rate we choose. Here, in the afterlife, you experience whatever you imagine. You are imagining all this. Yet it is very real, is it not?"

I had to agree. It was marvelously wondrous or terrifying what the mind could do unfettered by the body.

He concluded, "Fahd Abdul, you have been called, given a unique opportunity. What you do with it is entirely up to you. But now you must rest."

Fatigue once more overwhelmed me. My mind swam, and as

I began to slip into another deep sleep I saw him cock his head to one side again and I saw the ozone shimmer golden and silver around him. He seemed to be thinking together with someone: a female in a white hooded robe.

An image of Luna and Quenby began to form in my mind. *Quenby. What of Quenby?*

From the ethers, Aidan's voice reached Kirsan Tabiyat.

You're not telling him everything, Kirsan. Time is running out, she cautioned.

Not yet, the deceased Jabar philosopher responded. *He is not ready.*

But he must remember.

I can't make him remember. Only you can.

ALPHA

What you seek is seeking you.
Rumi

Two months earlier, before the explosions, before the deaths, just as the sun rose on Terra, Aidan and Robert Walker began their morning meeting. It was 6:45 a.m. the day after Pardek's revelations on the Krieg battle cruiser. Aidan and Robert had finished his cook's perfect eggs Benedict and were working on a silver pot of Jamaican Blue Mountain coffee.

Walker lifted a delicate white bone china cup to his lips and let the aroma linger before he took his first sip. Aidan's husband Michael was due back tomorrow from the Antal home planet Alvar. Michael was ironing out the details of a deal with the Antal firm Utlåanskhum to coordinate the construction of the Mars Base habitat with Spaceventure, Walker's construction company. Starbound, another Walker enterprise, was poised to oversee emigration to Mars, with major input from Aidan and her dead. Thousands of jobs and work orders would flow through Walker's holding company, Alpha, and another small fortune would be added to the Hardeman Trust.

Or not!

Robert Walker restlessly crossed and recrossed his legs under the table. He had to be prepared to meet this new threat. Not just his project, but Luna, Terra, Mars, even the Krieg homeworld, Kot, were in imminent danger.

Walker shifted uneasily in his chair and frowned ominously. He set his silver spoon down into the delicate china saucer with a little too much force and a nerve-pinching *pinnng!* He wanted to throw the cup against the wall with all his might, smash it into smithereens! "Aidan, my dream of creating a new world is either on the verge of becoming reality, or evaporating in a cosmic cataclysm the likes of which several worlds have never seen."

He desperately wanted to take action. ***No!*** *This goddamned plot is **not** going to succeed! Koscientzi must be behind it! I'll kill him this time!* He peered over the edge of his cup at Aidan knowing that she saw the ugly thought form raging through his mind. "I'm sorry Aidan," he half-whispered sheepishly.

He had become accustomed to her reading his thought waves. He owed her. He had come a long way, and she had been there all along the way to help him. Now, with Mars Base so close he could taste it, he needed her more than ever. He felt a surge of love sweep over him, and regret that she was someone else's wife. He fiddled with his shirt sleeves in embarrassment and noticed Aidan's white cheeks had a rosy flush to them. *Well, if it embarrasses her to know how much I truly care for her, so be it.*

"Aidan," he said, "You and I both know I could never have become the new person I am without you."

Aidan fiddled with the simple gold wedding band on the third finger of her left hand. "You worked hard at it Robert. Made yourself an honest man. And you know that I, and Michael, are both very fond of you."

Ouch. Touché.

Despite his unusually strong impulse control, he could feel his face turning bright red as the shame rose in his heart. He felt he had a lot to atone for. Redemption was not just a name picked out of a hat when it had come time to name the low orbit station. Most people thought it signified earth's redemption, and it did, but Robert Walker knew it was also a big part of his personal quest for salvation. But parts of the old Robert, like wanting what he wanted when he wanted it, and ruthlessly sweeping his enemies aside were still there.

His admiration for Aidan had morphed into something deeper, something he knew he could never act on. *But I can't help feeling what I feel.*

Aidan was one of the four intrepid souls who had risked the quantum intrusions to and from the Nord homeworld and successfully defended planet earth when it was a Krieg finger stroke away from annihilation thirteen years ago. They had saved the planet without him! It stung like a hot iron then and even today, it still made him want to weep! He wiped a tear away without caring that Aidan saw both the tear and the thoughts behind it.

"You know we could not have done it without you, Robert."

"But you did. You did just that! Because I was not worthy to go."

He had wanted to go with them, and still ached deep in his soul because Vitok flatly refused to allow him to undertake a quantum intrusion. Robert Walker was not used to being told he could not do something. In fact, telling him "You can't do that" was usually a certain way to see something done, soon. A lump rose in his throat and he coughed nervously as he recalled the alien's precise words, clear as day thirteen years on: "Individuals who have attained a certain status in Terran affairs, simply cannot shield their minds sufficiently from thought form contamination. I have scanned your mind. If you attempt the quantum intrusion you will spend the rest of your days in an insane asylum."

Walker knew what Vitok had not said: that one cannot rise to certain levels without committing highly negative acts of volition. And the quantum intrusion would crush the fragile shell that kept

86

such a mind whole.

Thirteen years, and it still haunts me.

"We all have our ghosts, Robert."

Yes, but how many of us have had the fate of the world hanging in the balance and been found wanting, not fit to take part? How many of us have been excluded from the most important mission that ever was?

"Yes. That's all true. But it's also true that we could not have done it without your backing to convince the tribunal Earth could succeed at transforming itself." Aidan paused. "And you transformed yourself in the process."

"Second chances should not be taken lightly."

It had spurred him on to work ceaselessly to redeem himself. He led the effort to remake the planet.

Robert Walker understood the contradiction between some of the things he did in the past and his espoused Christianity. He knew he had failed in that responsibility, become part of the problem that had brought the wrath of the Seven Worlds down upon the human race.

He was not about to give up any of his power. Only a fool did that. Robert never lost sight of the testament to what power and influence in the hands of an aggressive, courageous man could accomplish.

He was determined to take corrective action. He created the Hardeman Trust, free to fund whatever it chose among the things that balanced out the Terran drive for wealth against the drive for meaning. It was one way that Robert Walker tried to make up for what he had done when money and power had ruled him.

Yet, he knew that it would take years, if not generations for Terran societies to drop their long-standing prejudices and hatreds. He would work on earth, but the real hope for rapid change lay off-world. He would build truly ecumenical new colonies in space. The new fourth world would change the world with new ideas the way the original New World had.

Robert sipped his coffee, noticing Aidan's emerald eyes staring deeply into his, aware that she saw his thoughts, perhaps more clearly than he himself.

He had come to rely on that.

The past is the past, and I am a different man now, he told himself. For thirteen years he had walked the razor's edge between good and evil, moving men and matter, dealing with the uber-rich and powerful, and attempted to be the camel that passed through the eye of the needle.

But this morning, it seemed his past sins were breathing hot down his neck, and he felt overly apprehensive. Something truly diabolical, such as he had never experienced was afoot. Someone on earth was trying to blow up Luna City and the two space stations. Aidan had told him that the dead were implicated in the plot and that Pardek suggested Krieg dead military were involved, had shared power secrets with Terran dead and were agitating within the officer class about semi-sentient, Terran 'subspecies mercenaries' overthrowing the Empire.

And if that wasn't enough, from what the cruiser commander had so palpably revealed to her, a significant portion of the Krieg war fleet was all too ready to pull the trigger.

The Terran reprieve was now hanging by a very thin thread.

"Only a fool or a madman wouldn't be worried," Walker said aloud. "And speaking of fools and madmen, that viper, Koscientzi has been trying to get rid of me for years and take over. I can't shake the ominous feeling that he has to be involved in a plot this evil and massive."

He stood up suddenly, then sat back down and poured himself a new cup of coffee. *But why? And why now?* He racked his brain, seeking the answer to *why now?* His eyes darted all around the room, never settling on anything. Then he spoke. "We have finally obtained Seven Worlds' permission to return to Mars, and we beat Koscientzi's plan to set up a corruptible state where he could make unconscionable profits. That has to be the trigger event. But Luna is old news. How are the two connected?"

"You fought to begin creating a new society based on justice and freedom on Mars Robert, and that idea had to rankle Koscientzi."

He took another sip of the Jamaican coffee and made his mind focus on the present. He knew that the future, and true redemption for the sins of his past, lay in the stars. He was in his fifties. He did not want to be an old man, recalling the thousand and one times he caused harm, suffering those thoughts that keep returning over and over again, remembrance of things past, without the ability to right the wrongs. He intended to resolve them to his moral satisfaction while he was still at his most powerful. If Koscientzi was in the middle of this plot, well then, the time had come for the showdown between the new moral man and the old money-worshipping snake.

Rubbing one hand through his hair he stood up and began to pace, then decided he needed a smoke. Aidan rose precisely as he thought that, and followed him into the hall past the oil portrait of John Hardeman Walker, his grandfather. Ever the gentleman, Robert held the heavy mahogany door open for Aidan and followed her into the library. From within the portrait, the keen grey eyes of John Hardeman Walker monitored both of them, and behind those eyes, John Hardeman Walker himself.

French doors on the south side of the library opened onto a fieldstone terrace and an unparalleled view of several acres of lawn bordered by great swaths of high grass and then trees. Robert and Aidan heard the raucous crowing of a cock pheasant, crossed over to the French doors and watched Aidan's thirteen-year-old son Valerian stir up a pair of birds along the high grass edge of the field. They watched the boy use his super-senses to herd the birds through the high grass the way he'd been watching his Narr wolfcat, Shazam, do it, moving ahead of them again and again as they tried unsuccessfully to slink away, until they finally took to the air.

The wolfcat exploded straight up out of the tall grass like a white bolt of lightning. It leapt ten feet into the air, snapped its jaws shut around the cock-bird's throat, violently shook the bird to break its neck. Then like an aerial ballerina, long white ears sailing like wings, it did a back flip, whirled around to an upright standing position as if the air were solid ground, stretched out its long white legs and landed lightly on its feet.

Aidan and Robert watched Shazam gently carry the pheasant to Val, then raise its white furry head and lick the boy's hand with its long black tongue. Val bent down, hugged his wolfcat, which flared its silky plumed tail, licked his face, gave a soft satisfied wolf whine and gently nipped at the boy's ear.

Aidan sighed. She was watching a vicious, sharp clawed Narr mountain tavak nibble at her son's ear. Then she noticed Val and the tavak looking meaningfully, purposefully, straight at her.

Val was unique. Conceived on the Nord homeworld, Narr, the Terran boy with "the gifts," who had been a handful since, well, really since before he was born. The boy whom the Vita-Kor called the "Satt Kuwar," had returned from a journey to Narr a month ago riding a quantum wave that would kill most humans in a nano-second like a California surfer casually rides a three-foot swell, with a live tavak tucked under one arm. Not even Nord Va-Tor masters did that!

This long-legged, twenty-pound tavak, solitary predator that barks like a dog and howls like a wolf, but is capable of great cat-like leaps to bring down prey, had done what is only rarely done, chosen to adopt and look after Valerian, fulfilling the Vita-Kor prophesy, "The Yarr-Tun wolf-cat befriends him."

It will always protect you and the Terran boy and wishes to always remain with you, the wolfcat telepathized to Aidan.

Yes, she telepathized back. *I know. And it will.*

The wolf-cat flared its white tail once again. It might have been a highly efficient predatory carnivore on its home planet, ferocious when aroused, capable of killing humans but it was also hopelessly cute. And it appeared to know that.

And now the boy telepathized in turn. *Trouble on the moon, mom? Someone shooting down the space stations? How can that be? What is big enough to do that?*

He had seen what she and Robert had thought as they stepped to the glass doors. To Aidan and Val thoughts were visual, blazingly obvious physical things: solid, tangible, distinct, discernibly shallow or complex, casual or intense by color, pattern or shape.

She looked lovingly at her psionic, multisensory, Terran son who began life as a Nord fetus, conceived when his parents were deep in the psionic aftereffects of one quantum intrusion, who made the journey back to earth through the quantum waves in the womb and got a second full dose of quantum energy. The massive infusion of energy had created a being gifted even beyond the gifted Nord. "More Nord than the Nord" was what they said about both Aidan and Val.

Who was still a thirteen-year-old boy!

And Aidan saw Val's thoughts. "No," she said out loud for emphasis. "No. Absolutely not! You will not get involved in this."

Mother, he complained, *I saw what I saw. This is serious.*

Yes. It is. And that is why you will remain on earth.

Terra, the boy who persisted in referring to earth as if it were a foreign world, probably because all worlds were foreign to him, corrected her peevishly.

Valerian!

Mother!

The boy turned his back on her and began to sulkily head down the hill to the house that Robert Walker had built on the estate for his parents and himself, after they had become famous for their trip to Narr to defend earth.

That, she heard Robert think to himself, *is the future: multi-sensory humans taking their place alongside the other civilized species of the universe. And I have an obligation to see that it happens.*

Aidan turned. "You have a dreamer in one eye, Robert," she chided. "Val is more advanced than any Terran. He may well be the future, but right now he is a thirteen-year-old boy wanting to interfere in the dangerous affairs of adults. And if you want to have a future for him and the other multi-sensory children, you had best keep your other eye focused on the present situation." Quoting the Nord Jintu Kor, she added, "Do not mistake the true reality for that which you wish it to be."

With a crisp snap of her wrist, she pulled the long drape on the French doors closed. It was a signal to the boy to stop eaves-dropping, though it would do no good if he chose to ignore it.

Walker had learned to accept her terse admonitions to his thoughts. It was often unnerving not to have a hiding place. He could usually sense when she was probing his inner thoughts, and though she had asked him many times if he preferred that she stay out of his mind, had adamantly insisted that Aidan not do that. It was an exercise in trust that he shared with no one else.

92

Under the gun to form a real global community acceptable to the Seven Worlds to replace the irresponsible approaches of the past with a sustainable, rational world order that recognized man's inherent greed and irrationality without attempting to impose a moralizing ideal illusion doomed to failure, Robert had used his power to persuade enough of the uberclass that business as usual was suicidal and to form World Com with a recognition of rights and responsibilities.

Using the Sustainable Breakthrough Program he authored while still stinging from Vitok's rebuff as a starting point, he laid out measurable strategic and tactical objectives to expand the third industrial revolution into a worldwide transformation in the way humans did business.

With Krieg battlecruisers and dreadnaughts appearing at opportune moments to spread bat-like shadows across the planetary surface as a reminder of the alternative, it had been made much easier than it might have otherwise been. As the saying goes, "Nothing focuses the mind like a hanging."

Robert had taken the advice of several of Aidan's dead compatriots. The greatest minds that had ever lived on the planet joined the debate, and with the hindsight that finding oneself devoid of all material possessions can give, the deceased influenced the living Terrans to create a viable plan of action, a global market economy with a global ethic.

Robert turned and looked at the glowing holo of the seven-point outline shining in a silver base on his desk:

- an international competitive order,
- pro-growth, pro-change policies,
- recognition of the social and ecological costs,
- improved social safeguards to protect those displaced by rapid growth,

- a stronger link between the international flow of financing and the real economic goals of growth and employment,

- a balance between the drastic social and economic difference among the regions of the world,

- a legal entity with the power to stop excessive consumption of non-renewable resources, and protect the rights of the planet and its people.

Now Robert opened the humidor on the Chippendale side table, took out a Cohiba robusto, lit it and sat, fidgeting into one of the buttery soft Argentinean leather wingchairs. Blue smoke formed a cloud above his head, and then the auto exhaust sucked it silently away.

If only the enemies of change could disappear that easily, Aidan thought.

"What do we do about Natil, Robert? She intends to cut a swath of bodies in her plan to deal with the plot."

"Nothing, I'm afraid. You know how obstinate she can be, and speaking with Pardek will only antagonize her. Besides, Pardek has his own problems to deal with on Kot. He won't appreciate my interfering with his vice marshal."

"What if she decides to eliminate Koscientzi?"

"You shouldn't have mentioned Koscientzi to her," the man who controlled the World Com Board testily snapped. "That would be a political calamity!"

Then he shook his head. "I'm sorry, Aidan. Forgive me. I'm a bit tense. I'm sure you're right about Koscientzi though. His parting shot at the meeting bothers me: 'Something will go wrong on Luna,' he said, 'mark my words. A disaster will occur. And you will be the one to blame.'"

"Conventional wisdom still believes that force is required to maintain order," Aidan suggested.

Frowning, Walker added, "No, it was more the look on his face: so cocksure of himself. How could he be that damn cocksure if he wasn't behind it?"

"But what does he gain by destroying Luna and the space stations? And risking global destruction," Aidan queried!

Walker shook his head. He paused, took another long pull on his cigar, watched the smoke rise and solemnly announced "Natil would only kill Koscientzi if Pardek approves it. And that will mean the Krieg have decided to assume military control of Earth." He looked hard at his treasured assistant. "We need your peebs to come through for us now, as we've never needed them before, Aidan."

The deceased John Kenneth Galbraith materialized on the leather couch and stretched out languorously to his full six-foot-eight, making Robert start with surprise. His long oval face broke into a half smile as he added his opinion to the conversation. "Conventional wisdom. I coined that phrase Aidan," he said. "Faced with the choice between changing one's mind and proving there's no need to do so, almost everyone gets busy on the proof. Robert, you were proven correct on the Luna sovereignty question, as you will be on Mars."

The two incarnates welcomed their lanky friend from the other side, who still affected a casual business attitude, blue blazer over an open white shirt and vest sweater. "Hello Ken, what brings you here?"

"You do. You sent out a call Aidan, and all of us on the other side got busy." John Kenneth Galbraith's face turned serious. The specter cautioned them: "Koscientzi wants to make a fortune on Mars, using the conventional financial wisdom that the march of events has disproven. A free Mars means he would have to convince

95

that many more people to go along with his schemes. More people, more time, less for him. People of privilege will always risk their complete destruction rather than surrender any material part of their advantage. Intellectual myopia, often called stupidity, is no doubt a reason."

Robert Walker's eyes turned to angry slits. "He does not intend to stop there does he?"

"Worse than you know," Galbraith added ominously, "our friend Mao told me one of his contacts has credible, but unprovable, information that one of Vladimir's companies is involved with a group called Ahmar Saif—Red Sword, led by Faisal Hashim al-Wahab. According to Mao's source, this group has been planning some horrific action for many years. A number of people have been killed just for getting too close. In his anger at you Koscientzi may have slipped, and given us a clue to what they are planning. You need to check this out and quickly."

He vanished, leaving only the ominous sound of his last two words hanging in the room.

Outside in the field, Val had been eavesdropping. He'd heard everything.

STARFARER

You learn by going where you have to go.
Theodore Roethke

Later that same evening, two hundred thousand miles into space, Aidan's husband, Michael Good arrived on the high orbit station Starfarer and checked into one of the rooms permanently available for Robert Walker's Alpha Corporation in the star-class hotel. He had one Montecristo Petit Corona left from the box of Cuban smokes he had brought to the Antal homeworld, Alvar as unique Terran gifts. Michael really wanted a cigar, but smoking in the space stations was strictly limited to certain designated areas, and not even Robert Walker's special suites were exempt. He gently rolled the cigar between his thumb and forefinger, raising it to just under his nose, so he could enjoy the barnyard aroma of an unlit Cuban, and recalled that there was a lounge he could go to within a short walk from his hotel room.

"First things first," he reminded himself aloud. His eyes rolled upward and he saw Earthrise on the visi-screen. He sighed, reluctantly switched over to get the late news from Terra, then ordered the visi-screen to blank, unrolled the schematic of the Mars Habitat the Antal had prepared, called the music wave on, "Twentieth Century Terran jazz, Bill Evans Live at the Village Vanguard." The golden jazz age soundtrack began. He settled back in one of the suite's comfortable arm chairs to pore over the drawings again.

He laid them out across his lap: Utlåanskhum had done a truly remarkable design. *Beautiful! A city under glass built from the Martian sand.*

A golden dome reflected the craters it nestled between like a wadi in the high desert, protecting the red walled city against solar radiation. A meandering oasis of desert plants swept in, around, and through it all, creating park-like green space.

He marveled at the typical Antal elegance and simplicity. *Ahhh! Uplifting the spirit while form follows function seemingly without effort. Who but the Antal could create such a design? And function!* The dome itself was a solar energy collector that powered the entire city. The total surface area would be residential, recreation and social zones.

He turned the page to look at the architects' schematics of subsurface business functions, self-sustaining manufacturing and hydroponic food production levels all connected by near-silent Antal rapid transit tubes. Another page: six miles south of the city, a barely visible spaceport with retracting landing pads would welcome guests, shelter their ships from the Martian sand and dust storms and whisk the visitors underground to the city center.

Minimal footprints on the terrestrial shell. A true home for fourth world natives, thanks to Antal technology, he mused. *This is where the new world will begin!*

Michael allowed himself a moment of sheer pride of accomplishment. Robert Walker had sent him to complete a deal before the Antal winter hibernation and he had done it in style. He had successfully gotten a head start on the project that would undoubtedly save six to ten months, billions of credits.

In another month or so, the Antal would be underground for the long winter hibernation. The cold Helmar winter winds and snow would rage across the face of the planet, or rather moon, whipping the surface with hundred mile an hour, thousand mile wide storms for three months, during which the hibernating hive would be watched over by the precisely 14.2857%, the Fjortonde, who would take month-long turns keeping the machinery running at minimal level until the spring. Then the Jonan rains would announce the arrival of eight months of surface habitability.

The Antal lived on a homeworld moon twice the size of earth that teased the laws of evolution, circling the gas giant planet, Algot, as it took a thirteen-month long elliptical orbit around the system sun. A homeworld moon frozen solid for three and a half months in the winter, three months of which the sun is a distant star in the sky and the day goes from bleak to dark, that same homeworld a raging inferno for over a month in the summer. Having to hibernate twice a year gave the Antal a profound respect for nature and a grim will to survive.

They adapted by building three domed and one off-planet population center on Alvar. Because they had to devise their planetary domes and space city to survive sustained extreme temperatures, their materiel engineering was first rate. Antal quick freeze-quick thaw systems, heat and cold abatement systems, starlifters, shuttles, space stations were dependable, super safe, well-equipped, well-designed, simply superb, the best in the galaxy.

But the nature of their world also gave them a genetic cautiousness, a deliberate, measured, approach. He who is not prepared freezes in winter, boils in summer. They could be maddeningly reflective. Haste was not admired.

"We will think about that," was usually the best one could hope for from the Antal until they had taken their time to make up their minds about whether or not you and your project would be a long term positive venture of which their grandchildren could be proud. The Terran joke was that it was necessary to do it that way,

99

because it was usually their grandchildren who finalized the deal!

And though business was the lifeblood of the Antal, all business slowed down to a trickle over the summer and winter hibernations. The hive society remained the singularly most important thing to them. During *noka* hibernation, the Fjortonde are loathe to make any important decisions: the majority must approve of their actions after the *noka*. A misdeed would be terrible for one's reputation and standing in the hive community. Better to miss opportunities than make mistakes. And the surest way to not make a mistake was to take no action. The one exception, Antal intergalactic banks—computer driven—automated—were available all thirteen months of the year, mostly to keep off-worlders happy.

Leaning back into the comfort of the overstuffed chair in his luxurious suite, Michael ran a hand through his greying hair. Tomorrow he'd take the starlifter home and reaccustom himself to being the poor normal genius surrounded by his psionically-gifted wife and child.

He'd earned that cigar he was about to enjoy! *There were clearly things about the cautious, deliberate and proper Antal that we did not know!*

Yes, they were a curious race, a blend of enterprising communal capitalism, democracy, conservative liberality, and pensive hedonism. This hive culture had a monarchy, lords and ladies whose prime responsibility was to reflect proper manners and to uphold the Antal standards of principles, friendship and stimulating conversation, *renhjåalt, renskjåp*, and *rentjåal.*

Fairness and above-board dealings were absolutely required in their business and social lives. An Antal stood out by being intelligent, shrewd and a good steward, a good provider to the society. Conspicuous consumption was frowned upon: "Just enough—not too much" was one of their oft-quoted mottoes. Every business was owned by the government, itself a communal business in which each

100

Antal citizen had one share. It could be dissolved at their pleasure with a majority vote. Entrepreneurs got a bigger share of the profits and a high reputation.

And Michael had gotten thrown into the deep end of some aspects of the Antal hive-culture.

He and five Antal had negotiated for twelve days in Tarka, the political and business center. When they appeared to have a deal, the Utlåanskhum CEO, Lady Agaton, spread her silver lips and suggested with the slightest of smiles it was time to sauna. Her icy-hot grey eyes bored into Michael's.

He had a deal to close and he'd been briefed that it was a sign of trust among Antal doing a business deal to sauna then swim together, part ways and rejoin in the morning to conclude it, to cleanse oneself of business talk and then to finish the business appropriately, without rushing into something: to do it in the Antal manner, with proper caution and due deliberation. He'd been further briefed that an invitation to sauna by the Antal was like toasting the success of your venture with champagne or shaking hands on a deal prior to signing it.

But sharing a sauna with naked male and female Antal unabashedly interested in regarding his smaller, thicker, darker Terran body and displaying their own svelte, whiter-than-white, half-furred, half-smooth-skinned ones, had been, in a word, unnerving.

Particularly when Lady Agaton had languorously stretched her slender alabaster arms behind her head to pull her long white hair back and slowly twist it, displaying her two small silver-tipped breasts, reclined, presenting a sensuously slender waist and glossy abdomen ending in a silky pearlescent nest, staring all the while into his eyes with the palest grey eyes he had ever seen. Through the sauna window two of the gas giant Algot's lesser moons, Söti and Pårrl, shone pearly silver and pearly pink against a pale ginger daytime sky

101

tinged with coral pink, and aligned so that they appeared to be coming together, the sign of the deep kön . . . well, that was one of those moments of truth he had **not** been briefed on.

Then the naked dip in an ice-cold pond and back to the sauna house, where they dried off with large white towels. The unabashed Antal began with their hair and beards, then their arms, legs and finally their midriffs. Michael covered himself as best he could, wrapping a towel around his waist. The Antal were clearly sensually free and strikingly beautiful. Long white hair flailed, buttocks jiggled, breasts swooped in and out, thighs stretched out invitingly and he continually became embarrassingly aroused despite his efforts at self-control.

They noticed of course, and he felt five pairs of Antal eyes constantly glued on one part or another of his anatomy. Wishing not to give offense on their part, they giggled and chortled as inconspicuously as they could, chattering away in their native tongue. He heard the word råk, upright, used in a double entendre that seemed to amuse them no end.

Now, in his hotel suite on Starfarer, Michael shook his head slowly from side to side. *How can any male refuse anything to an Antal female in the kön? A seductive female in full kön could get a male Terran to do or say anything!*

He had only been able to decline Agaton's invitation because of Aidan's timely intervention. He recalled how the words in response to her irresistibly seductive invitation just seemed to magically form in his mind. "Lady Agaton, I have no wish to give offense to such a beautiful, enticing and desirable female," and looking down at the white towel around his waist, it was obvious he was being completely truthful, "but many of us still hold fast to the Terran *renhjåalt*, and *renhjåalt* compels me to share *älska kön* only with my true love, Aidan." He had never heard the words *renhjåalt*, monogamy, or *älska*

102

kön, union of mind, soul and body, with your true love, before! Then Aidan's face had appeared in his mind like a soft, cooling breeze. *I love you Michael. You're a sweet man and,* she chuckled, *an upright husband, and you needed some assistance.* Then she had flashed away.

If his psionic son wasn't constantly amazing him, his wife was!

He called up the link in his room and sent the following message to Robert Walker:

Success. See you tomorrow.

He was not about to jeopardize corporate security with any details. He rolled the schematic into its tamper-proof tube, sealed it with his fingerprint and placed it in the wall safe all the first-class rooms had. It was time to enjoy his success. He savored the aroma of the Montecristo one more time.

A dull fog eddied and swirled around the ceiling of his stateroom. As if it now held open the door to the dimension, a wave of slick, soft pliable grey mist rolled downward into the room. A large round man began to materialize, causing Michael to drop the cigar, which fell spinward toward the floor.

It was Bob Erickson, Michael's old chess teacher, a man who always had time for young players, always gave of himself, and died tragically young. He and Michael had enjoyed many games before and after his passing over. They had one going now: a kind of correspondence game where each player took up to three days to make his move and sent it via email—except that there was no email—Michael simply left the board set up in his study and would write down and make his move when he was ready. Two or three days later, he would discover that an opposite color piece had been moved and noted on the move pad.

But that was on Earth, not two hundred thousand miles into space. Leaving the planetary plane required tremendous energy. Very few of the dead could do it. "Bob," Michael sputtered. "What are you doing here?"

"I get around you know," Bob responded. "Now that I'm dead and not bothered by having to drag a body around, I go where I want when I want just by thinking about it. Lots of chess masters doing it. Why just last week I was in Riyadh, the week before in Moscow, before that in Rio." He moved his fingers in a discernable pattern, winked. *See the pattern,* he urged Michael soundlessly forming the words with his lips.

Michael wondered why Bob felt a need to be secretive. He stooped to pick up the cigar and returned Bob's wink. No reason to trust high orbit station security any more than one had to.

Bob nearly became invisible. He struggled to project his voice in discernable tones, ostensibly for anyone eavesdropping. "Your last move was a blunder. King to e5 will not save you. Queen to b4 and mate follows three moves later."

Truth had always been a malleable thing to Michael Good the administrator. Since "The Event," ongoing Nord and Jabar influence, and having a wife and child who could see thoughts, he had learned to be more straightforward. As a practiced dissembler however, Michael was near perfect at decoding facial expressions and interpreting voice inflections. Bob was overly concerned, possibly even terrified about something.

The connection was fading. Bob re-emerged one more time from the swirling mist. "This link is difficult. Appearing on Earth is one thing. Orbit is quite another. I've asked two trusted friends to join me tonight to help me bridge the energy gap between the living and the dead this far out into space." He looked around nervously. "I believe I'm being followed." He swallowed hard. "I'm afraid I have to speak plainly. What I have to say can't wait. Michael, old scores die hard. Some of the Muslim dead want revenge: a vicious group called

The Red Serpent Brotherhood."

"What do you mean, revenge?" Michael asked. "Who's involved on your side of the veil?"

"Some on both sides of the veil have joined forces to turn back the clock, undo the changes, remove Robert Walker as a player, any way they can make it happen. People on this side who got in their way have disappeared, can't be found, reportedly been hurled into a vile etheric effluvia. I have two bodyguards with me, but that may not be enough if they come for me."

"What about the Passed-Beyond Monitors?" Michael interjected.

"They'll act sooner or later. But the people you're dealing with are slick, way too slick."

Michael could swear he saw Bob begin to sweat. "Who are these people? What specifically are they planning?" he demanded.

Bob began to speak more quickly. "I don't have much time. I'm sure they're following me. Sabotage is being planned against Redemption, Starfarer and Luna City."

"What! Against all three? How do you know this?"

"I've been privy to a few indiscrete remarks over the chessboard. Whispered conversations off to one side of the room, unguarded PCD communications they thought I wouldn't understand or be able to piece together. But I've always been able to see the whole board and the **pattern** is there."

"Give me names!" Michael called out.

"Sssh. Please! Not so loud! I've heard 'al-Wahab', 'the Russian' and 'the boy genius from the wadi' mentioned frequently."

"What else do you know?" Michael asked in hushed tones.

"From the rumblings I've gotten recently, a major piece is now in place. I'm certain an attack is imminent."

"I need more. Tell me more."

"I have to go. You'd better have your boss's security services check it out, and quickly." He faded almost to a grey mist again, and then came back into view. "That's all I know. I think they may be on to me, but I'll keep looking and listening. And don't ignore the pattern!"

Bill Evans' piano kicked into the last mournful bars of My Man's Gone Now as the swirling mist evaporated.

Michael sat back and massaged his eyebrows uneasily for a few seconds while he committed the conversation to memory. He didn't know what to think. *Riyadh, Moscow, Rio? What could that mean? And why didn't Bob wait until tomorrow when it would be easier to contact me? Is Walker's estate under surveillance? How imminent is the threat?*

He took three long deep breaths and began to regulate his breathing as Vitok had taught him. He visualized the Jintu Kor before him, repelling fear, greed and sloth, to allow the true reality to wash away his fears, hopes, and desires about reality. Now he focused on clearing all thought from his mind, until he went into the Kir, the Nord trance state to allow the cosmic hologram free reign within the individual consciousness. Deeper and deeper, until he could no longer sense his own being as a separate entity and he had a flash of clarity. *Tell Aidan now.*

Michael slammed back into his body with a shock.

He took a moment to regain his equilibrium and strode purposefully out the door, down the hallway, and through the retro blue neon lined entrance into the Star Lounge. The otherworldly sounds of Yokohiko Kawashima's Night Orbit, ethereal lowing saxophone and bowed Antal lute, punctuated by sharp raps from bamboo hyōshigi clappers, just at the points where a listener might have drifted into the hypnotic reverie the music induced. *Well, I'm not the only Terran who's been entranced by the irresistible Antal.*

He ordered a glass of Kumla and waved the cigar at the short, pear-shaped Coryllim bartender, who smiled, "Welcome to the Star Lounge Terran friend," pointed one of his four stemmy hands at a table where Michael would be able to smoke while he reached for a stubby, fluted Kumla glass with another hand, the bottle with a third, and wiped the bar top with the remaining one. He clip-clopped daintily over to the table on four small hoofed feet, smiled obsequiously once again, said, "The Kot rabbit tenders go very well with Kumla. My Krieg patrons relish the combination," as he placed the glass of Kumla delicately in front of Michael with a six-fingered, half-webbed hand.

Michael shook his head, "*nnn, mymor.*"

"*pfirus abyt pyo infito, vob saggio Terran,*" the Coryllim responded in abyt, his small pink lips pulled back from beaming white teeth. Then, noting the panicky look on Michael's face, he switched back into Terran English. "Perhaps, one so galaxy-wise would prefer the pickled Kuldorian swamp viper?"

"No, thank you," a relieved Michael, whose abyt was restricted to three or four phrases, responded. "The cigar is sufficient."

The proprietor turned to face Michael and at the same time directed his rear eye toward the bar, where a slightly shorter Coryllim had replaced him. A sign passed between them. Michael assumed that was Mrs. C by the way the Coryllim behind the bar continuously looked at the two little Coryllim *saplini*, slightly over three feet tall, who pranced from table to table, bussing dishes and drink ware. Michael knew from their reedy greenish brown color and size they were not mature. The taller of the two was beginning to show signs of adulthood. Its ears and snout had turned light brown. Creamy cashew colored streaks ran vertically along its elongated body.

Good business: the little ones draw curious Terran stares, and doubtless-ly customers. Droids would have been efficient but not as effective a tourist attraction, and why spend money on droids when you had saplini who could learn the business while they grew?

He took a silver torch from his pocket, fired it, and lit the small cigar, watching the bluish-grey smoke rise upward into the dissipater. Through the ceralloy roof of the lounge, he had a clear view of Terra, blue and green and shining white.

He looked around as casually as he could manage. The Coryllim proprietor was scurrying off to the far end of the lounge, where the eye in the back of his head had caught a table with near-empty glasses. That eye now focused on a third table that might be ready for more business, and the tavern owner fluttered the fingers of one hand in their direction, signifying that he would shortly attend them.

No one was sitting near him.

Two Antal were engaged in meaningful glances at a table along the wall, obviously in the throes of pre kön foreplay. A group of four Jabar sat around a hookah at the other end of the smoking section. Their seven-fingered hands delicately lifted sliced succulents from a platter and dipped them into a bowl of olive oil and lemon while they gracefully passed the hookah hose. Almost all of the other patrons were Terrans.

Michael had kept one eye on the door. No one had come in since him. No one had followed him into the lounge. He took another measured pull on the cigar, pretended to look out the ceralloy window while he checked the reflected images, and slowly sipped the sweet blue liquor, sensing the increased awareness and concentration that Kumla produced as it warmed his mouth and throat. His perception amplified and he drank and smoked in silence as the Kumla-induced focus intensified until his own thought patterns were clarified waves and flashes of light.

Though the Krieg were able to resist the drink's addictive nature, Terrans had to go very gently with Kumla. Even off-planet, the Coryllim proprietor would probably deny Michael a second round if he ordered one, but it wasn't necessary. The effects would last long enough for him to do what he needed. Michael knew Aidan would be on the estate in Connecticut. He formed a solid picture of it in his mind, concentrated fiercely on Aidan, and sent her a piercing beam of thought:

I need you **NOW.**

He spent the next ten minutes pretending to enjoy his cigar and repeating the message every thirty seconds.

Aidan was sitting on the patio of the house Robert Walker had built for them on the estate, with their twenty pound tavak in her lap, gazing wistfully into the sky, trying to catch a glimpse of the HOS, which was like a bright star flashing across the clear night sky, and thinking of Michael.

A soft evening breeze gently moved her long red hair off her shoulders and along her back. Somehow it chilled her. She began to feel concern about Michael, as if he were in some danger. That was silly, she thought, he would be home tomorrow. But the feeling persisted.

He needs me!

Then she wondered, *am I seeing this because I'm prejudiced to see it this way? I need him and want him to need me?*

The tavak raised its white head and began to whine softly. Val stepped through the door onto the patio. He beamed, *is something wrong, Mom?*

I don't think so Val, but I would like to have some alone time, she sent back to him.

He retreated back into the house.

Aidan began to stroke the little wolf-cat in long, calming motions. But it would not relax and she could not shake the unnerving thought that Michael needed her. She looked at her PCD: The im-

109

pression was regular, there was a pattern. Every thirty seconds. She closed her eyes and focused.

Michael heard her voice.

What's wrong, Michael?

He breathed in relief. *Thank you my love. Scan the room. Do you see any telepaths in the area?*

There's a young woman at a table in the far east corner, she replied, *but she is clearly focused on the Eagle Legion trooper sitting across from her. Why the mystery?*

Michael relaxed slightly, but kept his mind taut. *Bob Erickson contacted me here tonight with a message he said couldn't wait until tomorrow. A message I can't repeat.*

You want me to probe you and deliver the message.

Yes. He brought the conversation into full consciousness.

He felt a jolt as Aidan entered his mind. Aidan took less than a few seconds to absorb the complete conversation, visual and mental images and emotional impacts. Michael shuddered as she withdrew and a chill breeze lapped across his mind.

I have it, he heard. *I'll get on this immediately. See you tomorrow my love.*

He felt the brush of a kiss against his lips as she melted away.

There was an inch-long ash on his Montecristo. Michael gently tapped it into the ashtray on the table, which sucked the smoke and ash down and away. His job was done. Walker would get a team working on this immediately. He took one last look around the room to satisfy himself no one had noticed or listened in on their mental conversation.

But someone had.

110

Val had perceived Michael's call to Aidan well before she did.

Concerned for the safety of his father, he had projected his mind up to the HOS, but seeing no immediate danger, in respect for the ninth Nord Jintu Kor Suggestion, "Respect the privacy of others," he had made no contact until his mother arrived.

When Michael asked Aidan to check for telepaths, Val shielded his mind, leaving an empty space that could have been perceived had she been looking for such a thing, but she was not. When their mental conversation continued, he watched the blazingly visual patterns and shapes and secured the entire picture in his eidetic memory, forever accessible to him. He had just come from six months in the Yarr-Tun with the Va-Tor Masters and with his enhanced Nord vision he saw beyond what Michael and even Aidan saw.

He considered that maybe he had bent the rule a little. *All right, a lot. But evil people on both sides of the veil are planning terrible things they're unaware of. I could feel them searching, reaching out for Bob Erickson, wanting to drag him into a hell world. My mom and dad are both in danger. I've got to protect them, whether or not they think I should. They may think I'm a child, but I'm not, and I have powers beyond either of them. They need me.*

VALKYRIE

Cry "Havoc" and let slip the dogs of war.
Shakespeare

Vice Marshal Natil had her own set of rules to play by. When Aidan called her to pass on the latest information her appeal to the deceased had brought, Natil growled, "You have confirmed what my own spies have learned. This Ahmar Saif is driving the plot. *Zadank*, Aidan Good." After she curtly severed the connection, she looked over at Shafat Bajar and snarled, "I will deal with this Ahmar Saif in the Krieg way!"

She dispatched a ciphered message to Marshal Pardek.

I will immediately seize the initiative, take the fight to the terrorists, hurl them into chaos and pandemonium and crush both Ahmar Saif and this plot.

"Bajar," she snarled, "it is time to show these dogs whom they have against them. Kill every Ahmar Saif cur you find!"

With a sober face, the commander of the Eagle Legion stood up smartly, strapped on his black weapons belt, slid the sidearm out, charged it with a precise movement of his hand and replaced it in its holster. "Vice marshal," he replied, "the Eagle Legion will become their worst nightmare. We'll hit them until whatever plans they've made are forgotten in their sheer panic to survive."

In a steady, lower-pitched voice, he added, "When they see

what we can do, formerly silent Ahmar Saif supporters will be eager to talk. And then we'll find and kill the Luna plotters."

On the streets of Al Hazm in Al Jawf Province, one of the most inaccessible regions of Yemen, a phalanx of thirty heavily armed insurgents hustled the Yemeni Minister of Health to a new location to hold him until the government in Al-Mukallah paid the agreed-upon ransom.

They had been moving the terrified, blindfolded minister every other day for eight days now. The men had learned their trade in Ahmar Saif's training camps and honed it to perfection in the ten-year-long civil war. Maintaining model military precision, totally dressed in black against the night, they turned down an alley to make the last four hundred yards.

There was no moon, not a breeze. It was pitch black, deathly quiet, only the hushed sounds of their muffled boots stirring the dust.

The hostage whimpered and a pistol was shoved hard against his neck to shut him up. The entire group froze, listening.

A short night bird call, *toowheet, toowheet*, barely louder than a whisper, whistled through the darkness.

Green laser fire, white needle flashes and red projectile tracers lit up the night with an apocalyptic roar, the ripping *sisss* of blasters slicing through muscle and bone, the terrible *thwack* of bullets penetrating flesh, howls of agony and the sickening smell of cordite and burning human tissue.

Then, as precisely as it had begun, the noise and flame ceased. It was pitch black and silent again.

Ten seconds passed in an eerie, disturbing quiet.

The smell of urine, vomit and feces, mixed with burnt flesh and death hung heavy in the chill night air.

A tall, dark figure cradling a laser rifle stepped slowly, stealthi-

113

ly over and through the carnage toward the cowering hostage, picking its way through shattered bodies that lay limbs akimbo, a few who had apparently held him, torn to pieces scattered around the quivering prone creature in pools of blood.

The figure in black bent over, removed the blanket and blindfold gently from the quaking man on the ground, who had completely lost control of his sphincter, looked into his tear-filled eyes that awaited the coup de grace, lifted an aramid hood to reveal a female Afro-American face, and said, "It's all right now, Mr. Minister. We've come to take you home."

Then she signaled with two fingers and at one instant, twelve men and women appeared out of nowhere and formed a squad of warriors in full black body armor completely surrounding the scene. She reached into a blouse pocket, extracted a piece of chewing gum and popped it into her mouth without the slightest tremor of her hands and signaled again. Two men in black and grey camouflage rushed in with a bot-lift, loaded the shaking, stinking minister on it, and hustled him away.

Two Kul military aircars appeared like howling black ghosts and swept the alley with arc lights turning night into day, recording everything.

A medevac transport with Bill Peebles and four of his medical exfil team aboard roared into the village square purposefully shrieking like a banshee. It was covered by two more howling Kul aircars as it descended and then lifted the incoherent ex-hostage up and away, to a hospital in Al-Mukallah, where they would repair everything but the one severed finger the insurgents had cut off and sent to the government along with their ransom demand.

As soon as the man was safely inside, Peebles took a pulse, checked his heart, injected a sedative and shouted over the siren noise into the minister's ear, in Arabic, "God is great. Cast all your

114

anxiety on Him because He cares for you."

I Peter 5:7, he left unsaid.

A black Kul transporter silently descended into the carnage of the alley and swiftly airlifted the warriors away. They took all the insurgents' weapons but left the bodies for the locals to marvel over. A playing card with the symbol of a black eagle was placed in the hands of a few of the dead, one in the bloody fingers of a severed arm.

Then there was nothing but silence.

The Valkyrie were gone.

Three hours later, the "Al Hazm Rescue Strike" was the eleven p.m. news lead story on every channel on the U.S. east coast: It opened with horrifying, high-def, full sound visuals of the carnage taken from howling Kul aircars. A brief, fact-laden narrative of the aborted hostage attempt and the three a.m. (Yemen time) strike was given. Eagle Legion units were identified, troop strengths and number of Ahmar Saif Zaydi dead specified. And the grisly severed arm with the death card in its bloody fingers closed every story. The next morning the story was blasted across European, African, Middle and Far Eastern visi-screens.

But the most terrifying part of the report was the interview with the Valkyrie. Vice Admiral Natil had calculatedly set up a press conference for nine p.m. in a large training room deep inside the North American Krieg base to make it so.

Her fierce brown wolf face was particularly terrifying when she grinned and allowed her long white fangs to show threateningly as she introduced Wingmaster Shafat Bajar, Commandant of the Eagle Legion and Lieutenant Amaka Alston who had personally led the mission.

On his part, Bajar seemed almost serene, but the cold eyes of a killer gleamed ominously through his dark brown face. "This was

115

an exercise of the Eagle Legion Valkyrie Group," he placidly announced to the world press invitees gathered there. "What we call a blackout surgical shoot." He nodded toward Lieutenant Alston.

"Greetings," she said, as the camera zoomed in on a café-au-lait face as beautiful as a fashion model and as hard as a blacksmith's anvil. "My name is Lieutenant Amaka Alston of Hostage Rescue Team Six. This," she said with a sweeping arm motion, "is my squad."

The lights reflected eerily on twenty-four white eyes showing through flexible armored aramid face masks, twelve men and women in full black body armor.

She extracted a small computer tablet from her pocket with the complete data captured by the Kul aircars, waved it so the cameras could see some of the information.

Her dark eyes were as cold as her voice.

"In thirty-five seconds this HURT team took out thirty targets surrounding a hostage they were ready to kill who was untouched by friendly or hostile fire and removed to safety."

The cameras panned from the close-up on her face, and focused on their state of the art personal weapons systems: laser rifles, blaster pistols, dart guns, machine pistols, around-the-corner shooters, sniper rifles, rpg-launchers, night sights, fish-eye long-range-short-range sights were visible.

She let her hand sweep along the line of weaponry, and added in arctic female tones, "And if this is what we're willing to let you see, consider what we're not showing."

The cameras were back on her face: the merciless tigrine look was too compelling to pass up.

"Terrorist, this is what will happen when we come for **you**," she hissed through an icy white grin.

Bajar made a nearly imperceptible hand motion and all power

to the room was abruptly cut, leaving the camera crews, reporters and the HURT team in pitch blackness. The hair on the back of the neck of nearly every newsy rose in apprehension. When the lights came back on a few seconds later the HURT team had silently vanished, leaving only a stone faced Bajar at the podium, a fiendishly grinning Natil seated to his right, and an apparently instantly disappearing HURT team on video.

The released vids made most Terrans who watched their visi-screen news feel the hair on their arms tingle with fright.

To Natil's delight, the sound bite of the beautiful, deadly woman had gone viral.

Even as the interview was being recorded, four Eagle Legion Valkyrie squads had swooped silently down on a supposedly hidden, supposedly impregnable Ahmar Saif training camp, killed everyone, left their death cards in mutilated hands and departed in less than two minutes. That would make all the private and public electronics. That was excellent, but this, this was a triumph! She snarled approvingly, "Well done, Bajar. Just-in-time intervention, minimal action, no messy heroics, no losses, no footprints save those we wish to leave." She chopped through the air with one black-clawed hand. "By-the-book, clean, quick, overwhelming force."

Folding his wiry arms across his chest in satisfaction, Bajar responded proudly, "Team Six is probably the best of the lot. But sending a woman to do the job had the added benefit of embarrassing them. It should also enrage them. I have doubled satellite surveillance. Some ill-conceived discussions should ensue. We should also expect some hastily conceived or poorly executed reprisal attempts within the next few days. I have put six Valkyrie HURT teams and three of Commander Peebles' PERD teams on alert," he added, turning toward his superior, who whirled about to clap him on both

117

shoulders in the Krieg warrior's greeting, an incredible honor.

"I expected no less from you, Bajar. You are a model of efficiency, a pleasure to work with: almost Krieg in your methods!" She released her hold on the man's shoulders and raised her right hand in a vicious, black-clawed fist. "We'll hit them again tonight, and tomorrow, in their safe homes, in their so-called unassailable secret locations. Again and again, we'll hit them until they lose all will to fight and think only of saving their worthless skins!" Natil slammed her furry right hand down on the desktop with a loud *whap!* "So much for the Terran-bound side of the plot. Now we need our spies or that witch and her minions to reveal the identity of the Luna plotters, and then . . ." her claws extended, cutting deep into the wood, "I'll personally rip their livers out!"

Turning away from the visi-screen where the interview had been repeatedly showing, she disengaged her hand from the wood, and leaned slightly backward. She thought a moment and stated, "Using Alston on this one was a deft touch, Bajar, one worthy of a Krieg wingmaster."

Praise from the demanding vice marshal was hard to come by and worth savoring. The small, dark Terran reached into his black combat fatigue, pulled out a pack of Mangalore Ganesh Beedis, lit one, sent a puff of aromatic smoke in her direction. "It is hard for these regressive elements to accept their own females as equals. But of course," he pronounced quietly, "soldiers are soldiers, and in any engagement, victory almost always goes to the side with the greater ability to inflict damage. With our training and technology we will always have that edge. Space, time and force are all on our side. It is an unequal chess game with only one assured outcome."

Natil liked his positive attitude, competence, military bearing, and adherence to orders, S.O.P., and the chain of command. He and Peebles were so different! She had to admit, both were Terran mili-

118

tary geniuses. But Peebles had been imposed upon her by direct order of Marshal Pardek. The all-Terran Eagle Legion had been a brilliant, brash suggestion from Peebles to Pardek: a way to use Terrans instead of Krieg battle droids to police the planet, to create a minimal alien footprint on what would otherwise be a hated planetary occupation, and of equal importance, a way to ease Krieg Military concerns about the emergence of a new warrior culture.

Marshal Pardek's brilliance in this concept shines brightly. The Eagle Legion is our cat's paw, striking where we need, keeping Krieg hands clean, avoiding any intimation of occupation. Her wolfish face broke out in a toothy grin that could not be contained, and she slowly nodded her head up and down. *But we maintain sufficient Krieg force on planet to deal with any major Terran threat, force sufficient to guarantee immediate destruction of the planet, a fact the Terran power elite remains well aware of. So we simultaneously aid and encourage the progressive elements to make all deliberate speed toward the desired goal.*

With a satisfied gleam in her yellow eye, Natil regarded her Terran Eagle Legion commander with near-reverence. "I am recommending you for the star of Kulzar, Bajar."

Then the smile disappeared. She added testily, "I'm relying on you to keep Peebles on a short leash during this operation. I don't want any more showboat heroics."

As much as it was possible for her to admire a Terran, even accept one as a near-equal, Bajar was that man. She had grown more than fond of him.

She had even begun to like the smell of those cone-shaped, tendu leaf cigarettes, tied with a string, which he persisted in smoking. She knew Bajar had picked up a taste for them as a very young man in the Pakistani-Indian border troubles. She assumed that there was some reason he always did his smoking out of the public eye, though she did not know that Beedi smoking was associated with low social standing.

Bajar carefully blew the flavorful smoke away from his commanding officer, who once again, irritatingly was reminded of Peebles. Although Peebles often played the doctor card and good-naturedly berated Bajar for his habit, Natil had noted that Peebles often stood directly in the way of the exhaled smoke, and when Bajar peevishly blew it away from him, moved into it. When questioned about this he had responded, "My doctors told me to stop smoking, but not to stop breathing." She growled softly under her breath. These Terrans had some behaviors she would never understand. And Peebles, *well, he did have his good points, but discipline was not one of them.*

But they had a victory to celebrate. Everything had gone off, in the Terran vernacular, "without a hitch" and her two commanders appeared to be ready to handle the anticipated reactions. Doubtlessly, the Zaydi would bristle at the insult that a woman had defeated them and make some foolish conversation or action. She would use the Eagle Legion to crush them.

Another sweet whiff of Beedi smoke assailed Natil's black nostrils. She looked down benignly at her five-foot-six Eagle Legion Commandant, reached out a black-clawed hand and grasped Bajar by the shoulder. *Hard as a rock. For such a little guy, he can really kick ass! He's brilliant, tolerates no fools lightly, speaks five Terran languages, and, he's learned Urtok.* Yes. He was almost Krieg. *Almost.* She tightened her grip on his shoulder, relishing the way he felt, caught herself imagining how the hard little Terran would feel in the heat of Krieg love-making. Natil brought herself up short, reluctantly released Bajar's shoulder. *Unthinkable! He's my subordinate. And a Terran.* Yet she thought it. Impossible as it might be, she longed to declare her desire to join in *Ravdok* with him, a desire that would remain unfulfilled as long as they wore the same uniform.

Natil retrieved her bottle of Kumla and two glasses. Bajar drank no Terran alcohol, but he made an exception for the mind-expanding Kumla, especially on the rare occasions when his boss offered him some of her private stash.

Above all else, Shafat Bajar was a realist who coldly examined his options. When the Krieg call went out for Terran Eagle Legion volunteers, Bajar, an Olympic pistol shooter and expert chess player, was a battalion commander of the Pakistani Special Service Group (SSG), the Black Storks, personally specializing in hostage rescue and special recon operations. He applied for two reasons: one, it would clearly be the best fighting force on the planet, and two, it would be a way to learn more about the ways of the Krieg, whom he might have to fight someday. And it is wise to know the ways of one's opponent. He joined the Eagle Legion.

He and Peebles met through a service-wide chess tournament, found a camaraderie of the spirit and despite their radically different approaches to military life became the closest of friends. If things went badly, they would fight and if need be die together.

But things changed. He admired Natil's no-nonsense leadership. She appreciated his unique abilities. He soon found himself in command and almost constantly in Natil's presence. Comradeship became companionship. He learned Urtok, even grew a Krieg scalp lock.

Though he now outranked him, Bajar remained the closest of friends with Peebles. He and Peebles reported separately to Natil. Peebles' Para Rescue Detachment was supposedly a medical-only unit, but as Commander in Chief of the Legion, Bajar knew its capabilities extended to armed combat if necessary. And armed combat was what the Eagle Legion was now engaged in. Irregular or not, Peebles was the kind of man one wanted on his side when the chips

121

were down.

Bajar puffed on his Beedi to keep it going and fingered the silver-grey skydiver and mountain warfare badges from his SSG days. Eagle Legion troopers were permitted some personal Terran unit identification symbols and Bajar treasured these two more than any others he had received. Soon he would have the Star of Kulzar to place alongside them, thanks to Natil. He wished she'd reach out and touch him again. He loved the way her strong, black claws made his flesh tingle.

He and Natil raised cone-shaped glasses of the blue liquid together. He could swear he saw more than admiration in her xanthic eyes. *Did the Kumla reveal the hidden truth? That she wants me for Ravik as much as I want her?* Then he too, dismissed the unthinkable thought from his mind. *She's my commanding officer!*

He made himself focus on something else, before the Kumla betrayed him, took note of the Knight's Star with Swords that adorned Natil's collar clasp. *Every Krieg warrior covets the Star of Kulzar. And she has put me in for one. That would place me above most of them. And then? Would I be worthy of her?*

He couldn't keep his eyes from hers. He could see it. And he could see that it would mean the end of someone's military career. *Could I give this up for her?* This? They were in the business of killing and being killed. He had no doubt his Valkyrie teams would be in action soon. People would die. Some of them would be his friends. Perhaps Peebles, or himself. They had both escaped death more times than any man should expect to. Sooner or later, their luck would run out. One mis-step, one move just a second too slow or too fast. This mission could easily be their last. *Will she weep for me?*

He pulled himself together, gave the traditional soldier's toast, "To our missing comrades," wondering whom that might soon include.

122

LUNA

A mind all logic is like a knife all blade.
It makes the hand bleed that uses it.
Rabindranath Tagore

A small group of coworkers from the magnetic mass mover sat in the Aérobleu Café for a late night party in the heart of the busy Luna City Mall. Uri Spiagin's recording, Agog filled the air with bouncy abstract jazz. Lively conversations in at least seven languages swirled and buzzed softer and louder to breaks in the music. The sharp, resinous odor of broiled bog lizard, a Coryllim delicacy Yuri Petrov, the Russian astrochemist was clearly savoring, nipped at Fahd's nose. He looked askance as Petrov pressed his face within an inch of the pungent dish, inhaling deeply. "Aaah, spiced with Glisan hot peppers! Hot, hot, hot! Nothing like them in the galaxy!" the stout Russian pronounced as stinging tears streamed from his pale blue eyes. He raised his big round head and in a deep basso, declared, "Half a day's wages, but worth it. One must live while one can, eh boys?"

Fahd rubbed his own eyes, waving one hand in Petrov's direction, pretending it was the fumes from the acrid, blazing hot Glisan peppers. *Live? For me to live is to die.* Unlike the adventurous Petrov, Fahd had a plate of broiled lunar trout, fried potatoes, and a leafy mixed green salad set before him. "They didn't tell us much about the food in Luna City during our orientation, other than we would be pleasantly surprised at the variety," Fahd said, regaining his composure and tucking into the unexpectedly crispy and green baby spinach in the salad. *Life. Yes. Precious life. How much have I left?*

He looked longingly at Quenby, sitting next to him, elegantly lifting white lunar asparagus one spear at a time into the air and slowly, gracefully lowering each spear across her silver lips without spilling a drop of the lunar butter she had dipped it into.

Petrov was forgotten. Every male eye was trained on the alluring Antal astrophysicist as she sensually chewed her way up the lunar vegetable, turning it into a beguiling performance.

The dark little man sitting across the table from Fahd suddenly brightened. Sitting up straight and raising one finger, he pronounced stridently over the music, "Yes, beautiful." He paused, grinned, overly displaying a full set of white teeth, took his eyes off Quenby, and said "lunar asparagus," as if that were what he was speaking of to begin with. Clearly pleased at Fahd's discomfort, Massoud Rashid continued his monologue. "Water may be a scarce and valuable resource here, but Luna City's underground aquaculture systems are nourished by human waste products." He went on, showing off, enjoying the attention of the others at the table, "including carbon dioxide. They produce a fine supply of grains, legumes, leafy vegetables, seafood, chicken, rabbit, and even some pork," he sniffed, "for those who care to eat such things."

Disregarding the reference to unclean animals like pigs, and Massoud's brash choice of dinner conversation, Fahd forked into the flakey brook trout with the omnipresent lightweight, plasteel Luna cutlery and popped a delicate bite into his mouth. He chewed slowly, wanting to savor the tender, perfectly done fish. But it suddenly began to taste dry and unpalatable. He had to work hard to swallow it. *I have to work with this envious, arrogant know-it-all every day at the mass mover, and God help me, die with him.*

Fahd's coworkers had sprung for some expensive Moonbeer. They all raised their plastene glasses and toasted Fahd's official assumption of the Launch Master position.

Except, that is, for Massoud, who consumed no alcohol. He raised a glass of expensive water and nodded knowingly at Fahd, who nodded back meaningfully at his co-conspirator in the plot to destroy Luna City and the space stations, the man whose curling lips spread wide across his olive brown face in more of a sneer than a smile.

Quenby continued slowly lowering asparagus spears into her eager mouth, while glancing meaningfully across the table at Fahd. It was impossible not to notice the hazy pink nimbus forming itself around Quenby. It gave off an intoxicating scent every time she looked at Fahd. She was going into the deep kön again and her silver-grey eyes sparkled in obvious anticipation of another night together.

Fahd began to smell that enthralling scent of jasmine again and looked around the table to see if the other men were feeling what he was. The conversation was lively and upbeat, but Fahd could see by the way they fidgeted in their chairs and cast envious glances his way, that most of them were succumbing to Quenby's allure. The pink halo surrounding Quenby made the clear white skin of her strikingly sculpted face more stunningly attractive against the glimmering whiteness of five feet of long, straight hair that danced enticingly as the Antal astrophysicist, taller than most of the men by at least a foot, tossed her head and laughed at the Terran jokes the men told.

Under the table, one of Quenby's long white hands sensuously stroked Fahd's leg, running her sharp silver nails along his thigh, and stopping every so often to gently pinch through the pants leg of his blue Moondust Corporation jumpsuit and watch his eyes grow wide with shock and pleasure.

He and Quenby had found reasons to retire early every night

but this one. Like all expatriate communities, the Luna crowd was a tight-knit group, where work and play were intertwined. It was as important to fit in smoothly as it was to make a new member welcome: animosity and discord were two things a confined population could ill afford.

The plaintive, longing sounds of an Antal harp in the jazz cut, *Alien*, struck deep into the emotional vibrato of everyone in the room. Conversation diminished.

Then the music stopped. Several large visi-screens outside in the Mall flashed on. Everyone looked up. The howling, shrieking sound of Kul aircars shattered the lunar evening ambiance. The Al Hazm carnage, the unnerving Valkyrie interview, and the chilling closing words, "Terrorist, this is what will happen when we come for **you**," echoed through the Luna City Mall.

The visi-screens blinked off. The music resumed.

A low murmur began to spread through the crowd inside and outside the Aérobleu. "What was that all about?"

Everyone at the table but Petrov seemed to have lost his appetite. The big Russian noisily chomped down a large bite of bog lizard, washed it down with one long guzzling gulp of Moonbeer, slapped the glass down on the table and proclaimed, "We Russians have a saying, 'Wolves eat dogs!' The Krieg wolves have just announced they intend to eradicate the Ahmar Saif dogs."

Quenby's long white fingers covered her mouth. Fahd blanched, laid his fork down, watched Massoud's face turn as white as Quenby's. *Oh shit! They're on to us!*

A few people rose and began to leave the Aérobleu Café. That was Fahd's cue. He reached over to run a dark brown hand through Quenby's shimmering white hair, soothingly over her ear and down the side of her neck. "Massoud and I have some pressing business to attend to, my precious one." He glanced hard at Massoud and sent his own phony grin out at the other man. "But we shan't be long, and then I will meet you at Sai'd bin Jubair's lecture."

Quenby's frown quickly melted away. "Whatever pleases you, pleases me, Fahd, but please do not be too long." She stretched out one long white hand to touch his shoulder and ever so enticingly leaned down to nip his ear as she rose to leave.

Fahd excused himself. He and Massoud began to walk toward Fahd's quarters, trying not to appear eager to arrive at a place where they assumed there would be no listening devices.

Fahd was the first to speak when they arrived. "What does this mean?"

"You heard the Russian fool," Massoud spat out. "The Krieg sent out a news flash to announce their declaration of war on Ahmar Saif. Why else would the Luna channels suddenly broadcast it across the city?"

"Why indeed?" Fahd murmured, "It means they know we're here and have some idea of what we're doing. But if they knew who we were we'd already be arrested or dead. So they're trying to get us to act precipitously or give ourselves away."

Massoud grimaced. He balled one hand into a fist at Fahd's breach of security. Still trying to speak in code as much as possible, still maintaining the iron discipline that had been drilled into him, Massoud said loudly, "Terrible people those terrorists. They deserve whatever they get."

Fahd snapped back into the drill. *Maybe we are under suspicion. Maybe we're being observed.* "Yes. Terrible people." He shook his head in false dismay and whispered "What if they kill al-Wahab?"

Massoud's eyes became cold, hard, flinty. Under his breath, he hissed at Fahd, "Then someone else will send us the 'go' signal. Whatever happens we will not give up."

Fahd blanched again. *Of course. I knew that. Am I having such sec-*

127

ond thoughts about doing this that I wish al-Wahab dead?

"Time is running out on whomever those fanatics are," Massoud declared.

Fahd looked long and hard at Massoud. *Is that what I have become? A fanatic like you Massoud?* But he got the message. *Go into action. Prepare. Maintain your cover story.*

"Well, that doesn't concern us, does it?" Fahd announced. He swung the door of his cabinet open, reached in and pulled a vid game out. It's another broken one," he winked. "I almost have it repaired. Maybe the two of us can finish the job with the parts from these other broken ones."

They both began to work together on his desk turning the vid game into one of the electromagnetic pulse devices they would use to destroy the space stations.

Massoud leaned so far in to watch he got in Fahd's way.

"Back off, you boob," Fahd snapped, "You almost got your nose caught in the nipper."

Massoud grumbled, but watched attentively as Fahd re-routed wires and attached chips in a seemingly incongruous maze. "Ah," he finally said, "so that is how it is done."

"Yes," Fahd replied, "it should work now."

Leaning in again, Massoud whispered, under his breath, "Ahmed is in the pay of the Russian infidel. He reports what we do. Beware of him."

Fahd, startled, blurted out, "Petrov?"

Massoud's chin came up. A sly smirk appeared, "Koscientzi, you dolt."

Fahd's head snapped back. *What?* "You tell me he is in league with Ahmar Saif?" he gasped.

A booming laugh. 'From the beginning. The son of a dog funds the operation." Massoud snorted contemptuously.

128

"How do you know this?"

Massoud sneered, hissed, "Just because you're in charge now you think you know everything? Do you think I've been asleep here? The Russian promises Ahmed ten times the death price, enough to make Ahmed's family very rich."

"But why?"

"The Russian plans to kill al-Wahab, you simpleton. But al-Wahab knows this. Do you not think that al-Wahab has his own plan to topple the Russian? Are you thinking of reneging on your sacred oath?"

Fahd shook his head, stunned by the revelation. *Al-Wahab is going to blow up Luna, Redemption and Starfarer for the infidel Koscientzi! They both plan to kill each other. The only way Massoud would know this is if he is al-Wahab's button man, the assassin: the one who will kill me if I do not go through with the mission. I must beware of you, Massoud, not Ahmed.*

Then he looked down at the table top in disbelief. *And I have just shown him how to wire the vid games! He no longer needs me to complete the mission. I must not let Massoud become even slightly concerned about my desire to complete the task. Well, the less he sees the better.*

Fahd turned to the desk and made a few rapid movements with the hot glue gun. "There. I have sealed the vid game against tampering. I will conceal it with the others." He pocketed the game. *And keep them out of your hands.*

It was time to strike a pose, to act completely determined to do whatever was necessary. Fahd reached out and clapped Massoud on the shoulders like a brother. "Well, Massoud, I only have one more vid game to fix and we'll be ready to hold that gaming tournament." His dark eyebrows squeezed together. *Time to separate myself from this assassin.* "I have a lecture to attend now."

Massoud stopped his chuckling and asked in hushed but challenging tones, "Why are you going to that infidel alien's lectures with the Antal female? You and **Doctor** Quenby seem to be so enamored of his lectures," he snorted, "you haven't missed one yet."

"I seek truth," Fahd replied simply.

Massoud flashed a cold smile. "Truth? From a seven-toed alien eunuch?"

So arrogant. Unwilling to open his closed mind to anything new. "They're not eunuchs. They are sexless except for the annual mating season."

"Then they become either male or female!" Massoud hissed. "What deviltry is that?"

"It is their way."

Massoud spit out air at the cabin floor in reply.

Fahd knew Massoud had been trained by the same people who trained him. He too, certainly had a family awaiting his martyrdom and the huge death price promised by Ahmar Saif. But the difference between them was Massoud sought only death, not truth. *Death is meaningless unless it is in jihad. And the greater jihad is the conquest of the self in the search for truth.*

But there was no sense in antagonizing a disciplined, determined man willing to kill you. *Willing and likely eager to kill me.*

Once more, he clasped Massoud's shoulders. This time he brushed his cheek against Massoud's both right and left and whispered in Arabic, "*Rafeek*, comrade, I swear, *wa-Allah-el-Adheem*, by Allah the Great, the honor of the Mahra is sacred. Nothing will deter me from keeping the Mahra honor pure. Believe me, if I choose to bed the Antal female, if I choose to listen to the Jabar master speak of truth, it matters not."

They separated. Fahd took the lift down to the mall level. He stepped out into the late evening crowd, the sounds and smells of gaiety, mulling over what he had heard from Massoud on his way to the lecture hall. He saw families walking arm in arm, children by their

130

sides along the brightly lit walkways. He thought of his family. *I have sworn a sacred oath. But how can honor require me to kill the woman I have come to love, the woman who has opened my mind to greater truths?*

He recalled a stanza from Tagore the Jabar master had quoted in his last talk: "The water in a vessel is sparkling; the water in the sea is dark. The small truth has words which are clear; the great truth has great silence." *Yes, the small truth is clear: Koscientzi drives the operation. But this makes no sense. Koscientzi is a billionaire, an evil man driven only by money. He makes millions off the space station and Luna trade route. Why would such a man destroy his own money-making machinery?*

He walked past what had been the old Osiris Grill, now being renovated. The sign in the window flashed, BIGGER, BETTER, RE-OPENING SOON. UNDER NEW MANAGEMENT.

Unless, unless he plans to re-build it!? He wants us to destroy it for him so he can rid himself of some partners he dislikes and rebuild it. Unless, of course, al-Wahab kills him before he himself kills al-Wahab. But what are the chances of that? Petrov said it: wolves eat dogs. He may already have turned on al-Wahab. **He** *may have loosed the Krieg on Ahmar Saif!*

Rage swept through him. *I have spent twelve years preparing for this? To do the work of a godless infidel bent only on becoming richer? To be the tool of a capitalist?*

Fahd nearly bumped into a couple of workers from the Lunar Oxygen Facility waiting to enter the clear-ceralloy observation tower that rose from surface level to the very top of the Luna City dome.

He realized he had been walking faster and faster. He slowed down. "I'm sorry, I wasn't paying attention."

"That's a dangerous thing to do on Luna, friend!"

Yes, very dangerous. "You're right. Forgive me."

Backing away, he noticed Massoud marching rigidly down the other side of the Luna City Mall going in the opposite direction. *Massoud's looking at me as if he would really like to put a blaster beam through my brain.*

He looked up at the ceralloy-enclosed elevator that stretched two-hundred-and-fifty feet up and provided magnificent views of the Luna City complex. *Massoud, you've just given me far more information than you should have. Ahmar Saif has built a tower of glass, full of clear words that are small truths. They have set me high up in this tower where I can catch a glimpse of the greater truth. The truth of jihad. The prophet said, the greater jihad is the more difficult and more important struggle: the struggle against one's ego, selfishness, greed and evil. But what must I do?*

He set out again. More carefully. Aware of just how dangerous inattention could be.

And then, as he neared the lecture hall, immersed in thought, a long white arm slipped into his from behind. Quenby. As they walked arm in arm along the Luna City Mall, Quenby lifted one graceful arm to point out the flyers spreading their beautifully colored wings and soaring inside the Luna City dome in Luna's one-sixth gravity. "They seek to feel what the birds feel. To be free."

Fahd wondered aloud, "We're all seekers after something here on Luna. I came seeking one thing, and now I seem to have found something else." He grasped Quenby's slender waist and gently pulled her closer to him. "Something I never thought I could have."

He looked up at the carefree moon flyers, dipping, soaring, flapping their plastic wings. Fahd could not shake the thought from his mind that he would die very soon. He could accept his death. For him to live was to die. It had been that way since his twelfth birthday when the men in black took him away from his home in the desert.

He wiped a tear from his eye. *Free. They say the truth will set you free. But it will cost me everything!*

FAHD

Death is not extinguishing the light;
it is only putting out the lamp because the dawn has come.
Rabindranath Tagore

Assalamu alaikum. Peace be upon you.

It's a strange and wondrous thing, this after-death reality. On this plane of existence, every thought has a direct effect. Just now, I recalled the perfumed scent of that western fruit that was always such a rare and delightful treat to a boy from the hot desert climate, an apple. That thought led to another and another. I could taste the succulent, white flesh and crunchy red skin. I became enmeshed in a lip-smacking sensory feeling and the sweetest, juiciest, reddest apple I've ever tasted appeared in my mouth! Through force of habit I reached up with my hand to hold it as I savored each bite, licking the juice from my lips before it fell to the ground. But of course, there was no ground, no apple, no hand to hold it, no mouth to eat it. And when that thought occurred to me, it all disappeared and I felt and saw myself as a being of pure light, dancing in an endless array of radiance.

I felt I would burst from joy. And on that notice of separateness I became aware of being Fahd al-Sharfa and I was myself again.

All one truly has over here is the mind and the personality. So it is that I have been learning to control my thoughts, to regard them as passing clouds in a clear blue sky, to choose carefully which cloud I shall focus on, for over here, thoughts are things more real than

133

they appear to be on the physical plane. And one can get lost in imagination.

Over here, we create by thought: we think it and it exists. We travel by thought: we think it and we are there. We communicate by thought: we exchange thoughts. Once you get the hang of it, it is extremely efficient. If I wish to "see" a person, I merely think of him, and I am with him. If I wish to be in the desert, I think it and I am. And if I wish to eat imaginary fruits, I think them.

But it all takes some getting used to. I have often been confused by what is happening to me. I have had many surprises. Perhaps the greatest has been that, just as on Earth, life beyond death is far from simple, though one can make it so, and many do.

For me there is no end of struggle. I have a sense of urgency, as if this fork in the road will appear as suddenly as the Kitab-al-kashaf appeared at Kirsan Tabiyat's side. And I must be ready.

Just as before, time eludes me and I cannot say precisely how long I have been here. I can say that the sage, Kirsan Tabiyat and a beautiful red-haired lady have come often to guide me through difficult stretches.

"Who are you," I asked, "and why do you assist me?"

"Who I am matters little, but since you ask, I am Aidan Ray Good, and I was involved in your past life on Luna, though you cannot yet recall the details," the red-haired lady said with a wave of her long white fingers. "What matters more is that the time for your decision draws near.

"Luna. Yes. I recall Luna, but not as much as I would like. I feel my destiny was sealed on Luna."

"No man can escape his destiny. You were destined to go to Luna, but what you did there became a matter of choice. By your actions you have brought certain things into being on the incarnate plane. And by the choices you made as an incarnate, you have be-

134

come entitled to make yet one more, significant choice."

My mind reeled. I felt a great wall of energy wash over me when she said these words. *Choices?* The myriad choices I made during my incarnate life swept over me like a tsunami. They overwhelmed me. I threw myself down upon my knees, pleaded with her "Tell me more!"

She turned her pale face away, as if seeking advice and permission from some higher source to respond, then turned back toward me, her dark green eyes shining like emeralds. "One often meets his destiny on the road he takes to avoid it. I can say no more about the choice you face, other than you must prepare your mind, for the time is short."

"Time? What time? And why is it short?"

She shook her head, "I am not permitted to say." And then she vanished into the ethers.

Unlike the red-haired lady, when Kirsan Tabiyat comes to my aid, he does not tell me what I should do or not do, except by giving me things to think about. I wish he would just give me direction, but I think I understand the wisdom of what he does. Destiny is no matter of chance: it is a matter of choice. I was chosen for something and must earn my place.

I know that I must prepare my mind for this, and constantly remember that in this post-death world I will only see what I want to see and think what I want to think, and so I have to make a continuous effort to not be seduced by one thing or another and always seek to enlarge my perspective. I know that keeping my thoughts disciplined is the only way to make progress. I always believed I was good at concentrating, but now I realize I can only maintain my concentration for periods of time and then I lose it and drift off into a personal reality, sometimes into illusion.

There is a feeling of ecstasy here, and there is soothing, healing light everywhere, but I can find no particular source. They just are. It is so easy to just relax and enjoy. So tempting! I can see now why it would be so easy for people to continue in this lovely state of reverie. It could be challenging to come out of it, though it really is quite easy when one is motivated. But it is so restful, comfortable, almost addictive to go along in a dreamlike state, just be in heaven. It is so easy to enjoy the ecstasy, frightfully tempting to stop striving.

You can fool yourself by creating your own reality. Some beings over here are well and truly stuck in their own personal spaces. Quite a few are living a life so similar to what they've left, except that there is no need to reap or sow, or earn money, unless you imagine it to be so, that one would hardly know the difference.

For the most part, everyone travels at his own pace. You are allowed to be as lazy or as diligent as you wish. The sages do not often intervene, but as I have been told, I have a task set before me, for which I have been given exceptional assistance.

One of the first things Kirsan Tabiyat helped me do was to rid myself of an all-too comfortable dream-like feeling. "Do not allow yourself to drift too long," he told me. "You must use your powers of concentration to pierce the veils that separate true reality from personal reality, others' reality, and illusion. If you become lost, merely think of me and I shall be at your side. But there is only so much I am permitted to do."

I asked why the Sages do not instruct and direct much as the Imams on Terra.

He replied, "Why do we leave you alone? Because all wisdom comes directly from God. When we go to the infinite source itself we leave the sway of personalities, institutions or writings. These are good, secondary founts of wisdom and truth," he continued, raising three of his seven crimson fingers, "but they are agents, not sources." Now the Kitab-al-kashaf appeared in his hands, and, laughing, he tore it apart. I was horrified. "God is the source," he declared, chuckling at my shocked expression. "Truth is truth. Truth is within your own self. It is through your own soul that God speaks to you."

At that, the red-haired lady, Aidan Ray good, appeared. Seeing the thought running through my mind, she raised a delicate fairskinned hand and said, "Then why do we help you at all you wonder? As Kirsan said, you have been chosen just as Kirsan and I have been chosen to assist you since you have much to learn and little time. Use your scientific training Fahd. Observe, question, clarify your mind so you will be ready to see the truth when the time comes."

Their words and the parting guidance from the two Yemeni sages, *Kun namla wa takul sukr,* has spurred me to work very hard.

In my quest to learn all that I must, I have noticed that most of the people here tend to gather in groups by vocation, community, or ethnicity: academics with academics, soldiers with soldiers and the like. And then there are others, loners, who seem to be going through an experience similar to myself.

I can see why the Terran peebs tend to stay here: it's too nice to leave. But there are so many human passed-beyond here! Kirsan Tabiyat says it is a cultural thing. Other worlds have had intense interaction over millennia with their dead. Terrans have mostly ignored the dead, until they essentially saw little reason to struggle to communicate where they could merely enjoy the fruits of heaven.

And Kirsan Tabiyat should know. He is over six thousand years passed-beyond. I enquired. He would not elaborate.

"Where are the Jabar?" I asked him. "I see only humans and some pet animals the humans seem to have willed into existence."

"There is an infinite variety of beings on this plane," he responded with a flurried waving of his fourteen red fingers, "but the species tend to keep together and each species occupies space in, around and about their home planets." And then his eyes darkened

137

and with a frown he added, "And the hell worlds deep within most of those planets."

"Hell worlds? Fire and brimstone?" This frightened me.

"Yes, worse than that, for these hell worlds are created and sustained by the very thoughts of those within them. Beings who choose darkness and suffering over light and joy." Sensing my horror, the sage spread one hand wide, then slowly closed his long red fingers together into a funnel and sent a powerful sense of calm, peaceful feeling to me, restoring my inner tranquility. "But you were asking about the Jabar and the other heaven worlds, were you not?" he queried. "Would you care to see these worlds? They are accessible by thought, but going across the void is not so easy as moving about one's own world."

"Oh yes," I responded in delight.

"Which of these worlds would you like to visit?"

I thought of Quenby. "Quenby," I shouted. "Is she dead or alive?"

He reached out a long red hand and soothed my brow with four of his seven fingers. "In time you will know."

"Then take me to the world of the Antal," I insisted.

He smiled. And I thought I saw some meaning behind his grin.

Our visit to the Antal was wondrous. I felt myself moved to tears of joy when I beheld them floating serenely in one great group physically enveloped in a sing-song, humming chant. This is difficult to describe, but imagine music, a hymn, having a physical form like a great swirling white cloud and the Antal floating, swimming, darting about within it. I felt their chant reaching into my soul, touching me, making my heart tingle. These tall, chalk-white translucent beings calling to me, beckoning to me to come join with them seemed so familiar. I almost felt I was a part of them. And when I saw them I felt Quenby's spirit swirling like a cloud within my own, calling out to me, caressing me.

Now, I feel a great aching desire to be with her. I wonder, but I cannot tell what it portends. And when I speak of this, Kirsan Tabiyat and the red-haired lady merely smile and make no reply.

I use words like "took me to" and "speak" to use your words but it is not like that at all. Thoughts are everything here.

I continue to have difficulty controlling my thoughts, which for me is strange. I would have described myself as completely disciplined in this way when I was in the body on Earth. But when I see others over here, I realize that I am a neophyte at mind control.

I can sustain concentration for periods of time, and with practice, I have been able to extend those periods but there are also periods where I cannot say if I have been awake or asleep. I cannot recall where I have been, what I have done, or what I thought. Like a drunk's blackout!

Some of the beings over here are very uncontrolled. If I let my thoughts wander, others' realities intrude on mine and I become enmeshed in their personal or illusory reality and confused. It is challenging. But I usually can work my way through without Kirsan Tabiyat's intervention.

I cannot honestly tell you how long I have been here, or how long I spent on any particular occurrence. That is another thing that makes the sense of time very slippery.

In a sense there is nothing but law operating here, a law so strong it needs no rules. Powerful in its simplicity. Every thought goes out and returns laden with thoughts of its own kind that it has attracted to itself.

Kirsan Tabiyat advised me that would happen. It's quite amusing! I didn't realize how much I would miss having a set of rules. I didn't appreciate freedom would be so difficult. But God

139

knows best!

I know that I spent periods of time being very angry with my-self, and very ashamed. It is a bit of a blow when one comes over here and looks back at parts of one's life and can see them objective-ly. Highlights, crossroads, periods when your life could have gone one way or another. I did not realize what it would reveal. Some of it was shocking. I saw and felt myself wanting to seek truth and love, but making bad choices over and over again. Some of the things I re-experienced were so powerful they sent me into one of the blackouts I spoke of.

It's like replaying a holo: you don't remember something, you replay it, only you're actually experiencing the whole thing again. You don't see and feel it in sequential order, rather all of it at once, yet selecting one bit to focus on.

It is difficult to describe.

I find that there are many things I cannot remember, or see clearly. I am experiencing difficulty remembering certain things about my earth life, like my death. I have an absolute aversion I cannot ex-plain to seeing it. When I draw near to the explosion that killed me, my whole being shakes and I lose awareness, waking up sometime later.

Once, I saw myself with Quenby. She was distraught; I was wiping blood from my face, but the emotion was so overwhelming I passed out.

I woke to Kirsan Tabiyat soothingly telling me "When you can deal with the emotion you will see it all clearly. Do not worry needlessly. Just keep trying. It will come when it will."

"But why does this happen, Kirsan? Please tell me why."

"There are certain areas of yourself that you must yet learn more about and explore more thoroughly."

I pressed him for details, but all he would say was, "Think

about the prejudices and fears we hide, even from ourselves. Pierce them and you shall pierce the veil of remembrance."

I find myself remembering Quenby more and more often. I know we shared a great love. I know it was on Luna. I can recall many more instances being with her. Some of them make me quite ashamed of myself. My fear, my lack of trust become glaring cowardly acts when I see, or rather, experience them on this side of the veil and at the same time experience the emotions she felt at those times.

I'm not sure if this is reality. It seems to be so. But I have to be careful of creating a personal reality from desires or illusion.

Interestingly, whenever I question the reality of what I am seeing at the time my perception of it alters. Given that my truly weak powers of concentration and my own lack of awareness are holding me back, I realize that I should have spent more time in contemplation. But I push on. Whatever this task that I am being prepared for is, I must do all I can to make myself ready.

Truly the possibilities of this afterlife are beyond comprehension, and the glimpses one gets of greater spirits are miraculous. I can understand now why so many who achieved spiritual advancement on the earth had to go off by themselves, for in helping others, there is sacrifice.

And Kirsan Tabiyat is one of those who have sacrificed their own advancement for the love of others. Thanks be to God, I have been blessed to have this man take such an interest in me.

I have almost limitless choices at this point. They can last as long as I wish them to. But I feel driven by an inner urge to go in one direction and I follow that urge, though I would be hard pressed to tell you what that direction is. I only know that I must go that way.

I find that my ideas are constantly changing. I notice that when my ideas and thoughts go through a major transformation, my surroundings seem to transform as well. This makes things difficult.

It's like the earth under your feet shifting, not being solid.

But I guess that's because it's not, is it?

I find explaining difficult.

I find words clumsy now.

There are different concepts here. I have difficulty conveying the sense of timelessness here. The temptation to linger, versus the urge to go on. I can see many changes in my personality, character, essence. A work undone. A thing remaining to be completed.

I feel closer to the knowledge I want. I feel a sense of urgency to face the unknown.

LUNIE

Love is the only reality and it is not a mere sentiment.
It is the ultimate truth that lies at the heart of creation.
Rabindranath Tagore

Quenby fussed over the pull-out cooking unit in her apartment. She was irradiating a müusarüuta and the scent of turnips, carrots, and potatoes flavored with a little rabbit meat, all produced on Luna, filled the room when she lifted the clear crysalite cover and bent over the dish flaring her delicately chiseled nostrils wide. *Yes. It smelled like home.*

She set it in the center of the silver silicate table that slid down and out from the wall with a tap of a touch plate, rearranged the black silicate chairs perched at each end of the dining counter for the third time, making a perfect cozy table for two, dispatched the cooking unit back into its wall compartment, and looked once more all around the room.

Her Third Level Luna City apartment had fifteen foot high ceilings, which made them particularly attractive to seven-foot tall Antal, several of whom resided on this floor. She reached up to the touch plate that controlled the lighting, sliding a long white finger from side to side until the ceilings were dark and softly star-studded, making the apartment seem outdoors. The entry was welcomingly bathed in a soft golden glimmer, the sitting room subdued and the dining area swathed in the golden glow of simulated candlelight. Her black tableware glimmered slightly.

She had the privacy level on the window wall set to opaque so they could see out but no one could see in. *Yes. Perfect.*

A soft bird-song whistle made Quenby check the new message on her PCD. *On my way. Fahd.* She strode into the bedroom, whisked off her apron and tossed it into the waiting clothes bin.

Then she reached back and untied the silver ribbon holding her hair up, shook her head gently to let the luxurious white tresses fall seductively down her bare back, and checked one more time in the mirror. Her sheer white silk gown hung from one shoulder across her breasts and swept sensuously down her long legs to trail ever so slightly above the floor. She set the bedroom lights to dim, strode back into the living room and looked around once more.

The apartment was inviting, quite a bit nicer, not to mention larger, than the Lumina Corporation bachelor quarters. Those were designed for six month to a year temporary occupation. This was luxury long term living quarters for Luna residents. Though both were constructed of waterless lunar concrete, Luna City residences had softly tinted colored lunar plastic covering, where the more utilitarian corporation quarters were concrete throughout. And in the luxury levels molded furnishings slid away into pockets in the high walls when not in use, maximizing floor area and creating a sense of spaciousness.

Quenby was a Lunie: a permanent resident; a lunar citizen. Antal usually came for eight month assignments, rotated back to Alvar for the kön and the *tunnelban noka* and reintegrated back into the all-encompassing Antal society.

But on her first rotation back to her homeworld, all the feelings of separateness and alienation she had felt as a young female hit her like a smothering blanket. She had always been a freethinker, skeptically regarding the accepted ways of the hive society. All her life, this had set her apart from the mainstream of Antal society, where service, duty, the society, and "fitting in" were prime directives. Only her absolute brilliance had saved her from becoming more outcast than she made herself and now that she had been on Luna, the culture shock of her return home proved it to her. She was ineluctably *egen anüt*: an outsider.

Her mother and brother had greeted her warmly, invited a large group of friends to their modest residence in a grand day and night *sämhallkomst* celebration to welcome her home. Like a massive swarm, her former friends, teachers, associates and lovers came by to offer companionship and conversation. She struggled with the desire to want to be like the others, took part in the group saunas, the naked swims, the kön, to no avail.

Desperate to bring her daughter home, her mother Petra had managed to get Quenby an appointment with Lady Gota of Utlåanskhum, who was quite interested in hiring the space-experienced young woman to work in space station manufacturing. The assignment would be on the off-planet city, Bodil. Petra and Gota hoped that being off-planet on Bodil would satisfy Quenby's need to be different. That need that was so painful to all who knew her.

Lady Gota gave Quenby star treatment: took her on a private company starlifter to Bodil, a mini-shuttle circuit of the great space yards where the next generation of space stations were being designed and constructed, and personally toured her through the professional engineering areas making certain she got a good look at the abundance of young Antal males who made a point of tossing their long white manes and attempting to make eye contact with her. A few were brash enough to wink in un-Antal-like fashion when they thought Lady Gota's eye was not on them.

In equally un-Antal manner, Lady Gota actually pressed her

case for hiring the attractive young aerospace engineer during the ride back to Alvar, while they sipped private-label Bodil Üle and ate delicate slivers of äskåarfiska on thin wheat crispbread.

In deference to proper Antal manners, Quenby responded: "I will think about it." But she knew in her heart the answer would be no, thank you. Yes, the work would be pleasant, and all those pretty males nice to have around, but in truth, despite the kön, they and Bodil were not foreign enough, not nearly wild enough.

After tasting the freedom of the overly-independent Terrans on Luna, she found she had an unslakable thirst for adventure, for experiencing other worlds, other species, sharing their strange ways.

Of all the Seven Worlds' peoples, the Antal were the most self-consciously well-behaved and civilized race. Terrans were savages, impulsive, primitive, irrational, prone to violence, uncivil. She found them raw and exciting and she wanted more. She could not pretend otherwise.

As the starlifter touched down on a spotlessly clean, well-laid out runway in a well-designed, efficient spaceport, Quenby knew absolutely she could not abide the not-too-much-just-enough Antal mores. She wanted to experience too much, to wallow in it, to sate herself. If and when she reached that point of satiation, then, only then, might it be time to return to safe, secure, predictable Alvar.

As soon as she reached her mother's home, she notified Lumina Corporation of her intent to re-up again as soon as the required four-week waiting period expired. Within another month, she was back on Luna.

There would be no underground three month *noka* for her. But Antal scientists had discovered that one week of *måaksnoka*, power hibernation, taken in intervals, like the Terran Churchill's famous noontime naps, sufficed to replace about three weeks of long hibernation. Quenby adjusted, as a few others had to other planets,

146

by taking a week every other month to sleep uninterruptedly in her quarters. Luna was on a fifty-two week year and a twenty-four hour day, like Terra, so four weeks of power hibernation was all she required.

And like most Antal, her need for sleep during a non-hibernation period was minimal. She could easily double shift at least one week of each month, which made her Lumina employers very happy. Since Lumina employees were strictly salaried, expected to do the work necessary to get the job done, someone who could double shift regularly was highly valued.

Finally freeing herself to admit her discontent with the Antal workers' paradise, she had not even pretended to miss home, to show any reluctance to sign on for a third and fourth tour, never stayed on Alvar for more than a month between tours, to do what would be seemly for appearances.

There had been times, rare ones, when she missed her mother, brother, homeworld, but they passed. She was truly happy living the expatriate life.

On her fourth tour she made the decision to remain on Luna. After two years on Luna full time, she applied for and was granted Luna citizenship, becoming one of the 100,000 dual nationals. Free to return to her homeworld at any time, and also released, as a formally declared non-resident, from the one-third Antal *skät* tax, she found herself in possession of entirely more money than she could spend in the fairly simple life she was living.

Experience too much, wallow in it, sate yourself.

In very un-Antal-like profligacy, Quenby splurged on a luxurious, two-room apartment in Luna City's prestigious Third Level. Located in the center of the six-story complex, with a balcony that opened onto the acrie, it overlooked the Luna City Park.

A gentle *ding-dong* chime announced Fahd's arrival at the en-

147

trance to the Luna City residential units. Quenby glanced at the over-door scanner and eagerly granted him entry, watched him walk through the lobby and enter the vacu-lift. On a sudden whim, Quenby chose to lift her window wall and step outside onto her small patio while he took the vacu-lift to level three. She arched her back and deeply inhaled the earth-like atmosphere inside the dome, rich, fecund, teeming with Terran sounds and feelings. The joyful cries of children playing in the greenery reached up to her. *Children!* She breathed in more deeply, as if she could take them inside her, share their unbridled joy for life. Her silver grey eyes swept out and across the great Luna City Mall to the entertainment complex and the throbbing lights of the shops, banquet halls, bars, cafes and game halls. Moon flyers sailed by level with her window wall on lightweight plastic wings. They wheeled like giant birds above her head with their brilliantly colored wings in the one-sixth lunar gravity. She felt free. *Free to be myself! Free of the hive! Free to go too far!*

She looked up at the moon flyers soaring higher, higher, al-most touching the overhead ceralloy dome, 250 feet above the sur-face, which used Antal technology to shield Luna City from the con-stant bombardment of radiation and mini-meteorites. Crawlbots skimmered over the external surface, eating moondust, keeping eve-rything sparkly clean. *Yes. Use the technology to make it safe and clean. But let me live!*

She watched the ultra-thin coverlets that simulated a Terran day-night cycle during the Luna twenty-eight day sunlight period slide another three feet into place over the dome, darkening the early even-ing sky. *Wondrous.*

But Quenby knew what made Luna most wondrous for her were the Terrans. Now in her eighth expatriate year, Quenby had a wide circle of Lunie friends, quite a few true friends, one or two con-fidants. There were a handful of Antal living full time on Luna, who were to Quenby's amazement and joy a lot like her. She never knew there could be any others like her so secretly desirous to do other than what the hive wanted. And the rainbow of Terrans that intrigued her. Overwhelmingly numerous but unlike the Antal, what variety! Just rising out of the cosmic zoo, primitive urges barely contained. Vibrant. Alive. Full of wonder at the advanced Seven Worlds' ways that seemed like magic to them. Over her eight years on Luna she spent as much time as possible amongst them. And filled her Luna life with rapturous sexual activity twice a year, until the kön passed, sampling one Terran genotype after another. *Was this going native*, she wondered?

And now Fahd! Fahd, whom she had fallen head over paws for.

A dome flyer swooped low, just slightly overhead, quite close. Quenby looked up to see the beaming, ecstatic grin on the pleasure-filled Terran. Let her eyes drink in his slim, athletic body, draped in a bright yellow skin suit that left little to the imagination. *Yes. There was more to life than the hive-like Antal way.* The sensor rang, the Terran bread was ready. Time to attend to dinner. She turned and left the patio, leaving the window wall open to the air. *And there was also more beyond mere pleasure-seeking. There was duty, yes, and principles. A being without principles is a lost soul. If one was free, where did one's duty lie? To whom? To what cause beyond one's self?*

She knew what duty and principles signified on Alvar. *But how does one define them when completely, utterly free to choose the meaning, in a mind-dazzling array of often conflicting ethics, values and beliefs on Luna?*

She had been seeking answers among others like her: expats living as strangers in strange worlds. She made a point of attending all the Jabar and Nord philosophers' lectures. She and Fahd had attended every one of Sai'd bin Jubair's lectures on truth and spirit.

Fahd. She glanced up to see his face on the flashing visi-screen, where she once again needed to electronically clear him to exit the lift and walk down the hall to her apartment. Yet, as she literally felt him coming down the hallway, she wondered how much her love for Fahd had to do with wanting to nurture that wild part of herself that the Antal society had so ruthlessly culled, that wild, primitive nature that the Terrans had in overmeasure. She had the strangest feeling that perhaps her duty lay assisting them in their reach for civilization, adding them into the cosmic mix of races, like hot pepper into a stew. Her delightful little primitives had avoided extinction by the narrowest of margins, and they were still on probation.

Even so, she thought, Fahd was different from the others. She knew from the beginning. *Yes, he was very other, very dark, brooding, hiding some terrible secret,* she could tell that, but there was something in his soul that drew her to him.

She could feel him coming closer, almost to the door. Quenby could explain away her first sexual encounter with Fahd as the kön, but she knew better. The omnigamous Antal were casual about sex and procreation, but they all knew of *älska kön,* those who joined for life, essentially forsaking all others, though few had actually sampled, experienced it.

Have I found "the one?" Of all things, a Terran, and a good foot and a half shorter than I?

She had spent most of the past week finding excuses to be with him, from the business of taking him to the mass mover, where they both worked, to steering him to what she considered the best places to eat and to play, to the latest Jabar lectures on spirituality, and bedding him as often as she could. She found herself growing unusually jealous of the time he seemed to want to spend playing vid games, toying with vid game boxes, speaking with other vid game users, one small group in particular. It was highly uncharacteristic of an Antal, even one as atypical as she.

150

Antal were not jealous. Yet she found herself so. *Was this a sign of ålska kön? But what was this seemingly unhealthy attraction to the vid games? It was as if Fahd was possessed, driven to do something!*

And his furtive glances when she "happened" upon him and another vid-gamer in apparent deep discussion of some obtuse aspect of their games! That disturbed her. *What was he hiding?*

But now she tingled with anticipation as she heard the entrance chimes and saw Fahd's face on the scanner. At the end of his first week on Luna, she invited him up to her apartment for dinner. Until then, she had contrived to meet him in one of Luna's clubs or restaurants and return to his quarters for most of the night. She was about to let him enter her personal space. She swept across the threshold into her apartment and closed the window wall with a trembling hand.

You're still Antal, like it or not! An invitation home is the ultimate declaration of renskjåp, what the emotional Terrans call love, though they seem to "fall" in and out of it with great regularity.

Feeling the kön spread through her body, she called out "Enter," in a gravelly voice that startled her for its anticipatory sexuality.

The door opened with a low *swisssh.*

Fahd stepped in, then stopped, stunned by the sight of a living alabaster goddess standing framed before a darkened window wall to the Main Plaza. He had been warned by his co-conspirator Ahmad that an invitation to an Antal home was more than significant, and he had a job to do here on Luna that he could not let anything interfere with, but by all that was holy, she was magnificent! He felt his resolve melt into desire. He wanted nothing more than to be with her, now, tomorrow, forever.

He fumbled with the bouquet of moon flowers that his friend from the MMM, the eccentric, romantic Russian Petrov, had insisted

151

he spend half a day's salary on.

"There are women, my friend," Petrov had growled, as they finished their last shot of vodka in the Happy Hour Bar and Grill, "and there are Antal females. When one so ugly as you or I is fortunate enough to have one of the latter choose him, he must not take anything for granted. Bring her something to warm her heart and then enjoy every fleeting moment."

Taking Fahd by the collar in his over-large Russian hands, he led him off across the mall to the small shop where he prevailed upon a diminutive Indian Luna City Tourism worker to create a bouquet of seven pure white tea roses. "One for each day you have known her," he grinned lasciviously. "I know you're not getting enough sleep my friend, but who cares!" Then Petrov turned serious and melancholy. "Treat her like the goddess she is, Fahd Abdul, for you do not know how long this will last."

How long indeed, Fahd mused, as he offered the white roses to a beaming Quenby, who bent over to plant a light silver lipped kiss on his dark brown lips and reached down to dishevel his jet black hair with her silver claws slightly extended, so he could feel them lightly scratch his temple.

"I have made *müusarüuta* for you," she crooned in her lilting sing-song. Then she let go of him, tapped a panel on the silver wall, which opened to reveal a selection of plasticene glassware, selected one, set the flowers in it along with a few ounces of precious water and placed it on the table while Fahd strolled as casually as he could over to the window wall to look out into the Plaza.

Thanks to Nord technology, even though the opaque window wall allowed limited light and vision into the room one could still see out. The view was unmatched. The shades above the dome were drawn to simulate a Terran night-cycle. Earth, blue and green and bright white, slowly moved along the dome on a huge visi-screen.

The cheerful lights of the Mall and the entertainment section glowed. People in light costumes strolled along the well-lit main walkways around the Mall on surface level and along twinkling paths through the greenery. Faux stars glistened in the roof panels. About a half dozen flyers whose eight foot long, bright orange, yellow, white or red wings reflected the various lights, swooped, climbed or circled lazily like giant human night birds.

Quenby came over to reach around him with her slender white arms and run silver tipped claws into the openings in his silk shirt and through the hair on Fahd's chest. He leaned his head back and they kissed longingly.

"We must eat the *müusarüuta* while it is hot," she breathed, disengaging her face, but keeping her hand busy inside his shirt. The heavenly aroma of the mainly vegetable stew reached them. Fahd stood on his toes to kiss her again, then reached into his trouser pocket to withdraw a two inch oblong pane of energy circuit recordings. "All my favorite jazz," he said, "would you care for some dinner music, precious one?"

She kissed him once again, this time letting her long silver tongue reply. She adored his Terran music.

Fahd's jazz collection: scanned, checked for bugs, contraband, scrubbed clean, sealed and delivered to him on Luna where he broke the customs seal. New stuff mostly, but some older golden age jazz. It had made him instantly popular. Jazz was the lingua franca, the common exchange of Luna. Every night the Aérobleu Club and Phoenix Café were filled with jazz aficionados. He hit the play switch, Abdul Abbas's Sand, Dream, Lazeez, Red Dust, and the classic Caravan, would give way to Jasmine, Moonstone and Solitude, then Antonio Sanchez' ECR Quadrant, with its sensuous Latin sounds. He could forget his mission. His duty. His death. He was in for a night of romance!

Quenby spooned some of the müusarüuta onto the black plate she had set out for him, and watched him as he first raised a forkful to his nose, appreciating the aroma, then ate appreciatively, savoring each mouthful.

"Exquisite," he said, gazing across the table at her with his big brown doe eyes.

She was pleased, but not a fool. *I'm glad he likes it, but I could have served him snow wolf dung, and he'd have said the same thing. Nonetheless, it's sweet. And the flowers, beautiful things, but what romantic fools these Terrans are!*

In between forkfuls of the white porridge-like stew, they munched a little thin crisp bread and chick pea spread which she had made because she knew it was familiar to him.

Halfway through the meal, she looked meaningfully at the boy from Wadi Shiban and brought out a bottle of outrageously expensive and potent vita-åska imported from Alvar, mostly for the Luna tourist trade.

They tossed it back in shots, Antal style, with the traditional Antal drinking toast she taught him, *May the wolf never find your hidey-hole!* Over and over again they shouted in sing-song Änska, *Må ulvor alltida ut om gömhål.* Then Quenby stood, reached across the table, scooped him up into her arms and carried him into the bedroom.

The chimes gently woke her just as the dome began to glow. Simulated sunrise blushed bright orange through the window wall, and the ceiling shimmered slightly. Quenby stirred. Her long arms shone white against Fahd's dark, hair covered body. Alvar and Beck were thankfully distant. She gently disengaged herself, rose from the bed with one last lingering look at her coffee colored Terran lover, and let her long legs carry her into the ultrasonic, high pressure cleansers in

154

the bathroom.

Fine, suspended droplets of dry detergent mist sprayed past her forcefully in a warm air stream. She stepped out clean, dry, and slightly scented of lavender, slipped into a flowing robe woven out of a smooth almost see-through fabric and stalked silently back through the bedroom into the living room, where she opened the food keeper, withdrew a container of dried hjortberry juice for herself and dehydrated coffee for him, drew off six ounces of water each from the tap, and heated his coffee in the radiator.

Then she glided into the bedroom with her hair swept back from her forehead falling in simple white straightness all the way down her back.

Fahd was half awake now, and once again permitted himself to savor the stunning sight of her seven foot tall thin white body, clearly visible through the robe as she coasted along the floor toward him, black coffee in a black handle-less cup.

She perched like a great bird on the side of the bed and sipped the slightly bitter hjortberry juice as he gratefully blew across the surface of the hot coffee to cool it slightly before he drank. He reached out to stroke the silky white fur of her lower legs. She smoothed his black hair with her hand and soothingly caressed his worry-lined forehead. Her pale grey eyes stared deeply into his and he saw that she intended to question him.

His face turned apprehensive, murky with anticipated harm. He shifted his eyes from hers to the coffee in a vain hope to avoid a confrontation. But she reached out with a slender white hand, cupped his face in it and with gentle, but unresistable strength, raised his eyes back to hers.

"You must tell me what is bothering you, dearest Fahd," she sighed. "I can see you are burdened with a dark secret. You must

155

share that secret with me, and so release yourself from its imprisonment."

The coffee cup shook in Fahd's trembling hand. The strength of Quenby's hand and the look of pity in her icy grey eyes startled him. He felt her reaching into his soul, making him want to tell her everything. He wanted to. But he said nothing.

"We cannot go far forward if you cannot trust me," she warned, gently stroking his face with her long, seductive fingers.

Fahd's mind reeled. *Say something, you fool. Say anything. Do not insult her with silence.* He struggled against the feeling, but he could not bring himself to break the years of training and divulge the secret he had so successfully hidden from so many for so long. Droplets of sweat broke out on his forehead. *Lie to her! Tell her anything! Mean it when you say it!*

But he could not bring himself to lie to her. They were more than intimate, more than just lovers. He knew, as surely as he knew that Allah existed, alien or no, this woman was his one true love.

"Surely you know that I love you as no earthly female ever could," she cooed. "Why can you not speak this thing to me?"

He tried to speak, but again, his voice failed him. He'd been mentally and physically abused, beaten and mind-whipped into keeping this secret against all possible inducements. Only a thin, rasping "ahhhh" came out of his mouth.

She soothed his head with her long white fingers. "My poor lover, you must clear your mind."

Fahd's mind control was failing him. *It was a mistake to fall into this female's snares.*

But they are so sweet.

I cannot speak of it, he wanted to whisper, but he could not make the words come out of his mouth. I will tell you, but I must wait yet awhile, he tried to say. But again, his voice failed him.

Then he gave up, hung his head and would not look her in the eye.

She stroked his face with three long white fingers, kissed him lovingly with her silver lips and drew her head back, waiting.

He met her gaze, and broke.

"I have an obligation of honor that I cannot speak of but must complete."

Her silver lips pressed hard together. She lifted a single silver eyebrow. "Honor? What could honor possibly require you to do that you fear to share with me, who has shared everything she is with you?"

"I cannot speak of it," Fahd mumbled.

Her eyes began to chill. "I thought you valued truth above all things? If you are ashamed to speak of this, how can it be honorable?"

"It is a thing I have sworn on my honor to do."

Quenby straightened up archly. Her silver-grey eyes burned. "I have heard Terran males and the Krieg speak of sworn oaths and honor. It is usually a testosterone-induced male fantasy that makes them do misguided, foolish, stupid things that harm themselves or others." She cocked her head to one side, raised her voice a pitch. "What harmful thing are you misguidedly sworn to do?"

Fahd fidgeted under the covers. *I have sworn to do this thing or lose my family. Al-Wahab and al-Yasir tell me that dying in jihad is not suicide and there are no innocents, that all who contribute to the Great Satan's work are evil. But how can this woman be considered evil?* "It is not misguided," he responded. "Honor requires that a man keep his sworn word."

"Not if he has committed himself to do harmful things!"

Now Fahd's face reddened. He put the coffee down on the bedside table with a *whap!* and snarled, "What about defending that which you love? Would you not kill one who seeks to kill you or your

157

family?"

"Kill?" she gasped. "You speak of killing? To me?" She let out a low moan of betrayal. "I thought I knew you! To strike out at another being is *felsmen!* Insanity!"

Fahd was taken aback by the ferocity of her response. He knew the Antal were pacifists, considered how she would react to mass murder.

He broke eye contact and shrugged. "What about honor? What about defending those you love?"

"Honor? We have no word for honor in our language. We have 'true, just, honest, decent, decorous, upright, and proper.' That is honor for us. Honor does not compel us to murder other advanced sentient beings. That is *felsmen.* How do you Terrans justify it?"

He cleared his throat. "Ah, we consider it the lesser of two evils."

"*Fels* is *fels*. Stop there. How can *fels* be *rens*, wrong be right? That is insanity, *tökmyck.*"

Fahd stared, shocked at the simplicity of the thing. She was right! But he had taken an oath on the honor of the Mahra. What did a man have if he had no honor?

She pressed him. "Just stop at that. Wrong is wrong! Wrong cannot be right! That is *rens*, truth. Have you not been listening to Sai'd bin Jubair when he speaks of truth?"

Fahd felt like he'd been struck in the face. He and she spoke often of truth. Now his doubts assailed him like hungry ghosts tearing at his vaunted mind-control. In truth, *ah yes, truth, the sine-qua-non of Islam,* he enjoyed modern conveniences, jazz music, fast cars, intoxicating beverages, moondust brownies, the freedom to be who and what one wanted to be, the freedom of western and Antal females.

Was he truly *takfir?* Had the play acting at disbelief become real? It had been easy despising the west and its modern ways in

Asim al-Yasir's house but was that because al-Yasir was so obviously a hypocrite?

His training in science had taught him to question, to demand proof of propositions, to seek truth. Now she was telling him that his "truth" was insanity!

I was taken as a child, taught as a child, did I remain a child? Was my childhood ignorance replaced by a more insidious, sophisticated one? Have I accepted insanity for truth? Is it that simple? But no! I was sold! To the man who will kill my family, my entire clan if I do not do this thing! That is truth! And to save them I will kill innocents. That also is truth!

Fahd's shoulders curled in over his chest. He turned his back on her. "Truth? What is truth?" he asked.

Quenby rose, sipped her hjortberry juice and slowly shook her head.

AHMAR SAIF

It's not enough that we do our best;
sometimes we have to do what's required.
Winston Churchill

Peter Larson, Robert Walker's personal security chief, shook his head and frowned into his cup of strong, dark Kona coffee. Black. No sugar. He watched with practiced eyes as Aidan arrived at the main house. In the time it took Aidan to walk from her cottage, Walker's butler had managed fresh cannolis and an exquisitely aromatic coffee service in silver serving pots.

But neither the coffee nor the pastry had taken the edge off his boss's indignation. Larson quietly sipped as Walker venomously castigated Vice Marshal Natil's killing spree. "Damn her! That wolf-bitch is liable to kill everyone who might be able to finger the men behind the plotters. She'll crush this plot, but there'll just be another after it. And she wouldn't have done this without Pardek's tacit approval, so we have to assume he's getting ready to make a move of his own that could include an occupation." He wheeled around angrily, pointed a finger at Aidan and demanded, "Tell Peter what you found out."

Larson was not pleased as he listened to Aidan reveal what she had taken from Michael's mind. He knew Aidan had some very special abilities, *but mind-probes, two hundred thousand miles into space!* This was all too "Ooogah-booogah" for the ex-Presidential Secret Service man.

Larson adjusted the Beretta .38 in his shoulder holster, drained his cup in three gulps, immediately filled it once more and began listening intently, not wanting to miss a single nuance. But the woman was spinning a tale of intrigue that had only half its roots on planet earth with foes he could physically touch. *There are dead involved!* Some group called the Red Serpent Brotherhood. And to make matters worse, since it involved the space stations and Luna, he could not rule out extraterrestrials. Even dead extraterrestrials.

Larson smothered a groan, squinted, rubbed his forehead. *Not again!* He looked longingly at the bottle of cognac on the shelf behind his boss. He would like to add a healthy shot to his coffee. He did not look forward to dealing with peebs. In his business, death was the end of the affair. It was either to be avoided, or brought down upon your enemy.

And aliens! Was Aidan about to make him deal once more with aliens like Vitok who could make a mockery of the most sophisticated security systems in the world? Like his boss, Larson still smarted from Vitok of Narr's visit to the same room in the estate thirteen years ago. On that unhappy occasion, he had been incapacitated, disarmed, and his boss had been outnumbered and trapped within his own library. A phalanx of the best-trained security guards in the nation, state of the art internal and external motion, heat and sound sensors and the hovering security helicopter, armed with air-to-air and air-to-ground missiles, had been unable to detect or prevent the arrival of a five-person party that magically materialized inside the library——at least according to his boss. Larson was unconscious the entire time. One minute he and Mr. Walker were sitting there, he with his gun drawn, a bullet in the chamber, and the next minute, Mr. Walker was relating an unbelievable story of how an alien had simply bypassed all the systems and infiltrated four humans and himself into the library.

None of the security systems indicated that anything had happened. None of the cameras in the library had recorded anything. None of the security teams had seen anything. Unbelievable, except that he, Peter Larson, the best in the business, had somehow lost three hours in the blink of an eye.

His impeccable security had been breached, he had been down for the count, and the large glass of two hundred credits a bottle Lagavulin Islay Scotch Robert Walker had given him with the tale had not stopped all his internal alarms from ringing.

As Aidan spun her story, an irritated Larson cocked his head to one side, looked up at the mahogany ceiling fan. The slow whoosh, whoosh, whoosh of the blades echoed the whirling agitation of his mind. No, he did not like dealing with aliens, alive or dead.

When she finished, he shifted in his chair, glanced once more at the slowly spinning fan paddles and forcefully shook the cobwebs out of his thoughts. *Okay. At least now I have something tangible to go on. Ahmar Saif, Faisal Hashim al-Wahab, Vladimir Koscientzi,* he already had quite a file on that bastard, *a boy genius from the date palms, a pattern involving Riyadh, Moscow and Rio, the Red Serpent Brotherhood, ugh,* and that word he didn't care for at all, *"imminent."* But he was the consummate professional, the best of the best.

Robert Walker drawled thoughtfully over his coffee, "I think it's obvious that people in high places includes Koscientzi. Peter, check Red Sword, al-Wahab and Abbas through your friends in the CIA and NSA, and find out who the boy genius from the date palms is. The Riyadh, Moscow, Rio pattern should give us a clue to what the plot involves and who specifically is mixed up in it." He drew a breath and took another long gulp of hot coffee. "But this Red Serpent Brotherhood, and possibly alien dead," Walker pointed at Aidan, "We'll need some help from your sources."

When she nodded and calmly replied "Vitok," in between delicate bites of a cannoli, Larson shuddered involuntarily.

"White Willow," Aidan added. "Possibly Mao or Galbraith. I know Bob Erickson will give me anything he finds out, but I don't know how much more that will be. He seems to be on the run."

Robert, somewhat calmer now, and pensive, was fiddling with one of the ivory pieces of the mid-nineteenth century chess set on the Chippendale table. "Someone is counting moves to mate, it seems to me. Time is of the essence," he hastened to append to the conversation. Frowning at Aidan, he announced, "You will have to stay off the web and make no references whatsoever to this on your PCD, since we must assume that whomever it is has someone sur-veilling you. You can bet Natil's murder spree is shaking them up, and if they decide that our sources have tipped us to their plan, it could cause them to move up their timetable. My tracks will be cov-ered," he added, "and Peter can give you a completely untraceable, scrambled PCD for this."

She responded with a nod of her head that sent her long red hair tumbling downward along her blouse. "Thank you Robert. I'd appreciate that. Most of my work will not require electronic para-phernalia, but when and if it does, a unit like that would be very nice to have. You're a very resourceful man, Peter."

"When I'm awake," Larson quipped, trying to add a bit of light-heartedness to an otherwise sobering situation. "How about sur-reptitiously beefing up security on the three targets?" Larson put in.

"Whatever we do must be done without tipping our hand," Walker responded. "All we know now is possible targets. Are they going after one or two or all of them? From what we hear, we can assume that they're going after all three, if so they would have to con-struct a complex, well-timed plan of attack. We need to do some re-search before we make a move. Then we might know where or when the first attack will occur and possibly the second and third."

Walker took a bite of one of the cannolis, thought for a moment, and said, "We need to see the whole board, not just the immediate threat to the King, before we decide on a countermove. We need to identify the pattern. And not needlessly antagonize Natil or Pardek in the process. They can make the military power we may need available with a minimum of attention-drawing activity."

Peter Larson put down his cup. "Okay. I'm running." And with that he rose, turned on his heel and aggressively strode out of the library, down the hall and down the stairs to his operations room.

Aidan reached for another cannoli to disguise her sudden agitation. Her inner sense was tingling in a way that meant someone was reaching out into their conversation.

She raised one finger to her lips to signal Robert to silence.

She scanned the room, then the hallway and the patio, then the field. But whomever or whatever it was, was way too quick for her and she was left with an empty-handed feeling.

It was gone now. Whatever it was, she was certain it would not show up on Peter Larson's sophisticated sensors. She had felt it discern her searching it out. Maintaining silence, she chewed thoughtfully. This was not a physical presence. *We might have to do less talking out loud and I will have to speak with Kor and the Vita-Kor Sisterhood about this. Now who would be in the best position to intercept a passed-beyond link to Ahmar Saif? The Jabar, of course. And of the peeb Jabar, who better than Kirsan Tabiyat? But not directly. I should contact Vitok, share it mentally with him and have him reach out to Kirsan for me. That way it would be untraceable by whatever means whoever is listening in to my conversations has.*

"We're dealing with some sophisticated people Robert," she half-whispered. "They may be blinded by revenge, but they are neither dim-witted nor lightly prepared."

164

He nodded solemnly.

"Robert," she said in calmative tones, "I'll be at the cottage."

She opened one of the French doors and walked out onto the patio and across the lawn toward her house. As she passed through the wooded area separating the four-house complex from the main house, she stopped, folded her hands in the Vita-Kor Sisterhood way and went deep into a trance. A gust of wind scattered her red hair in a nimbus around her head and Kor the Wise appeared before her.

Probe me sister, Aidan thought, and focused hard on the recent conversations with Michael, Peter Larson and Robert Walker.

Aidan rocked slightly as Kor implanted a phrase into her mind. Kor nodded, and with the parting thought, *my sister, more Nord than the Nord, mwuk Nord wal Nord, another prophecy will be fulfilled,* the leader of the Vita-Kor Sisterhood vanished as quickly as she had come.

As she made her way along the path, Aidan called on Vitok with the words Kor had implanted in her mind, *Saarp kaawta, wal fwuup a hahpa.*

When she reached the cottage, Vitok was seated in the living room, having assumed the familiar embodied form of a young Terran man with long golden hair in a flowing silver robe. Val was sitting attentively with his legs tucked under him on the couch next to Vitok, the tavak was licking Val's hand. It stood up on its long white legs and barked happily at Aidan, who reached down to stroke the round white head and floppy ears. The tavak gently took and held her hand with its two sets of fangs and made soft little greeting whines.

Vitok extended his arms in the Nord sign of pleasured welcome, which Aidan returned.

"You're upset about something again Mom," Val complained.

"Yes dear I am," she replied, smoothing her long red hair into some semblance of order. "And I would like to speak privately with Vitok, if you don't mind."

Val's eyes slitted into irritated little slashes. He forced a smile, swept the little white tavak up and said peevishly, "Of course, Mother. I'll take Shazam with me." As he stalked out of the room, he protested, "You will permit me to learn something of this, won't you."

"Yes, of course, Val," Aidan responded without thinking.

And that was all he needed. He hadn't said how he intended to learn and he now had her unwitting permission to eavesdrop. With a self-satisfied smirk, as soon as he reached his room, the boy sat and immediately went into the Kir.

In the living room, Aidan switched on the Nord-installed security system that encompassed the entire house. She knew that no place is perfectly secure, or secure for more than a few minutes or hours if someone desires badly enough to penetrate it, but the house should be adequately protected against intrusion of any kind for at least as long as she and Vitok needed to talk. That done, she once again focused on the conversations and thought, *Probe me Va-Tor brother.*

Once she had passed on everything she had learned, they spoke, putting their trust in the Nord security system.

"*Saarp kaawta, wal fwuup a hahpa,*" Vitok began. "The viper strikes but the eagle shall eat it. You will be involved in killing a man, or many men, but whether or not you do this before the viper strikes remains unanswered. And the fate of two worlds lies in the balance."

"You see the dilemma," she responded. "We need to intercept a passed-beyond link to Ahmar Saif, to ascertain who is behind this, the precise nature of the threat, and the timing."

"And you believe that Kirsan Tabiyat is the way?"

"Yes. And I have also put out a call through Kor to White Willow," Aidan replied.

"And Mao Zedong?"

"Yes."

"I will speak with the Krieg passed-beyond," Vitok added pensively. "They also have many ears in many places on Terra, though this is not generally acknowledged."

"I was unaware of that."

Then the hair on Aidan's arms rose up. A grey mist settled into human form on the couch next to an intensely alert Vitok, opposite Aidan.

"Well beheld, White Willow," the Nord spoke. "It is good that you could join us so quickly."

"Well beheld, Vitok of Narr," the hazy human form replied. "Hello my beloved Terran disciple," she added. "Kor of the Vita-Kor has made me aware of the situation. I have come as you requested and will do what I can to assist you in your hour of need. But you both must know that my work is within the realm of integrating the dead with the living in peaceful harmony. I am not privy to the comings and goings of underworld characters."

"Yet you served us well when we needed to contact Terra and seek out a group of just humans to appeal the Terran cause before the Council, White Willow," Vitok replied, opening his arms wide. "You are a capable being, and we owe you a debt of gratitude."

"Kind words, Vitok," the specter responded, "It was well within my purview to let Aidan know she would be called upon to serve, and to guide her in the direction of her true love, Michael Good. But I fear that you must rely upon others for specifics in this matter." She turned toward Aidan. "My beloved student, there is something I can do to help, but only if you are willing."

"What is it?" Aidan queried.

"I can harness Vitok's and my energies to enhance your intuitive ability and focus it upon this matter. Such a plot must have much

167

accretion. It will be highly unpleasant, negative as the thought forms of those who would do such things must be, but thoughts are energy and as such can be accessed within the cosmic hologram. You should be able to pluck something out of the ether."

Aidan considered what was being proposed. White Willow and Vitok would be there to protect her, pull her out if necessary. She agreed.

The three joined hands. Vitok went into the Kir. White Willow softly chanted. Aidan focused on keeping her breathing steady. White Willow focused the energy toward the targeted thought forms. Aidan felt her mind swirling, eddying, dissipating, gathering again, moving through a great, foggy, buzzing multitude of thoughts, searching.

A jolt. They had made contact.

Aidan's body shook violently. She was riding the whirlwind, shaken by what she saw and felt. She spoke in a quivering voice, "I see two men dancing on a red sword: one man, dark, lean, messianic, and maniacal, in a dishdasha, the other, pale and calculating, in a grey suit. The sword is balanced in the air above what looks like a great cannon, miles long, on a grey plain. I see, in the minds of these persons, Starfarer Redemption and Luna City exploding, no, imploding, collapsing into themselves. I see thousands dying, gasping for their last breaths."

Her right hand seized a pen and began to write the word **Деньги.**

"It covers the man in the grey suit. Their faces are hidden from me, but he calls the other by name, Faisal and asks for the progress of the plot and, he whispers, al-Sharfa. I feel a great evil power narrowing its intent and activities into a small dark man on Luna. But there is something about this small dark man. I hear a voice saying, 'You will find him. You will kill him. You will work with him,' and another voice, but it's fading I can't make it out . . . It's gone. The door is closing."

Aidan suddenly lurched forward as if released from the grip of a terrible fiend. Vitok caught her and soothingly enveloped her in a soft blue aura until her glazed eyes returned to normal and she slowly shook her long red hair from side to side, mumbling, "There was more. The dead were helping me, but I was not permitted to see into it."

"You wrote something down," Vitok gently prodded.

"I did?"

Reading it upside down, "It is the word 'money' in Cyrillic," Vitok announced. "So, at the heart of this conspiracy we have a traditional Arab named Faisal, and a modern Russian who is covered by and obsessed with money. They intend harm to all three entities and will use a man named al-Sharfa, which can be translated as 'the gun' to achieve their purpose in a suicide mission somehow connected to a long cannon on a grey plain. The very name al-Sharfa might be an allusion to a cannon, not a person. Yet whatever they do, they plan to implode not explode Starfarer, Redemption and Luna City. And you will find this small dark man on Luna, kill, and work with him, all three, but in what order we know not."

He released Aidan gently. "I find it hard to conceive that you should kill someone. Yet you say the voice said so."

"I know the being who spoke," White Willow interjected. "I am not permitted to divulge his identity at this time, though I can attest to his veracity. All three things shall occur." She heaved her shoulders and sighed, "I believe I have done what I can for the moment. I must take my leave, dear student and dear friend. Adieu." And she was gone.

"I will go to Kirsan Tabiyat and the Krieg. Perhaps Pardek and Natil will rethink whatever they have in mind if they know the

Nord are involved. You must now see what your Mr. Larson can make of all this," Vitok advised. "The estate security systems have been enhanced by Antal and Nord technology. Do what you do within the confines of this property, as much as possible, but be aware no security is foolproof," the Nord cautioned. "It appears you are once again yourself. So I shall be off." And he too disappeared.

Aidan sat silently, committing all of what she had seen and heard to memory.

In the other room, Val did the same. When the time came, he told himself, he would do what was necessary.

MOONDUST

And ever has it been known that love knows not its own depth
until the hour of separation.

Rumi

The magnetic mass mover was operated by Moondust Corporation, a subsidiary of Lumina. Located at the Main Mining Center on the plains of Mare Nubium, twenty-five miles from the outer rim of Crater Ptolomaeus where the ceralloy dome of Luna City reflected golden in Sol shine.

And that is where Fahd al-Sharfa was, at his regular job, getting ore off the moon. He absentmindedly fiddled with the vid game he was disassembling during a break in his work schedule, looking wistfully out through the ceralloy window of his small office at Luna City's golden dome. He could not keep his thoughts from wandering. *Quenby's over there. I want her so badly, I am incomplete without her. But now she must detest me. And what right do I have to involve her further in the deadly game I'm playing?*

He watched a bot move along the ceralloy window, digesting moondust, clarifying what he could see. Moondust clings tenaciously to everything. It is especially bad for moving parts like hinges, light screens and the bots are constantly moving to keep it clean. When they reach saturation, their programming makes them find a way inside to get emptied and recycled.

171

Clearing moondust was essential to keep the solar energy driven magnetic mass mover working. The two mile long linear synchronous motor in the shape of a huge tube, raised by degrees rear to front with two large power hemispheres at its base was connected to a vast solar field just east of the structures.

Outsized crawlbots sucked dust off the solar collector panels, bots repaired micro meteor punctures. Without the bots, moondust would quickly render the magnetic mass mover inoperable.

Fahd watched as cargo buckets were delivered by moon movers along rail lines that ran from the manufacturing pods, loaded like cannon shells into one end, levitated by cryogenically cooled, superconducting magnetic fields, ready to be accelerated through the tube at more than 100 g's and catapulted thirty-two thousand miles into space, where they would be caught by the mass catcher in high lunar polar orbit, packed into freighters and shipped to LOS, HOS, or Mars Base.

As the mini-bot cleared another strip of his window, Fahd pondered how much his own vision had cleared since the Antal female came into his life *like a white angel.*

With one loud tap on the office door Petrov pushed his way into the office with a wink, a nod and a steaming cup of coffee for Fahd. Since he met Quenby, Fahd had slept well only in her arms. Apart from her, he tossed and turned and slept poorly. He noticed the envious look on the man's face. They had all heard of Antal wilding during the kön. They all wished they were in his place. Massoud and Petrov both ascribed his need for caffeine throughout the day to all night sex with Quenby.

"Lucky dog," Petrov said to him for the second time that day, "you have the rest of your life to sleep."

Fahd grinned, nodded, took the coffee, and watched Petrov barrel back out the door to his own post. *The others think that she and I make love all night long, and yes, we have, but they don't know we've talked and talked, often into the sunrise, and made me question things I never have before.*

Walls were coming down in Fahd's compartmentalized mind. He was allowing himself to entertain opinions and feelings he had cast aside in the past. This woman had made him question what he took for granted, as she disciplined herself to do. *Could Luna free him as it had her? Could Lumina, the mass mover, lunar mining and the space stations be lifesaving creations, enabling us to progress into the next evolution? Could they be good, not bad?*

Now his right hand closed around the two vid games in his pocket and he cast his eyes downward. *I have seen and felt the impossible here on Luna, and Quenby has been the instrument of delivery. Yet I am sworn to destroy her along with all these others. A man of honor must keep his sworn oath or be forever disgraced. And along with him his family and tribe.*

A cold and terrible fury grew in his belly. He no longer wanted to die. But he must. For such a betrayal al-Wahab would have the right to vengeance against his family, the honor of the Mahra would be sullied and the name al-Sharfa would come to stand for traitor and coward.

But in his heart he knew he could not kill Quenby.

He watched the bot clearing the window, imagined he could see her apartment through the golden dome, longed for her company.

Fahd glanced at his reflection in the window, stretched a dark brown hand across the worry lines on his brow. *I have worry lines and dark circles under my eyes now. I knew what I believed when I arrived on Luna. Yet how much has this alien female changed me with her words and with her example? She was not just talk, she took action! She freed herself from a rigidly controlled society and sought to free me from false obligation.*

The bell of truth rang when she spoke, and some of the old truths of al-Wahab sounded tinny and hollow, empty, when he repeated them on Luna. But what was truth and what was moondust?

How could this be happening to me? My mind was like a steel trap. Now . . .

No one knew the inner turmoil he endured. He was in love with an alien creature! *A non-human! Not the same species!*

But did his association with the Antal female put him under suspicion?

Perhaps.

Though everything was ahead of schedule, Massoud had questioned him this morning about his progress in transforming the vid games into device packages and the amount of time he spent with Quenby. He had given Massoud a look and said, "It's all part of my cover," but he had begun to doubt that himself.

Had she been the cause of his becoming apostate, takfir? No! I'm not takfir. I'm more Muslim than I ever was on Earth. I'm a real truth-seeker now! Quenby was the trigger, the moment of truth when the whole gestalt became re-vealed.

He sipped the coffee and turned back to disassembling the vid game. He had two devices completed, one remained to be done and one more for a backup. *What am I doing? The prophet said, the greater jihad is the more difficult and more important struggle: against one's ego, selfish-ness, greed and evil. And Sai'd bin Jubair, to whom she brought me, clarified that for me.*

He prayed for guidance. And like a stroke of lightning, knew what he had to do. *Of course. Quenby was right. It's so simple. Wrong is wrong. Truth is truth.* He bit his lip. *And so I must die, but she must not.*

He switched one connection on the vid game he had been working on. There were two more in Quenby's apartment. He would have to fix those two as well.

The buzzer sounded. "Launch in five minutes." Fahd laid the vid game aside and refocused on his visi-screen. All systems went into secure status. Open doors shut. Connecting tubes were sectioned into blast-proof segments. Sensors swept every passageway with full visuals. Six green lights lit up one after another on his screen. Everything was in order. He spoke into the mike below the screen. "All systems go. Countdown initiated. Launch in," he checked the clock, "four minutes, twelve seconds."

The computers managed the process. He merely stood there, in case something went wrong. It never did.

In between launches, he and the other "wetware" types fussed over every little piece of the mass mover, refining the tolerances, checking for abnormalities, making certain that nothing would ever go wrong.

It was the last load of the day. After this, he could go back to Luna City. He ached for Quenby. The terrible secret between them made him shudder involuntarily and rub a hand hard along his worry lines.

How could he tell her that he had to die to save her?

He waited nervously as the clock ticked down, continuously checking his databoard. Nothing was amiss, as usual. A siren sounded and the big gun began to emit a soft whirr that would grow louder and louder until it was a roar, or would have been in an atmosphere, but here on Luna the only sensation was a slight trembling of the platform, that soft whirr inside the pressurized sections and then an abrupt nothing as the visi-screen showed the pointed end of the silver bucket leaving the tube on its way to high lunar orbit.

Shut down procedure took another hour. Everything had to be checked and rechecked, made ready for the next day's launches. Seven million tons a year was the quota and God help the wetware if it wasn't met.

At last, the red shut down lights all flashed white and clear and Fahd gave the command to end shift.

He walked to the door, let the sensor scan his retina and open it for him, strode down the hallway past two more visi-scans, and placed his palm against the handprint scanner to access the tube system, where he joined a small crowd of Terrans and one Antal walking to the tube station. One more palm and retina scan permitted each of them in turn to enter the carriage that would take them the twenty-five miles to Luna City via mag-lev in about twenty minutes. He fiddled with another vid game, maintaining his persona, and noting the wry looks some of the other Terran males gave him. It was no accident that Petrov had delivered a cup of coffee just shortly before fourth launch and the end of the work day.

Four scans later, Fahd was in his bachelor's quarters, enjoying an ultra-sonic, high-pressure shower in the tiny bathroom. He turned off the warm air stream by hand once he felt suitably clean. Not as fine as the unit in Quenby's apartment but it sufficed.

He picked up his PCD and hit the speed dial for her number. Her voice, cold as the winter wind on Alvar, came across the connection: "What do you want?"

"I want only to be worthy of your love." He waited breathlessly for what seemed an eternity, then added, "You are right. *Fels* is *fels*. I have a plan. Can we meet at Le Club Aérobleu for wine and a bite to eat? We can talk afterwards."

Again, the time seemed to drag forever, then the soft, lilting Änska tones of, "Oh Fahd, dear man, I would love to," filled his ears. "Shall I meet you there in five minutes?"

"My beautiful darling, I love you more than life itself," he responded, melting before her voice. "Two minutes would be better but five will do," he said, as he imagined her in his arms once again, perhaps for the last time.

Then he clicked off, hurriedly put on his best white trousers and a black silk shirt, and walked to and through the mall to the

Aérobleu, the definitive moody jazz joint on Luna. Fahd took Quenby there several nights a week.

The Coryllim manager trotted down the side aisle displaying the stripe on the four black trouser legs and sleeves of his black silk maître d' outfit, guiding Fahd to a table in the back along the wall.

"Feel it. It's real syrpo de seta fabric from Glisa. Just the thing for romantic evenings on Luna. I can get you some. My brother will tailor it to perfection."

Fahd declined.

"No? You're missing a rare opportunity. But speaking of romance," he winked his one large frontal eye ostentatiously, "the oysters are particularly succulent tonight."

He handed Fahd the wine list, and with a "Bon apetit, mon ami," Efis trotted off to another table of customers his back eye had noticed looking at the suit. Bruno Orelli's recording, Star Dancer, one of Fahd's favorites, was playing. He envisioned himself and Quenby drinking wine to Earthlight, followed by lunar oysters to Soul Lament, a baked lunar fish or shellfish coquille to The Moon Is a Harsh Mistress and then lunar coffee to Precious Jewel and finally a slow walk along the promenade.

Oysters. Not halal. Do I eat them to keep up my false persona, because I like them and have become takfir, or because she adores them and I will do anything to make her happy?

She made her sculpted appearance in the doorway about three minutes into Earthlight. He had counted. Long white hair drifted languorously in the mall breeze as she paused to see if he were already there, then flashed a pearly silver smile. Her fine boned hands fluttered delicately as she raised them to wave to him in that cultured way of the Antal who walked as if dancing, and floated toward him on her long legs in a diaphanous white robe that revealed more of her body by covering it than if she had been naked. Every male Terran

177

who wasn't blind looked longingly at the Antal female in kön.

She settled into the booth with a swirling motion, reached one long white arm across the table and tenderly stroked the worry lines on Fahd's brow.

Fahd was spooning crème brulé through Quenby's delicate silver lips when she stared deeply into his eyes and sat straight up in that Antal fashion that made them look like living alabaster statues. "You must tell me everything. Tell me about the vid games. And this dark secret of yours."

The spoon trembled. Quenby looked questioningly down at him. "Do you not wish to be completely truthful with me, as I am with you?"

The look of dismay and turmoil that spread across his dark face made Quenby wonder if she was in one of those bleak, depressing Terran vids where everyone dies or wishes they were dead. *He was going to lie to me! This human is intolerable!*

She rose, standing, signaled Efis with flashing silver grey eyes, wheeled about and began to sweep toward the door on long swirled strides, a confused Fahd walking double-pace to keep up with her.

All the way to her apartment, Quenby looked straight ahead. Fahd trailed behind her like a kicked puppy. Not a word passed between them. She paused by the entry door. Her emotions were feral. Only eons of Antal self-control enabled her to not explode in rage. She had never felt this way in her life, had only occasionally seen another Antal in this state.

Quenby's eyes burned into Fahd's soul when he dared look at her. "You will enter," she demanded discordantly, "We will talk." He obeyed.

Bots swept slowly across the golden ceralloy Luna City dome above Quenby's apartment, eating moondust, letting a brighter light shine into the living room. In the side table by the dropdown couch were two reassembled vid games Fahd had left there. Two vid games capable of destroying the space stations.

She ordered the privacy level on the window wall set to opaque. Then walked into the bedroom and dropped her flowing robe to the floor. She turned to face Fahd, who had pocketed the two vid games, and now stood, gape-jawed at the vision she presented.

"Tell me what you want!" she demanded in very un-Antal-like agitated tones. "Am I sex or am I *älska kön*! I wish to know!"

She ran one long white arm chillingly along his shoulder, slightly nipping his skin with her razor sharp silver claws every inch or so. Then she swept both her arms down and to her sides, chalk white palms outward and half-shrieked, "You observe the similarity among us. Antal are like other Antal. Krieg like other Krieg. One common language on each of the harmoniously united, civilized Seven Worlds. But you Terrans! So variant, tribalistic, uncivilized!" She growled, "So attractive."

Fahd stared up at her, unable to speak.

She raised her arms high above her head like a flashing white banshee, showing silver fangs to him and hissing. Nothing had prepared Fahd for an Antal displaying this kind of emotion. It was beyond belief. All her manicured Antal smoothness was gone. She accosted him with an icy challenge: "All your life, you've sought approval, been driven by it. But have you loved? Have you been loved? Or have you been used!" She reached out to tenderly touch his cheek with one silver claw. "Have you been free? On Luna, we are free. We choose our own paths to redemption. Our own guiding principles. The ties of Terran and Antal society no longer bind us. No other rules or promises save those we choose to make. The past is gone. The future is but a dream." One arctic white hand pointed at him, then pointed at her own heart. "All we have is this moment, this hour, this day!"

She appeared to be nearly hysterical.

"Love me Fahd. Be mine as I am yours. Oh Fahd," she hissed, silver teeth nuzzling his neck, "you are making yourself live in hell when you are in heaven. Luna is the most wonderful thing in the galaxy. Without Luna City, I never would have escaped from my gilded Antal prison, never become a free person, never been able to think my own thoughts proudly, without a sense of guilt that I was an outsider, a stranger in my own land. So could you. Lumina, the mass mover, lunar mining and the space stations have freed so many people they are all *brå vak* creations. It could be so for you as well, if you let it."

She grasped him by the shoulders and looked longingly into his dark eyes. "I am yours. I have given up everything to love you. I know when I came here I was running away from Alvar. From the hive. But now I run to something, to you. Why will you not share with me this dark secret that makes you so miserable! Why will you keep from me, who loves you, what she desires?"

Tears streamed from his eyes. He looked up at Quenby. "Believe me when I say I love you more than life. But I cannot tell you what I must do, my love," he quavered, "for you would hate and detest me."

She looked into his beautiful dark languid eyes. Something had changed in her, she was becoming more and more emotional. She felt her very body chemistry had altered. Not just twice a year in the kön. That would be understandable, but these changes were unique, as if her body was in turmoil, rebellion. She could not understand it. *Do I deceive myself?* she wondered. *Have I gone native, become like them? It is the Terran! He makes me crazy! No, he does what he does. I permit myself to become crazy. First jealousy, then anger. What is next: violence? What is happening to me?*

180

She looked imploringly at him, but there was a set to her pearl white jaw that was an ultimatum. "Whatever it is, Fahd, you must tell me."

Fahd began to shake. His hands trembled.

He told her.

Of the wadi, his father, al-Wahab and al-Yasir, the plan to destroy Starfarer, Redemption and Luna City.

She stood there, as if struck by lightning. Looked quizzically at him, as if he were a new kind of creature, not entirely pleasant to encounter. And then he told her of his plan, to make the vid games malfunction, to die without blowing up anything.

"But surely you cannot do this. Surely you can abandon these vipers, tell all and save yourself."

"They will kill my clan if I do not go through with the plot."

Her voice sounded flat and lifeless.

"You will die."

"I do not care," he said, but he knew and she saw he was lying.

Quenby looked away into the distance, at the sky flyers soaring through the air like giant birds in the Luna City Mall. *Who was this man she thought she knew?*

"You came here to kill thousands, hundreds of thousands of innocent beings," Quenby said icily.

"I will let myself be killed," he croaked.

Her head snapped toward him whipping her long white hair. Sizzling grey eyes burned into his. "And leave me to mourn?" she spat.

He looked down

"Answer me!" she commanded.

He looked away. His eyes were arid, cheerless.

"You appalling puddle of excrement!!" she shouted, shocking

him with the violence of her voice. "Do you want me to wail for you?" she shrieked, slapping him across the face hard enough to drive him backward against the wall.

He staggered, reached up to his face, where three long silver claws had slashed him. He dropped a bloody hand to his side pocket, reaching in to feel the vid games.

Blood sopped through the white handkerchief he held to his cheek.

"I must die," he hissed, "so my family, so you may live."

Her hands were at her own face now, aghast at the way this man had brought violence out of her, that eons of Antal non-violence could be overcome through the emotions surging through her body. Quenby winced as she felt a sharp pain in her belly. Like she'd been kicked. She lifted her face skyward and let loose a keening howl that made Fahd's skin crawl. *He is going to do it. The little fool. The little arrogant Terran monkey!* She felt her hand rise up once more, claws out and shuddered as she felt rage and grief surge through her body. She lowered the hand to her side, retracted the claws. "If you truly care for me, love me, then you will not do this hateful thing," she gasped through silver lips curled with pain. She felt another sharp jolt inside her, put one long white hand over her mouth to keep from crying out and whispered, "I beg of you, do not do this thing to us."

But he was silent.

Everything in him wanted to say, Yes, to her. This beautiful being had opened his eyes, his heart, perhaps, in the fullness of time she could have saved him. But he was beyond help. It was too much to ask.

He said nothing, turned so she could not see the tears streaming down his face, went out of her apartment, out of her life, toward his predestined appointment with fate.

KULDEN

Never, never, never believe any war will be smooth and easy,
or that anyone who embarks on the strange voyage
can measure the tides and hurricanes he will encounter.
The statesman who yields to war fever must realize that once the signal is given, he
is no longer the master of policy but the slave of unforeseeable
and uncontrollable events.
Winston Churchill

Dirtside Kulden base teemed with activity. Kul military aircars darted to and fro, transporters hovered soundlessly like black ghosts on maneuvers over the parade grounds, two ready to land and disgorge HURT teams, two more departing on missions. Six more Valkyrie and three PRD teams were on alert. Terran defense teams in the towers peered into visi-screens for intruders while their comrades in the barracks viewed training simuls and cleaned weaponry one more time. Vice Marshal Natil had declared extermination war on Ahmar Saif.

As Krieg warriors dragged a disheveled human out of the prisoner pen toward the interrogation center, a few sullen prisoners stared blankly out through razor wire but hastily looked away. The man was blubbering, "Allah, Allah, Allah!" He tried to claw the troopers with fingernails he had bitten to the quick, gasped for air as they tightened choke holds on him, his bulging eyes tried desperately to make contact with his comrades, but they all ominously avoided meeting his gaze, lest they be targeted for the next round. With a trembling chin he bit down violently, convulsed in wild, drooling spasms and died. The two wolf-warriors looked down with unsympathetic yellow eyes. "Poison pill in his tooth," one of them growled. "We'll have to get another." They began to drag the body off to a mass grave.

Vice Marshal Natil watched the episode from her office window. She was out to crush Ahmar Saif. The few traumatized prisoners she took were subjected to Krieg interrogation methods. They usually told all they knew, but so far, that had not been enough. She still did not have the identities of the Luna plotters. She tapped her razor-sharp black claws angrily on the windowsill. *That one might have known something. But it means we are getting close. This barbarian subspecies cult will crack. And then I will finish the job.*

Shortly after noon a large blue life-form broke through the sophisticated base defenses without security even noticing and apported directly into headquarters. The two startled, but well-trained headquarters clerks both reached for side arms, thrust themselves behind cover of their desks and hit alarm buttons in one smooth motion. The quicker of the two fired his blaster at the intruder. To his shock, the green bolt of energy crackled its way right through the heart of the creature, and burned a three inch hole in the reception room wall. With a flashing digitation of his left hand, Vitok of Narr froze both clerks in mid-motion, disconnected the alarm and raised his right hand in the universal sign of peace.

He greeted Peebles, Bajar and Natil with a grin as they burst open the office door and came tumbling out into the reception room, weapons drawn.

"Dammit to Hell, Vitok," Bajar cried out from his prone position on the floor.

Natil growled deep in her throat and thrust one immobile six-foot-four guard like a snack sack through the air toward their uninvited visitor. "Do you not ever tire of your jokes?"

When the Nord sent an infuriated Eagle Legion guard back through the air without so much as touching him, Natil snarled "*Kavlak Kavvuul*" in outraged Urtok, Stop this foolishness! and reached for the blades in her sleeves. They would be useless against the Nord, but she would have the pleasure of watching them pass through his heart.

Her legendary Krieg edginess slackened considerably when Vitok's grin turned into a grim slit. "It was necessary," he declared, releasing the clerks from their frozen positions, "to arrive unannounced, with no waste of time."

The outer door burst open and a HURT team poured into the room. Once again, laser and blaster fire hissed right through the blue Nord and made a shambles of the far wall.

"*Kavlak!*" Natil barked, and they all halted where they were, jaws agape. The acrid smell of smoldering wood silently filled the intense quiet that had come over the room.

"The drill is over. Well done. Dismissed," Bajar told them, picking himself up off the floor, holstering his blaster and dusting off his otherwise immaculate uniform.

With a grim look, Natil made it clear to the Terran troopers that the official explanation had just been given. "*Kondok*," and then in English, "carry on," she said as she exaggeratedly bared her fangs and extended one long furry arm to invite Vitok into her office. She waved Peebles and Bajar off. "I would speak to the Nord ambassador in private," she growled.

She closed the door behind them, wheeled around, shoulders rising ominously, making her lupine body features all the more fearsome. "Explain, Va-Tor."

"I come directly from Marshal Pardek," Vitok stated with a simplicity that underscored his authority in this matter. "The plotters have inserted a critical agent on Luna. He will be the trigger. Krieg High Command wishes you to dispatch Terran Eagle Legion troopers to Luna to stop him."

Natil touched her communicator.

Vitok stopped her with a wave of his hand.

"Covert action only until the signal is given. No troops should be sent to the low or high orbit stations. You must make it appear that your Terrans are on Luna in a routine practice mission. Our information is that this will be a suicide mission, conducted from Luna."

"And your information is from?" Natil demanded with a tilt of her prognathic jaw, white fangs gleaming.

"Terran intercepts. Confirmed by Kirsan Tabiyat of the passed-beyond Jabar. A Terran dead group called the Red Serpent Brotherhood is involved. And of course, there is a wider circle to the plot than just this one man on Luna."

"And the Terran who must be stopped, is?" Natil demanded with a low growl.

"We are narrowing that down at the present time."

She turned to face the window, unwilling to permit the Nord to see the consternation in her face.

But the amply apparent dismay in her thought forms was all too visible to Vitok. "Time is of the essence, we are informed," he stated as placatingly as he could, "so you should dispatch one Valkyrie and one Medevac team to Luna immediately."

She continued to look away. Then she spat on the floor and whirled about, snarling. "To prevent what we cannot categorize further, against a terrorist or terrorists we have not identified, within a

186

timeframe that is running out."

"Precisely."

She balled her hands into fists in front of her face. *He was so damned calm. He was giving her an impossible task, in an indeterminate timeframe, with only the barest amount of troops! Nord never lied. But, but by Kulzar, how had Pardek agreed to this!?* She took a deep breath. "Only two teams."

"Yes."

Orders were orders. "I will make it so," Natil stated. Adding with a snarl, "I will dispatch them directly to Luna in a cutter within one hour."

She waved off Vitok's frown with a sharp gesture of her own, cutting the air with a slashing set of black claws. "Time is essential, you say. Speed might make the difference between success and failure. The arrival of two Eagle Legion teams in and of itself would cause ample stirring of the Luna grapevine. A cutter will not add much to that. But it will carry battle transporters and aircars that will enable us to carry out our impossible task more speedily." She cocked one yellow eye glaringly at the Nord ambassador and snarled sarcastically, "There remains the danger that the terrorists will act sooner than your sources think."

Vitok nodded assent.

"I will be certain to include at least one assassin," the Krieg Base commander added in icy tones.

"We appreciate your usual thoroughness, Natil," the Nord responded evenly, "and you shall have any and all information as soon as we have it." He gave the Nord sign of deep gratefulness and apported away.

Natil shook her dark brown head, touched her communicator and called Bajar and Peebles into her office. She related what she had been told about the plot to the shocked Eagle Legion officers.

Peebles stormed around the office gesturing and muttering under his breath about fools and reactionaries, and more than once slapping a large brown hand down hard on the desk. When Natil gave him permission to speak, he shouted, "So we're supposed to find a dust mote on the moon?"

Bajar remained outwardly impassive, like the perfectly professional soldier he was.

Natil looked hard at both her subordinates. "We go there," she declared. "We pretend to train. We reconnoiter. We remain ready to strike at a moment's notice." She paused, "Your cover story is practice for Mars."

"Yes, vice marshal," Bajar responded, snapping to attention. "We'll need three teams each. One to search, one on alert, one to sleep."

"One team each. Those are the orders. Select your teams. They leave at 1300 Terran time."

"One team each! That's cutting it pretty thin," Peebles snapped back, adding at the last possible moment, "vice marshal."

Natil froze both men with an icy yellow-eyed look that broached no further comments. Both men saluted, turned on their heels and strode purposefully out of the office. Bajar grumbling softly in Urdu to himself, Peebles, more vociferously in unintelligible ghetto. They parted ways and reconnected at Landing Site Alpha with their chosen teams where a shuttle awaited to lift them to the cutter in low orbit.

"Patterns, Shafat, indicators of moves to come. That is all we will have to go on," Peebles said as the cutter moved off with twenty four troopers plus Wingmaster Bajar and Commander Peebles.

Both men had chosen to take the best of the best and to personally accompany them, Bajar to make sure military procedures were followed, Peebles, Bajar thought, to make sure they'd be broken when necessary.

On their side of the cabin, Peebles' First Para Rescue Team, "First of the First" was sitting stoically. Across from them, Bajar's Sixth HURT Team fidgeted with their weaponry. Lieutenant Alston, the HURT Team leader, slapped a blaster cartridge into her sniper rifle with a sharp *crack* and turned her merciless tigrine look upon Peebles, who met her eyes unblinkingly with his own. It was clear to Bajar that Peebles, a doctor, would rather save lives than take them. Peebles had wearied of killing. Alston had not.

Bajar leaned in against Peebles chest, with his grim face coldly turned upward. "Peebles," he hissed softly, "your people may be more para than rescue this trip."

"One does what one must, wingmaster," the stone-faced, larger man responded. "No one on my team will quail." He raised his voice so everyone in the cabin could hear. "If the need arises, One Perd will kill as quickly and efficiently as Sixth HURT, though we would prefer to leave that task to you."

"It looks like you and I might get along just fine," Lieutenant Alston muttered in undertones through her icy white grin. She looked spaceward. "We're coming for you," she said aloud to whomever it was on Luna.

Peebles reached out across the aisle, put a large brown hand firmly on her shoulder. "And if we must come for you or yours, lieutenant, never fear, we shall get you out."

Bajar, always placing duty above personal need and always dedicated to the mission, interjected, "But we could wish for a bit more information, could we not, Commander Peebles?"

The cutter flashed moonward.

Vice Marshal Natil tracked it on her visi-screen. In keeping with the mission's covert status, she had ordered the cutter to make three-quarter speed, fast enough to arrive on Luna within four hours, but not cause the commotion that a flank speed appearance might. The screen shifted to interstellar, and the cutter became a flashing green dot, moving rapidly toward Luna. "*Virt Inz Kuldai Zwar,*" she growled, May your knives be swift.

Her communicator buzzed.

"Shuttle arriving cloaked at Landing Site Bravo. Base security dispatched."

It buzzed again.

"*Haal! Pardek Dis Kulden! Int Zutu Pixnot Gu Ky Konzulen! Kulvak Natil. Zorg. Virt Not Tek!*"

"Belay that security team!" she barked back at her Terran traffic controller. "Dispatch an automated aircar. No driver. No guards. Clear the area. Now!" and clicked off.

Well, well. One Terran hour after he sent Vitok, Grand Marshal Pardek wishes to inform the base commander that he and two Konzul guests have arrived. Aircar requested. No formalities will be observed. Two Konzul! He brings Krieg dead with him!

She stepped quickly into the anteroom where she checked her impeccable field uniform. Something more was afoot! Dirtside Kulden was about to get much busier! *By Kulzar! I should have known Pardek wouldn't just knuckle under to the Nord!*

She watched the aircar draw up in front of her building, where the Terran sentries popped to attention. Pardek stepped from the car, snapped a fist in Krieg salute and hustled his two semi-transparent companions inside the door one of the Terrans had clicked open.

Natil strode into the outer office. One set of rapid footsteps signified her three visitors had swiftly ascended the stairs to the second-floor. When Pardek opened the door, Natil saluted smartly, fist to chest. The clerks stood at stiff attention as Pardek returned her salute and whisked his pellucid cohorts through the open door into Natil's private office.

Once inside, he extracted a small flask of Kumla, handed it to her, walked to the window and stared out. Quizzically, she sipped. No one spoke.

He had not introduced the two discarnate counselors who stood motionless, diaphanous yellow eyes taking the measure of the vice marshal.

When he surmised the Kumla began to take effect, Pardek turned. *"Ravkut Dengor Dis! Virt Not Sirsens! Zka Urtok!"*

Clear enough: Homeworld security conversation. No recorders. Speak Urtok only.

Vice Marshal Natil ordered her immediate area audiovisual units off and activated an energy seal. What followed would be known only to the four Krieg in that room. *Pardek feels this discussion will be sufficiently sensitive to disable any technical substantiation and speak entirely in Urtok! And Pardek wants me to have enhanced mental acuity to satisfy myself that all words spoken are accompanied by truthful thought patterns!*

Natil had a sick feeling in the pit of her stomach that she was not going to like what she heard.

Pardek reached a furry brown hand for the flask, took a sip himself, handed it back to Natil and began. The silent shadowy figures, he informed her, Konzuls, were senators and advisers to Proconsul Ardut, the planetary Leader and Commander of the Armed Forces.

He paused and let that sink in.

Both Konzuls were involved in the long-range plan to inculcate Nord philosophical and ethical principles into the educational curriculum and senatorial leaders of the burgeoning movement to reduce the amount of militarism in Krieg society.

191

The taller Konzul began, "The Krieg are and will forever be a warrior race," he growled. "But like Marshal Pardek," he added, making it clear they were of one mind, "we believe that gradually one generation after another, we could engender a kinder, gentler warrior race, if such a thing could be."

"Some Krieg doubt the wisdom, even the possibility of that," the other Konzul acknowledged. "I have heard from discarnate Garka friends who work only with the dead, that a counter-movement has gained strength and was fomenting dissatisfaction among the general populace. A significant portion of our people still distrust the violent Terran nature and question the wisdom of training Terrans in *Kuldok*." He looked sharply at Natil, "And the recent recommendation for the Star of Kulzar to a member of the Eagle Legion, has given fuel to the fire of fear and hatred of *Khlyvak Wokulen*."

Natil stirred at those words. "Wingmaster Bajar is a uniquely talented and deserving," she began.

Pardek cut her off. "You will recall our conversation about the reactionary Kulgarka splinter group which is agitating among the junior officers about your Terran Eagle Legion, Vice Marshal," Pardek growled.

"Yes sir!" a simmering Natil responded.

The taller Konzul continued. "A small, but not insignificant portion of our people would still incinerate or occupy Terra. Recall that seven out of ten of our computer simulations concluded with an eventual Terran attack on us. This group still believes that antiquated data. They carry the argument to absurdity, I agree, but they still hold sway over many Krieg who believe that violence is part of the Terran genetic, and that, once given the opportunity to attack, they will."

Natil shifted uneasily. She was an outstanding soldier, but somewhat naïve politically: too honorable to twist the truth that the Krieg military could easily defeat any Terran force.

Pardek raised one clawed hand to the side of his face, exhaling sharply. "In the past five thousand years Terra has had forty-eight hundred years of recorded war. They have demonstrated a willingness to use any weapon to slaughter their own kind, why would they hesitate to slaughter us? That is alien enough to be used by this group to inflame the fires of fear."

Natil nodded. "*Zadank!*"

The second Konzul now informed Natil, "Another reactionary Garka splinter group has learned of the involvement of Terran dead in this plot to destroy the space stations and Luna City. They have passed that information on to senators friendly to their cause, who are now waiting for the Terran Eagle Legion to fail. We believe they will use this failure to turn back the clock, call for the elimination of the Terran Eagle Legion and if not able to achieve that, replace all Terran Eagle Legion officers with Krieg friendly to their side."

Then why did you not allow me to send six teams to Luna?

The Kumla betrayed Natil, and her thoughts were clearly seen by her three visitors.

"I allowed you to send Eagle Legion troopers as a concession to the Nord Council." Pardek interjected. He held up one clawed hand to stifle Natil's objection, "Only two teams because we cannot allow the Eagle Legion to fail in a sole attempt, and you know there is the possibility that, given six or even twelve teams, you do not have sufficient intel to identify the plotters and take action. Failure on such a scale would be catastrophic."

Almost transparent yellow eyes flashing, the Konzul continued in an agitated tone. "We cannot allow the destruction of the space stations to occur, even if what we do embarrasses the Terrans or jeopardizes our relationship with them. It will be embarrassing to the Terrans to have us intervene, but contrasted to the embarrassment of the loss of both the high orbit and low orbit stations, it would be as nothing, *Spu Gi Ksum*, Spit in the Ocean! Embarrassment is better than occupation or destruction."

Occupation or destruction?

Shifting their gaze from Natil to Pardek, who nodded, then back to Natil, both Konzuls spoke as one voice. "That is precisely what this cabal wants. If the stations are destroyed, there will be Krieg senate calls to eliminate or gut the Eagle Legion in the face of simultaneous calls to occupy or destroy Terra."

Elimination of the Eagle Legion? After all I've done to raise it to a level worthy of fighting side by side with the Krieg? Natil stared hard at Pardek.

He slowly shook his head from side to side. "The reactionary groups would use Gor Thab on both planets to destabilize the situation. This could thrust Kot into a protracted political battle or worse, military civil war."

Natil stiffened. This was mindboggling. *The military divided? Civil war on the homeworld?*

The Konzuls looked hard at Natil and then, again with one voice, growled out their orders: "You must take decisive action to prevent either Terran space station from being damaged. Luna City may be another situation entirely, since we understand that there is already an agent or agents onsite, but there you must limit any damage to inconsequential. We will not presume to tell you how to do what you must do. But you must do it."

They paused, locked eyes once again with both the incarnate Krieg, and then left the office, presumably to wait outside while Pardek and Natil conferred on tactics.

Pardek wasted no time. He switched to English, so the Konzuls would not understand what he said, had they some means of advanced listening device.

"They are politicians. If you succeed, they will take credit for

194

the strategy. If you fail, they will deny ever doing anything but meeting you to inquire regarding the progress of the Eagle Legion." He sighed heavily. "You are out in the cold on this. I will not be able to protect you from disgrace." His yellow eyes narrowed to blazing slits. "Tell no one, but act. Particularly do not allow the Terrans to learn of your actions." Now he tilted his lupine head skyward, raised his bushy black eyebrows and gave a glassy stare. "Dispatch a cloaked warbird from orbit to cover LOS, a cruiser to cover HOS and three up gunned cutters to Luna. Krieg crews only. Take up intercept positions via Luna and the two stations," he once again focused sharply on Natil, "and if necessary, destroy **anything**, Terran or not, that appears to be showing hostile intentions."

Natil slowly shook her head from side to side in dismay. She couldn't believe this was happening. *Politicians! How could Pardek hang her out to twist in the wind like this?*

But the Kumla was still working! "I do what I must to preserve the homeworld," Pardek snarled, baring his fangs. "When and if you ever rise to full marshal you shall have to do the same, regardless of whom you sacrifice, or not call yourself a warrior!"

Pardek's words hit her like a slap in the face. Natil snapped to attention. "Understood sir!" Her eyes went vacant. The air in the small office suddenly seemed suffocating. She swallowed hard. *Like it or not, she had orders to carry out.* Her mouth went dry. "What of my Eagle Legion teams on their way to Luna?"

"They are Terran. Expendable." Pardek took note of Natil's slack expression and waving one clawed hand in the air, softened. "Let them do what they can. Assist them as you can. Perhaps they can ferret out the snake before it strikes. That would be the best of all outcomes." Then his voice hardened, "But if they appear to be failing, take decisive action from orbit. If you must destroy part of the lunar complex to save all of it, hesitate not."

"And what of Vitok, through whom you sent the orders to dispatch the two teams?" Natil queried with a shake of her head.

Pardek snarled once more at the potential impertinence and Natil snapped to attention again. Her yellow eyes burned, but straight ahead, not at her superior officer.

Pardek sighed.

"At ease, comrade-in-arms. As you may still learn, politics is the unfortunate attendant to rank, difficult decisions the prerogative." He placed one furry hand on his subordinate's shoulder. "I will speak with Vitok when this sad episode is over. If we succeed, perhaps he will understand. If we fail, then he and I will have hard words, for my allegiance must be first and foremost to the homeworld, *Ravkut*, and," he growled, "we may soon be fighting our own people." He gripped Natil's shoulder hard then released her and stood tall and straight. "Any other questions?"

"None, sir!" she barked. "May honor be with us!"

He saluted. "May your knives be swift," he added, turned, left the room, gathered up his two Konzuls, and sped off in the air car.

Natil watched the air car head toward landing site Bravo, and brought both fists down hard on the desk. *Damn all politicians! Why did I allow Bajar to go with that irreverent, unconventional, hell-jumper, Peebles! Bajar, the best of the best, the one Terran worthy of Krieg desire. I should have ordered you to remain behind!*

Natil might be out on her own in this misadventure, but they were truly dancing on the laser's edge. They were now expendable.

"May the stars protect you," she sighed through clenched teeth. "Nothing else will, Terrans."

STONEWALLED

Power is not revealed by striking hard or often, but by striking true.
Honora de Balzac

"I'm sorry, Peter, but that's all we have." Peter Larson's friend in the CIA raised his eyes toward the ceiling, indicating the camera recording their conversation. They had hit a stone wall of refusal. "Hopefully this will help," he said, shuffling the pile of photocopied pages and handing them to Larson with a nearly imperceptible second shift of his eyes toward the door.

Larson got the message. "Thanks for your help George." He placed the papers into a well-worn, tan leather briefcase, snapped it shut, and spun the four brass combination lock dials. "I'll be sure to tell Mr. Walker how helpful the Agency has been." The men shook hands. Larson paused, reached one arm after the other into an expensively tailored camel hair blazer and pretending to notice the time, said, "Hey, you've been at this with me all morning. How about a quick bite of lunch--on me."

"Sure. Cafeteria's just downstairs."

Larson's old friend straightened out his silk blue and red striped tie, reached behind him to grab his grey suit coat from the desk chair, and said with a grin, "You bet it's on you. You private sector guys pull down a lot more long green than us civil servants." They both laughed. As they strode out, the man in the grey flannel suit paused to press his thumb against the double lock key pad on his office door.

In the elevator, as if it had just occurred to him, Larson suggested "Let's go to a nicer place than the cafeteria. How 'bout the French café just down the road?"

"Sure. As long as I get back to my desk on time."

And get back on time, he did. After he had informed Larson just who had put the kibosh on giving him any more information.

"So you're being stonewalled by an Assistant Deputy Director?" Robert Walker declared, tapping his foot on the lush oriental carpet.

"Yes sir. And George affirmed it's not the first time. Anything that leads to a certain Russian company seems to stop cold right at this guy's desk."

Walker picked up a black bishop from the chess pieces on the chess table in his library. "Mao's source uncovered that company connection. Bob Erickson overheard conversations linking a Russian, al-Wahab and the boy from the wadi. It leads inexorably to Koscientzi."

"Probable, but since it's only one of his companies, as yet unprovable, boss."

"Not yet. But if it walks like a duck," Walker grinned, reached out with his other hand, picked up a black pawn and waved it in the air, "that AssDep has to be Koscientzi's man in the CIA. He's probably on the line to the snake right now."

"Very likely."

He put the pawn down. "So Koscientzi knows we're getting warm, hot even. But he isn't called the snake for no reason. He's too cold-blooded to panic." He picked up a black knight and stared at it. "But al-Wahab might. Suppose we did something to startle al-Wahab, to let him know his cover's been blown. . ."

198

Larson fidgeted in his chair. "He'd probably pull the trigger. Either give the 'go' signal or abort the mission and kill anyone who might talk."

Walker continued to stare at the black knight. "He won't abort. If he aborts now, we'll have more time to track them all down. He'll know that. He'd have to kill all his men on Luna. And he knows Koscientzi would kill him for such a blatant failure. But maybe he'll move without thinking and give us a provable direct link to the Snake."

Larson turned rigid. "You're going to increase the risk?"

Walker set the black Bishop and black Knight on black squares on the chess board and placed the white Queen on the white square directly in between both of them. "*Zwischenzug!*" he declared. "An unexpected move! I'm going to use their own sources against them, raise the threat level and put them both off their game." Walker seized his PCD, punched one button, then a second. A mellow male voice on the other end announced, "President Wilson's Office," and paused.

"Please inform the President that Robert Walker is on the line and would like to speak with her."

"Sir?"

"Robert Walker. W-A-L-K-E-R."

"Yes sir. Please hold."

Robert put the PCD down on the chess board and poured himself a small glass of Lagavulin Scotch whiskey. He sipped it slowly. In less than one minute, the male voice on the other side of the line responded. "Mr. Walker, the President of the United States."

"Bobby! You old dog! You never write! You never call!" Margaret Wilson barked into the air. "Except when you want something! I've got the Russian ambassador cooling his heels outside my office. So what is it?"

199

"Maggie, you never change. I need a meeting."

"With whom? And when?"

"With you. And the heads of the CIA, NSA, FBI and Military Intel. Today."

A low whistle. "Today. You're the one who never changes. This better be good." The line went silent.

A very short time later, the male secretary was on again. "Mr. Walker, the President will see you today in the Oval Office in exactly one hour for a fifteen minute meeting."

"Thank you." Walker disconnected. "Get my aircar ready, Peter. I have an appointment one should not be late for."

The four men in the room glowered at Walker when he walked into the Oval Office. None of them enjoyed being abruptly pulled out of his routine, summoned to the White House on short notice, and when the President's Office informed them there was no agenda, but there was a visitor, Robert Walker, they were not amused. They hated being unprepared and whatever the Chairman of World Com was going to spring on them in such short notice would not be pleasant.

They were correct.

Robert Walker calmly took in the room. *Yes. They've all made a rash of calls to deputies trying to find out what this is about. And that AssDep at the CIA is chewing his fingernails down to the elbow right now. Zwischenzug!*

Margaret Wilson entered from a side door. Everyone stood. "Sit," she commanded. "We have fifteen minutes. So no bullshit, no excuses, just facts." She cast her iron stare around the room. "Got it?"

"Yes ma'am," four voices replied at once. Robert Walker just smiled.

200

"Mr. Walker, the floor's yours," the President declared.

"Thank you Madam President. I'll get right to it."

"Please do," she ordered as she sat behind the Lincoln desk.

"Yes Ma'am." He turned to face the men in the room. "Two days ago, the CIA hacked into the computer of one Asim al-Yasir and extracted a video of a young man announcing that he was on Luna and going to blow up the two space stations and Luna City. I, or rather my security chief, was given visual-only access to that vid, but denied access to further data. Apparently, the plan is to use an electromagnetic pulse to fry the computer circuits." He turned an ice-cold stare on each of the men in turn. "And it's about to happen."

"Shut up and sit down, Bill. You too General," Margaret Wilson signaled the CIA and Military Intelligence Directors who had risen angrily to their feet. "Robert, cut to the chase."

Walker continued. "I need access to all the information each of you has and I need it now." He turned to the President. "Madame President, this threat is real and imminent. Time is now critical. You can believe what I say or watch both space stations and Luna City explode."

Margaret Wilson leaned back in her leather swivel desk chair and slowly rocked three times.

"Leonard," she said softly to the three-star General from Intelligence, "give Mr. Walker personal access to the SCIF." She sat the FBI and NSA Directors back down in their chairs with a scowl, waved a pointed finger at each of the men in the room. "The room where he can access what each of you has on file. All of it. Today."

The room was silent.

"Dismissed, gentlemen. Mr. Walker, remain seated."

The Directors filed out.

Margaret Wilson came around from behind her desk. She walked purposefully over to where Robert Walker was sitting, reached out her right hand and gently stroked his left cheek. "It's been a long time, Bobby."

Walker flushed crimson. "Yes, Maggie, a long time."

"They were good times, weren't they?"

"Yes, they were."

The President of the United States leaned over to press her lips against Robert Walker's. "Just wanted to do that one more time, Bobby." She turned, ran both her hands through her blonde hair, shook her head vigorously, and, with her back still toward him, said, "You'd better be right about this Bobby."

DIRTSIDE

If you shut the door to all errors, truth with be shut out.
Rabindranath Tagore

Deep underground, in a secure, secret location in Virginia, a stiff-backed Marine sergeant stood at attention outside a triple-locked, tempered steel door with **ULTRA SECRET** painted in large red letters on it. Robert Walker was locked inside, in his shirtsleeves, working furiously. He was running four programs simultaneously on a large screen, flipping from one to another, muttering to himself, ignoring the cameras recording his every move and the scowling Marine colonel with the sidearm locked inside the room with him.

Walker was in one of the most sensitive and well-guarded rooms of a Sensitive Compartmentalized Information Facility, called a SCIF by the intelligence community. No one lower than a Department Director was permitted access to the data inside that room. Except for someone personally authorized by the President, like Robert Walker, who was beginning to sweat profusely. He pulled hard at his loosened necktie until the knot came undone and the tie hung limply down his sweat-soaked shirt.

Walker turned to the screen section that held the NSA data, swore under his breath, just loudly enough to cause the colonel's face to redden, "Goddamn never-ending, inter-service war for money and resources. You'd think these imbeciles would have learned by now to

203

share the toys in the sandbox with each other!" His eyes whirled to the top right section, where a bright yellow flashing slice of information caught indicated a search hit, muttered angrily, "There! The FBI had that data last week." Back to the lower left screen segment. "Sun-

uv-a-bitch! The NSA had this! And never shared it."

He turned to the colonel: "Look at this," pointing to a video running of a young man in a red and white checked keffiyeh, on the lower right hand screen segment. "The CIA got this two days ago," he growled in seething, low-pitched wrath, "and this," switching over to a video of a woman in a white lab coat, "The FBI had a psych profiler analyze it and shared that with no one."

Walker reached to his left, seized a bottle of water and took a long pull. "And you, your Intel people had a Luna Security vid of two guys assembling a SIED three days ago." He raised his face high, tilted the plastic water bottle up to drain the last few swallows and then angrily tossed it across the room in the direction of a waste basket. "Well, you're all in shit up to your necks, because I **will** discuss this with the President." *But not World Com. Not yet.* He checked his PCD. *Yes. By now that AssDep at the CIA has been chewed out about the hacking leak and has alerted his contacts for Koscientzi and Ahmar Saif. The shit is about to hit the fan.*

Walker pressed two buttons on his PCD. He was now transmitting live from inside the SCIF to Marshal Natil's secure line at Kulden Base. That had required additional Presidential authority.

The wolf warrior immediately opened the channel.

"I found what we're looking for, Natil," Walker stated simply.

Natil moved one black claw along a series of buttons. Tapped one and patched him in to the cutter on its way to the moon.

Walker's flat monotone totally underplayed the impact of his repeated words, which were received with a rare, toothy grin from

Natil, and a "hallelujah" from Peebles, on the cutter.

"This is absolute top secret," Walker began, "All Source Intel, ECHELON and CARNIVORE stuff. There are maybe six people in the world who . . ."

"Cut the crap, Terran," Natil barked, "I'm impressed. Just give me the data."

"My, we're having little stressy fit are we?"

Natil slashed a hand in the air across her throat, claws out— yes, she was stressed, and Robert Walker was fortunate he was not within reach of those claws.

Bajar intervened. "Sorry Mr. Walker. The stakes are high, we have blessed little information, we're personally involved, and we need a break."

"How many people are on the channel?" Walker demanded.

"Just Commander Peebles and I in the cutter," Bajar responded.

"*Wom Puk!*" Natil swore. "Time is running out. The data!"

"Well here it is. Ahmar Saif, Red Sword, under al-Wahab, began recruiting workers for Moonbase, now Lumina Corp thirteen years ago. Six month techs. In and out. They each took with them several e-games, one of which had the components of an e-bomb. Got right past security. Why shouldn't it? Passed the x factor games from one temp worker to another. Leaving vid games at Moonbase was SOP, worth more there than they were on earth. Took them thirteen years to gather what they needed. Then they sent the man who could put it together."

"To do what?!" Natil snarled.

"To take one specific piece of redundant electronic from specific vid games, and put it together into," Walker pronounced the next eight words slowly and carefully, "an explosively pumped flux compression generator, an EPFCG."

"A what?" Peebles interjected from the cutter.

"An electromagnetic pulse generating device. One small and light enough to be easily concealed by a person. It works by compressing magnetic flux and could produce pulses in amperes and terawatts that grossly exceed the power of a lightning strike. The concept was conceived as early as 1951 by Andrei Sakharov in what was then the Soviet Union. Apparently, someone in Russia got hold of the plans."

"Lord have mercy," Peebles muttered.

"But, the device can be used only once as a pulsed power supply since it's physically destroyed during operation."

"A lightning strike on a space station! You don't need more than one!" Peebles exclaimed. Then, "How could they hide such a device from Luna Security?"

"The device would be approximately the size of a hand-held vid game, so they could hide it in plain sight. This version is triggered by a minute amount of nitrogen trichloride. The chloride compound can be readily found on the moon, and we send in tons of nitrogen with which it could be combined, so it would give off no unusual chemical signals."

"How do they plan to use it?" Natil demanded abruptly.

"Nitrogen trichloride is a dangerous explosive, sensitive to light, heat, even moderate shock. Once armed the device would explode on the slightest provocation, sending out an e-pulse that would fry every computer circuit for miles. No computers, no life support systems. Back-up systems would also likely be fried. Everyone would die. But that's not the worst part. Without their systems to manage the pressure, the targets would likely implode in the vacuum of space."

Natil broke an electronic stylus in half in frustration as she listened to Robert Walker's calm description.

"And two days ago the CIA captured a vid of one Fahd Al Sharfa telling his father how he planned to use the magnetic mass mover to fire a projectile at the two space stations and then destroy Luna City and enter paradise."

"*Wosh!*" Natil snapped her fangs together.

Bajar, Peebles and Natil could not see Walker scratch his head in puzzlement.

"So we know how they plan to take out both space stations and Luna City and in what approximate order. But how they plan to use the magnetic mass mover to get the stuff to HOS and LOS is beyond anyone's conception. The MMM launches cargo in a capsule to a lunar mass catcher, where it's loaded onto space freighters for the trip to mass catchers at LOS and HOS. Even if they could fire it from the MMM, which I'm told is theoretically possible, this stuff would explode when it hit the mass catcher. But, that's the plan as I know it."

He reached behind him, transmitted the al-Sharfa video. "And the man who knows how to put the EMP device together is al-Sharfa. An extraordinarily bright aerospace engineer. Educated at Riyadh. Demonstrated pro-western lifestyle and leanings. He must be *takfir*. He probably has two or three others working with him."

"Your security is pathetic," Natil said crossly.

"No security system is impenetrable, Natil. You know that," Walker snapped. "Lumina screening security was apparently good enough to keep the number that could slip through the net to a minimum."

"And this was discovered when?" a provoked Natil demanded.

"Four days ago a security camera caught al-Sharfa and Massoud Rashid putting parts together from a couple of vid games. Not altogether unusual, a way for scientific types to spend downtime, but

207

a circuitry pattern matched a Sophisticated Improvised Explosive Device—a SIED configuration. And the alert flag went up. The rest of the data is as old as can be or as recent as this morning."

"So eliminate them, Terran! Kill the ringleaders!" Natil snarled.

"Not a good idea," Walker countered. "We've put nano-tracers on those two, so we know where they are at every moment, but there are others. We need to find all of them."

"*Wom Puk!*"

"You can kill as many as you want, Natil," Walker said irritably, "when your Eagle Legion arrives on Luna. But not before they reveal who the others are and begin to do what they plan to do. We must penetrate the plot, or they will merely be replaced. I don't believe for a moment it is coincidence that the EMP device originated in Russia. I want to trace this plot to the man behind it."

"Then have Luna Security capture these two. Make them talk. Offer al-Sharfa and the other man money, glory, women."

"You think terrorists ready to die will talk? Really, Natil, haven't you learned anything about Terrans in twelve years? And," he added, "there's another complication: an Antal female involved somehow, possibly just as al-Sharfa's unwitting lover."

"Kidnap the Antal bitch. Threaten to kill her if al-Sharfa doesn't talk."

"We don't work that way, Natil. We don't become what we are trying to eliminate."

Natil picked up the nearest heavy object and hurled it savagely against the wall. "What I have learned is that you Terrans are maddening!"

"Hey! I found the information we need. You'd be working in the dark without it." He turned on his most persuasive voice tone. "Natil, work with me and we'll succeed. We'll stop the plot, and get our link to the men behind it."

"And just how will we do that, Terran?"

"I'm still working on that," Walker admitted.

Natil slowly tore four long strips across the desktop with her claws. "Aaarrh! Send me all the images, the e-files, the holos," she growled.

"What do you think I'm doing," Walker replied coldly.

The data began to stream across the vice marshal's private scrambled channel. "Natil out," she said abruptly and cut off the voice conduit.

The *hummm* of the data stream was far less maddening than talking to Terrans. Natil paced angrily around the floor until two short *beeps* signaled complete reception. *He hasn't worked **that** part out yet, and he expects me to **wait** on **him**?* Time was passing all too quickly. And she had a duty to perform.

She tapped the red logo in the upper right hand corner of her PCD twice, to summon her personal staff to her office, *SURK,-IMMEDIATELY!*, and then then with one middle claw opened a scrambled channel and ordered a cloaked warbird and cruiser to launch from orbit and take up intercept positions via Luna and the two stations, and three cloaked cutters to Luna orbit. "Full battle speed. Krieg and battle droid crews only."

She wanted to see the whole file, not just Robert Walker's summary. She turned her attention to the psych profiler's holo Walker had transmitted. A translucent Terran female in a white lab coat with the initials FBI over one breast, stood in the center of a pale green room, referring often to the databoard she held in her left hand. "Overly romantic tendencies, sky high IQ, personable, friendly, but tends to spend time alone when he can. Thoroughly westernized, obviously a cover. If he's a confirmed terrorist—and I have no reason to doubt this, he hides it very well, suggesting a seriously compartmentalized ego." The FBI profiler raised her face to look directly at whoever was viewing the holo. "Which means he could be capable of anything, good or evil, depending upon which sub personality he had admitted/allowed to the forefront."

How did he get past the security checks, Natil wondered, but she already knew the answer, and there it was on the databoard now displayed on her visi-screen at the same time the FBI tech was reading it.

"Subject has outstanding mind control. Slipped through the security net by putting the right sub personality forward. And he is absolutely custom-made for the MMM: an irresistible education, personality and training package. Designer-made for precisely that job. Aerospace engineer, whiz-kid, no serious attachments on earth, very physically fit, eager to go into space, capable of working alone or along with others and able to deal with long periods of isolation. Irresistible applicant," the profiler concluded.

Natil's Aide opened the door, waved a frowning Chief Engineer and glowering Chief of Security through and stepped artfully after.

She let them view the ECR's and the holo. After the initial fiery Krieg response to the information, she turned their attention to the al-Sharfa vid, already on its way with the rest of the data via scrambler to the cutter speeding toward Luna.

Raldar, the Chief Engineer, angrily dismissed the vid as pure fantasy with a slashing movement of his left hand, claws extended. "*Kavvuu!* You might be able to launch the projectiles without blowing the magnetic mass mover," he grumbled through his fangs. "I doubt it, but even so, they have only one place to go, and that's the mass catcher. And they would blow up there when they were caught."

"So," Natil's Aide, Sibune inserted wryly, in the manner that had earned her the nickname, *Khut Zlot*, Ice Heart, for her ability to coldly assess situations and ask the questions that eluded most hot-tempered, impatient Krieg, "Assuming they have or will have the devices, and plan to use them, and we can assume that, how could one get two devices off Luna and to the LOS and the HOS? And how does the MMM fit into this?"

"From the mass catcher!" Raldar shouted, responding in Krieg manner to the precise question posed. "The mass catchers have three man Terran crews. They could get the devices to the mass catcher via Terran carrier. Then that Terran could place the device in a freighter aimed at LOS or HOS!"

"That would give us an approximate time of delivery," Sibune added.

Chief of Security Kildar was already on a scrambled channel to Luna Security. "I need to have a list, **now**, of everyone who has gone to the mass catcher in the past week."

"You got it, Kildar," a smiling Luna Security officer replied as he pushed a button.

And there it was on the visi-screen. Yesterday morning, Massoud Rashid made an in-and-out inspection tour of the mass catcher. He was now back at Luna City.

How much time do I have? "How often do they launch freighters?" Natil snapped.

"I need a freighter schedule for the mass catcher," Kildar stated, keeping his voice calm.

Are we too late?

"Four a day to each site," Raldar responded, punching in some numbers on the console in front of him, lifting his head in thought as he calculated something.

"How long does it take the freighter to reach LOS? And HOS?" Natil asked.

Raldar politely waited until his commander had finished the question and barked out "Two hours to LOS, Four days to HOS."

Reading another visi-screen, "LOS freighter has already arrived," Sibune coolly affirmed, "So Redemption is safe for another four to six hours today. HOS package might have been launched first though. How will we know which freighter the packages are on?" she asked.

"When one of the mass catchers explodes," Raldar growled.

"Unless we blow up every one of the freighters," Natil declared to the shocked threesome. "And wouldn't that set the Terrans howling! They'd probably assume it was an act of war!" She responded to their worried expressions with a snarled, "On my own authority I've dispatched a cruiser and a warbird from orbit to take up intercept positions via Luna and the two stations, and three additional cutters to Luna orbit. Full battle speed. Cloaked. We could destroy the freighters, the mass catchers, even the mass mover if we had to."

No one stirred. They knew the vice marshal had gone way beyond her authority. The Terrans would take destruction of their freighters, the mass catchers or the MMM as an act of war because it was.

Natil broke the shocked silence. "*Virt Not Sirsens!*" She turned away from them to face the window. With the recorders off, she revealed in hushed English, which they all spoke well, "If I fail in what I am doing, I will be disgraced at the very least. You may withdraw from the room now if you wish, with no repercussions."

But they were loyal to a fault. When she heard no footsteps, she turned smartly on her heel, grinned wolfishly and commanded, "*Virt Sirsens.*" Now she spoke for the record in parade-ground Urtok. The words "*Zwis Inemz Ravkul Zot! Int Kors Inen Tut Gi Ti ZyAmak!!*" echoed off the walls of the room. "You are sworn to obey. I order you to assist me in this action."

By making it clear that duty required them to obey and ordering them to assist her in this action, Natil hoped to spare them disgrace if she failed.

Outside, the setting Terran sun swathed the parade ground in blood red shadows. The plangent voice of the color guard's Kot flutes was sounding afternoon recall, a mournful, dutiful song from her home planet. The sense of purpose it inspired was clear. The three officers snapped to attention, saluted fist to chest and shouted, "*Ravkul! Kulrav! Ravkul!*" Duty! Honor! Homeworld!

Natil cocked her head to one side. The flutes suddenly brought Peebles to mind. Peebles had remarked on that song, the same he had heard when he was ushered aboard Pardek's flagship twelve years ago and Terra's fate hung in the balance. He had given her the words to a corresponding Terran tune, The Minstrel Boy to the War has Gone.

She began to pace.

Why would that song and Peebles come to mind? Why?

And then it hit her. *Break the rules! The one faithful sword! Kumla!* It was still running through her mind! She could see the connections! "**They** know! We'll find out from them," she shouted.

"How, vice marshal?" a querulous engineer asked, cocking his head to one side.

"You do not need to know," Natil leered, shocking all of them again.

Her best Terran Legionnaires had already been written off. Everything she'd worked to achieve for the past twelve years was in jeopardy. She was out in the cold. Exceeding her authority. *So be it!* She slammed a sharp-clawed hand down on the table. *By Kulzar's Zorx! I am going to seize the initiative! I am going to break the rules!*

She snatched her sidearm and holster from a desk drawer.

"Kildar," she barked to the most aggressive of the three.

"You're in command here in my absence. The ships are to make maximum speed toward their arrival positions. Any, repeat, any interference should be considered hostile action. They will take whatever response the commanders deem appropriate."

With a decisive *whap*, she armed her blaster.

"Sibune, you're in charge of communications. Keep a scrambled channel open to me at all times. Prepare scrambled channels to both Terran space stations and Luna City HQ, but do not open them until ordered to do so."

She pinned a battle communicator onto her grey battle cape.

"Raldar, find everything you have about the Terran space stations, the MMM and its mass catchers and explosively pumped flux compression generators. I want to know precisely how a high power electromagnetic pulse would affect them. And if you were going to set one off, from precisely where you would do it to maximize damage?"

Wrapping her cape around her shoulders with a swirl, "Now get me the fastest cloaked battle shuttle we have!" she growled as she stormed out the door toward the waiting aircar and Launch Site Alpha.

INCURSION

In those days a great snake shall strike at the moon,
But the eagle and the wolf will fly together against him.
And she who is more Nord than the Nord
Shall set her foot upon his neck, binding him straight.
And the wolf shall pierce him through with a thousand teeth.
There will be blood on the moon
And two new stars will blink out of the night sky.
Book of the Vita-Kor 3:10-17

At that moment, Alam bin-Selim was running through the night as fast as he could. He darted into an ominously dark alleyway, flung himself at the heavy wooden door of a forbidding wall and began to bang furiously on it with his fists. A burly, contemptuous guard jerked it open, seized bin-Selim by the dishdasha, dragged him inside and hurled him to the ground in one motion. Slamming the door shut with a booted foot, he thrust the barrel of a Russian Makarov pistol into bin-Selim's face and shouted, "Shall I shoot this fool now?"

"No, no, no!" the terrified man screamed. "I must speak with al-Wahab. We have been hacked!"

The guard kicked the blubbering computer analyst in the ribs, hauled him to his feet, slapped him across the face and snarled, "Stop sniveling you piece of dung." Two more guards frisked him roughly, grabbed him by the shoulders and hustled him across the courtyard and through the doorway into the house, where two more guards seized him and half carried, half-walked him through another door, and then a third, where two more heavily built guards looked askance at the procession.

"We have been hacked," the man repeated, "I must report what I have learned!"

"This better be good, Selim" one of the men sneered, "We will have to move to another location because of your stupidity. You made enough of a racket to wake the dead," he flashed a cold smile, "whom you will soon join, if it is not truly critical news." He opened the door and roughly pushed the man inside.

Faisal Hashim al-Wahab sat in the dark at a small desk, engrossed in the screen of the tablet in his hands. He was not pleased with this disturbance. He looked up with cold, enthusiastic eyes that said he believed in nothing yet had absolute faith in what he was doing and growled, "Speak bin-Selim. What is it that has caused you to break all the rules?"

"My leader," the little man implored, "spare me! I bring news that could not wait a second more!"

"By the camel's hump, then," al-Wahab said disdainfully, "spit it out, or I'll fry your liver." If Hashim al-Wahab's darkly ominous face was not sufficiently terrifying, the brooding silent bodyguards caressing the triggers of their AK-58's were. Bin-Selim dared for a moment to meet the eyes of one man and saw a viper eager to strike.

His voice quivering with fear, the terrified computer specialist burst out, "Asim al-Yasir's computer has been compromised! Documents have been copied! The video of the boy from the wadi!" The dark little man cringed, awaiting the blow that did not come.

Al-Wahab's face turned darker, serious. He had come too far

216

along to allow anything to stop him. Now he had this fool bringing him the news that his security had been pierced. *Had someone turned? Was this a cover story?* "How do you know this?" he demanded.

"*Al-Hamdolillah*, wise one, not two hours ago I dreamt that agents of the Great Satan had pierced the security at al-Yasir's home." He cringed again as al-Wahab's left hand rose to strike him.

"Allah sent the dream to me!" he cried out, ducking the blow that stopped in mid-air. "I rose from my bed and went immediately to al-Yasir's home, ran a diagnostic on the tablet, verified that entry had been made and the documents copied. I ran all the way here," he panted.

Al-Wahab looked broodingly at him. In the frosty tone that usually preceded someone's death, he queried, "How do you know of the contents of this vid, bin-Selim?"

Now the computer specialist fell to his knees, shaking. "Al-Yasir showed it to me, wise one. I swear on my father's life!"

"And you are certain the vid was extracted?"

"May Allah blind me, I am certain."

Al-Wahab turned on his heel and spit on the floor. "Blind that buffoon, al-Yasir! I told him to erase that vid! But his ego would not let him do it. Now we are compromised!" He swung around. "Where is the fool!" he thundered.

"He has fled, my sheik," the little man replied.

Al-Wahab's saturnine eyes glowered like black coals. "We shall find and deal with him, but you," he turned and took a step toward the quivering little man, "you have done well, Alam bin-Selim. He stroked the man's head and neck like that of a faithful pet dog. "Now tell me, how quickly you can send a coded message to Luna."

"Immediately, my leader," the quavering tech responded.

"Immediately?" al-Wahab asked scornfully. "Am I a credulous idiot? I see no transmitting device in your hands."

The little man put both hands to his mouth in terror. "For-give me, my sheik, I will rush home and send whatever you wish!"

"Good, Alam bin-Selim. Mustapha will accompany you, to keep you safe. You will send one message to Fahd al-Sharfa and an-other to Massoud Rashid on Luna. Sign both, Cousin Ahmed and then report back to me." He slapped the man's cheek lightly, "Clear?"

"Yes, sheik," the terrified man affirmed, glad to be alive.

Al-Wahab brushed the sleeve of his black dishdasha where it had glanced against bin-Selim's cheek, and adjusted his black taqui-yeh. He raised one finger in the air. "Wait here, while I write the mes-sages down. Mustapha! Come!" He whirled through the door into another room.

Rubbing the barrel of his AK-58 along bin-Selim's quivering cheek, where al-Wahab's dishdasha had been, "You fortunate dog," another guard declared. "Al-Wahab is feeling generous tonight."

Generous! The little man quivered. *He said I've done well. Gave me the names of two lunar agents! And coded messages to send! Generous!* Bin-Selim dared to hope it must mean al-Wahab trusted him and would reward him well.

Al-Wahab appeared with two notes in his hand. On one was written the phrase *Lateef Ahwe*, on the other *Ghali Shai.*

"Send this one to Fahd al-Sharfa and this one to Massoud Rashid. Send no more, no less than these words. Sign them both, Cousin Ahmed. Then burn both these pieces of paper and come back to me here." He patted bin-Selim on the shoulder and smiled.

Bin-Selim nodded and turned to go. Al-Wahab's cold eyes met those of Mustapha standing behind the man. Bin-Selim would not live long beyond sending the messages. The two men left. Al-Wahab walked into the garden, turned on his PCB and rang up

Koscientzi. He sent off the precomposed text, **Wedding tomorrow,** and clicked off.

In Connecticut, in view of the revelations from Erickson, Galbraith and Vitok and Aidan's disturbing work with White Willow, the whole estate was on alert. Security teams prowled the perimeter.

Aidan was away from the hubbub of the main house, in the living room of the house Walker had built for them within the compound, in deep meditation. She focused on breathing regularly, in and out, slowly bringing herself out of the trance state inch by inch until her thoughts became nearly tranquil. Through a haze, she saw Val sitting quietly across from her in an armchair, stroking his tavak, Shazam. Aidan had told him to remain in his room, but he had slipped into the living room after she had entered the trance state.

Her PCD beeped at the same time as the outer courtyard security alarm began to wail.

Shazam launched himself off the armchair twenty feet to the glasteel patio door and stood snarling, fangs bared and the hair on his back bristling.

Ignoring the PCD, Aidan leapt off the couch, placed herself between the door and Val, blocking his own rush to the door. With her hands spread wide to her sides, she turned.

A naked female Krieg officer was down on her belly, staring eye to eye with Shazam through the glasteel!

Aidan recognized Vice Marshal Natil, speaking softly to the Narr wolfcat, whose fur went back down as it cocked its head to one side and regarded the brown, two-legged version of itself. Off the patio, a Kul battle shuttle was recloaking! She watched the battle shuttle disappear and returned her attention to Natil and Shazam.

Still speaking softly in Kumlar, the Nord tongue, Natil slowly rose, stepped into her grey trousers and turtleneck and offered Aidan,

219

Val and Shazam the arm spread Nord gesture of welcome.

With a look at Shazam, Aidan ordered the door to open.

Natil remained where she was. Then she stepped forward on long brown furry feet somewhat incongruent under her uniform, onto the soft carpet of the Good's house.

She inclined her head slightly then looked directly into Aidan's green Terran eyes. "Greetings," she said in English. "I seek your assistance. I have much to say and little time to say it. Probe me."

Aidan hesitated for a full three Terran seconds.

What?! A Krieg field marshal willing to display the contents of her mind? Unheard of!

Aidan shook her head from side to side, long hair whirling in a red haze. *This was an unbelievable request.*

"I need you to do this, Terran," Natil said assumingly, and in a more urgent tone, "and now."

Aidan saw Natil's worried expression, and noted the way the wolf-warrior kept one eye on the slowly circling tavak. "Well, then, vice marshal, since you insist," Aidan folded her hands in the Vita-Kor method and sent a probing beam of thought straight toward the spot between Natil's gleaming yellow eyes.

Both their heads snapped back. They each took a staggering step backward as an excruciating shockwave hit them. Shazam's claws sprung out and it tensed, ready to spring.

Squinting hard to relieve the pain, Aidan shouted, "Shazam! No! It's all right!" The wolfcat became less agitated, but began to pace in a tighter circle around Natil with its claws unsheathed.

"Your imperial conditioning is too hard to penetrate, Natil," Aidan said with another slow shake of her head, "I cannot do this."

The wolf-warrior rubbed her furry fists against the pain in her eyes.

220

"Yes, of course. The imperial conditioning. It is of the utmost importance that you try again, Terran. I shall give you all the mental assistance I can."

Aidan refocused on the spot between Natil's eyes.

Natil's furry head jerked back a quarter inch in trained response, and then by dint of will, relaxed. Natil felt the energy enter her mind like a sensible wave, then a chill breeze and a pop like she had just been preoccupied and had returned to the present moment. She checked her timepiece. It took less than three seconds for Aidan to absorb the visual and mental images and emotional impacts. *Good.* She thought. *That will do.*

"What will do and why, vice marshal?" sprung out from Aidan's mouth like a lightning bolt.

Natil paused, clear about what she had to do, and decided to speak again. "Pardon this intrusion Aidan Good, but as you can doubtlessly surmise from what I have permitted you to see, we have what you Terrans call a situation and I am put in a near-untenable position."

She gazed down at the wolfcat. "May I," she asked, inquiring if she could pet it.

"Certainly, vice marshal," Val responded, gently stroking the tavak's back and taking its long white plumed tail in his hand to assure it everything was all right.

Natil stretched down and tickled Shazam's white head with her claws. Shazam did not move away, but neither did he sheath his claws nor take his eyes off the Krieg warrior's throat. "I have had the good fortune to behold a Yarr-Tun tavak in action. It tore the throats out of two Kuldorian assassins faster than I could have dispatched them with my Kuldai. I did not wish to give it cause to mistrust me."

Aidan felt Val reach up to run his hands along her temples, gently,

221

then firmly, and felt the pounding headache she had gotten from the arduous mind probe dissipate. She breathed a sigh of relief. *Yes, Val the healer was here. Thank you Val.* She shook her head. *Val?*

Aidan's deep green eyes grew cold. *Val, you should not be here.* But Val wasn't going anywhere. *We'll talk about this, young man!* He merely stroked Shazam's long tail. *Then please keep still.* She swung her head around and locked her eyes challengingly on Natil. *And I will not let you change the subject so easily, wolf-warrior.* "I would not bet my life on the swiftness of my blades against that of the tavak, vice marshal. Why are you here?"

Natil swallowed hard, rose to her full height, came to near-attention. "I needed to feel the impact of a mind probe to determine if it could go unnoticed. I believe it cannot, but can easily be dismissed as atypical thought. Hence, we can use it. I ask you to accompany me to Luna, where I would have you probe the mind of one of the key plotters."

Aidan shook her head in the negative. "You ask me to violate the ninth suggestion of the Jintu Kor, to disrespect another being's privacy."

Natil's nostrils flared. "You have probed me w. . ." she began to say "witch" but a hard stare from Aidan and a low growl from Shazam changed the word to "woman. You know what Robert Walker has told me. You know what the threat is and who the main plotters are. You know I must stop this threat at all costs. The aim is to learn the plan of attack and the timing thereof without being discovered. In this manner, I can make my strikes surgical and thwart the plan with a minimum of destruction."

"And when I probed you," Aidan retorted, "I could also see that Marshal Pardek told you not to share with any Terran the information to which you allowed me access." Aidan paused, shook her head slowly from side to side, "Yet I can see that you are not attempting to deceive me." She put her hands on her hips and stated bluntly, "So you are defying Pardek and disobeying his direct order."

Natil groaned softly, "The politicians have their objectives," she responded, "I have mine. You have probed me. You know that I will not allow the Eagle Legion," she raised her voice, "which I have labored twelve long Terran years to raise to the level of Krieg warriors," her speech quavered, "to be disbanded."

Aidan could see the wolf-warrior's blazing yellow eyes mist over slightly. *Sentimentality toward one Terran in particular: Bajar! Natil is in love! In anguish from the obligation to never consummate that love with an officer under her command, and now torn apart by the call of duty, to stop this threat **at all costs**, even if that means killing Bajar in the stopping.*

Natil regained her composure, cleared her throat with a *harruuumph*, returned to Krieg directness. "I feel I must disobey that order to obey my other orders in the spirit with which they were given. If I can neutralize the plot with a minimum of destruction, using the Eagle Legion then it will remain viable." She passed one clawed hand across her brow. "But I must not allow the two space stations to be destroyed, so if you will not assist me, I will not know where and when the strike will occur and will have to destroy every freighter leaving Luna orbit until the plotters are neutralized. This will cause great consternation among the Terran tribes."

Aidan winced. A massive Krieg intervention without the foreknowledge of Terran authorities would be calamitous. She had probed Natil's mind and knew that the Krieg vice marshal would do just what she said she would, even if she had to create an interglobal incident. The Terran reaction would be outrage. And forces on Kot would use that to create Gor Thab on both planets. They were risking civil war on Kot and occupation of the Earth.

Natil pressed the issue. "Knowing this would give you pause, I permitted you the full knowledge I had of the matter, though that is a violation of my own code. If you assist me," she urged, "and we succeed, then Pardek may forgive me. He has always placed a high value on initiative."

And you might wind up with Pardek's job as well, might you not, you sly wolf? Such a show of initiative will not go unnoticed in the halls of the Krieg Council, will it? I know that has occurred to you.

Aidan scuffled her bare Terran feet along the carpet. She knew she had to act. But she also knew that she wanted all the help she could get. "I will do what you ask," she demurred, "but not without sharing what I know with Robert Walker."

"Not Walker. No."

Aidan raised a hand to stop Natil's interruption. "It is as necessary for you to bring Walker into this as it is for me to bend the Jintu Kor. There is an old Terran saying, 'all in'. It means that the game will be won or lost on this play of the cards. Natil, you and I both know, whether we like it or not, we are at that stage."

White fangs gleaming in pained thought, Natil slowly thrust her prognathic jaw forward, and then she nodded agreement. "I must, as you say, go 'all in.'"

At that moment, Shazam began to snarl. A Walker security team had surrounded the cottage and were about make verbal contact.

Natil turned, barked, "No Pixnot" and the shuttle decloaked with a menacing *whhoooosh* to display its deadly armament. The out-gunned security team leveled its weapons on Natil. One of them would kill her, even as they all died.

Aidan instantly stepped between Natil and the security team's weapons. "Everything is all right, ladies and gentlemen," she said in her most calmative attorney's voice. "Vice Marshal Natil is not an intruder. She has come to offer assistance."

Shazam growled menacingly, bared his fangs. His black eyes

danced back and forth between Natil and the security team.

"I think we should walk over to the main house, Natil," Aidan suggested, "before someone decides one of us is in danger."

"*Kavlak*," Natil growled softly into her transmitter, standing down her own firepower. She put her arm around Aidan's shoulder in the Krieg manner of comrades-in-arms and when Aidan reciprocated, strode purposefully toward the main house, all but ignoring Robert Walker's security teams.

Val slowly rubbed his hand along Shazam's ears. He had, of course, surreptitiously intruded on both the mind probe and their thoughts. He too, was Nord who was not Nord. He watched the security team follow his mother and Natil toward the main house, stared out at the weapon-bristling battle cruiser on the patio. *Adults! You're all in deeper than you can handle. And you think I'm just going to sit here?*

MAKS TAK!

Plato is dear to me, but dearer still is truth.

Aristotle

Aidan and Natil arrived at the main house, to see a phalanx of security guards moving from one position to another on or near the patio with laser rifles, blaster pistols, shoulder-fired missiles, and the old Terran standby, M-24's.

"*Wom Puk*," Natil snorted in Urtok, then added for Aidan's edification, "Worm Excrement! My battle shuttle would sweep them aside like dust before the wind."

But Aidan had seen her raise one furry black eyebrow at the hypervelocity Arrow Missile partially concealed behind the bushes. Having noted the murky grey edge of doubt in Natil's aura, Aidan retorted, "Perhaps not quite that easily after all, eh, vice marshal?"

Aidan watched Natil's notoriously volatile Krieg thought forms flare with crimson anger.

Natil turned, glared at the Terran she intended to use to probe the terrorists' minds. Her xanthic eyes blazing, she bared her fangs, snarled, "Are you reading my mind again, witch?"

In a red blaze of flying hair, Aidan whirled toward the Krieg warrior, her face inches from Natal's black snout. "I am an extra-sensory human, with what the Nord call, the eye, not a witch. Get your hackles down you dolt, before Walker's security decides to burn

226

your butt. And show me some respect," she added.

Natil made a point of visibly backing off and showing a fang-filled grin. Through her teeth she growled, "Vita-Kor witches make my hackles rise, and you, Terran, more than most!"

Aidan put her hands on her hips and leaned forward to hiss, "First, I would not probe you without permission. Second, your thought forms were so feral even a Terran child could have seen your apprehension when you saw that missile!" And then added testily, "Do you want me to work with you or not?" She turned on her heel, led the way past the twitchy armed men and women on the patio, stood silently for a moment at the French doors, with a grumbling Natil in tow. "Well?" she demanded of a scowling security guard. With one hand buried inside his bulging Kevlar jacket, and his eyes never leaving Natil, the man cautiously swung the door open wide enough for Robert Walker to see who it was.

Robert Walker was finishing his second round of summarizing the array of menacing information he had been made privy to.
"An electromagnetic pulse weapon," he stated flatly to Peter Larson. He chopped the air with one hand. "It would fry every computer circuit on the space stations and Luna City: we could only stand by helplessly and watch the catastrophes."

Walker turned, then nodded slowly. As the guard swung the door just wide enough for Natil and Aidan to enter one at a time, he welcomed the glaring Krieg field marshal with a smile. He reached for a bottle of cognac and poured a snifter for her. "Your sudden arrival here has caused quite a stir, Marshal Natil. Please refresh yourself with this Terran libation. From the look on Aidan's face and yours, I can see we are about to have a most interesting conversation."

Natil extended a furry hand, claws carefully retracted, and re-

227

plied, "A short one, Mr. Walker. I have much to do and little time to do it." Her yellow eyes blazed as she tossed down a splash of the fiery amber liquid.

"Aidan?" he queried with a raised eyebrow.

Reaching out a slender hand for the second snifter, Aidan swirled the glass, raised it to her nose to inhale the honeyed richness of the rare cognac, and stated softly but firmly, "The vice marshal wishes me to probe the mind of one or more of the terrorists on Luna to ascertain their precise plan to use the weapons, so she can execute her response most effectively."

"**Her** response?" Walker queried.

"She has orders to prevent the destruction of the two space stations at any cost."

Walker's hand tightened on the brandy snifter he had filled for himself. His blue eyes burned. "**I** have worked long and hard to prevent just such an uninvited Krieg intervention, vice marshal. Am I to understand that Terran pride, lives, even Luna City are expendable in the eyes of the Krieg?" He turned a murderously cold stare on the vice marshal.

Natil irritably met Walker's glare with one of her own.

Peter Larson's right hand twitched involuntarily and inched ever so slightly to the left as his other hand unbuttoned his blazer exposing the Beretta in the shoulder holster.

Still holding the brandy snifter, Natil crossed her arms, deftly resting her hands on the Kuldai blades in her battledress sweater.

Aidan sensed the explosive atmosphere. She had to act quickly. "She has permitted me to probe her mind," Aidan added matter-of-factly. She took a sip of her cognac and watched the stunned expressions spread across Larson and Walker's faces.

Robert looked sharply from Aidan to Natil and back again.

"She did what?"

Aidan's green eyes locked grimly with his. *Time to drop the other shoe.* "She had a visit from the Krieg dead. Two senators, to be precise. They informed her that reactionary *Kulgarka* groups have enflamed the Krieg concern about the emergence of another warrior society."

"Kulgarka?"

"Yes. These reactionary dead say, "Natil's Eagle Legion Terrans are being advanced ahead of Krieg warriors. One of them has even been put up for the Star of Kulzar.""

Natil winced.

Aidan continued, "They say these subspecies mercenaries," she rolled the words angrily with her tongue, "having been trained in *Kuldok*, the way of war, will soon take other ranks properly due to Krieg officers. And once they command the battle droids, will overthrow the Empire."

Robert Walker took an astonished half step backward, eyes widening at the ramifications of what he'd just been told. "Is this so, Natil?"

"So I am told," the vice marshal replied icily. "There is growing hostility within Krieg forces to the all-Terran Eagle Legion. But this supposed coup is sheer fantasy."

"Yet, they have managed to stir up concern on Kot and within the armed forces," Walker remarked.

"There was more," Aidan sighed. "The senators told Natil if the space stations are destroyed by Terran radicals, reactionary groups of the living and the dead would destabilize the situation on both worlds. Calls to gut the Eagle Legion and remove Terran leaders would be followed by calls to occupy or destroy Terra. The **predictable** outraged Terran reaction to that would undermine the tenuous probation, produce more Krieg cries for annihilation, and throw both

229

worlds into protracted political battles or civil war." Aidan took a long breath. Now she let fall the unkindest cut of all. "Grand Marshal Pardek accompanied the peeb senators."

Natil took a sip of her cognac to stifle the growl rising from her throat. "You go too far."

Aidan sighed, sent back the thought like a lightning bolt, *Not far enough, vice marshal!* "Pardek ordered her to exceed her authority, take any necessary action--and **not** discuss this with **any** Terran."

The brown fur on Natil's neck rose. She tossed down the rest of her cognac, placed the glass on a walnut side table, and folded her arms, positioning her hands on the hidden Kuldai blades. "I allowed this Vita-Kor witch to probe my mind because I have little time to do what I must and I wanted to avoid as much collateral damage as possible. She insisted on this meeting with you. I can see this was ill-advised." She turned her head to glance at the French doors leading to the patio, then back toward Walker. "My ship is right out there, Mr. Walker. I will now proceed to destroy whatever I must to stop this lunar plot. Do we need to see if your bodyguard can prevent me from boarding and your Arrow missile can stop my battle shuttle from taking off, with or without me? Or do I just walk out?"

Peter Larson's right hand slid ever so slightly closer to the pistol inside his jacket. Natil's brown furry hands tensed on the Kuldai blades inside her battle sweater.

But Robert Walker had not become the man he was without awareness of the way to seize the opportunity lurking beyond the danger in high stakes, high pressure situations. "There's no need for any unfriendliness here. Of course, I will let you do your duty vice marshal."

Walker slowly gave himself a judicious portion of cognac, retrieved Natil's glass from the side table and poured another fragrant splash into it. With directness and a naturally deft touch he respond-

230

ed in the inimitable soft-spoken, self-confident, unfailingly polite manner that made heads of state take notice. "But I think you would benefit from a short word or two with me before you do what you're going to do."

He handed Natil her glass. "Vice marshal," he quietly asserted over the rim of his brandy glass, "it appears that you are out in the cold." To the quizzical expression that wrinkled the brown fur on her wolfish snout, he replied gently, "You have been swept into the world of politics, and left to fend for yourself. You could find your career ending here."

Natil had one sharp-clawed hand on the brandy snifter, the other slowly rubbing the elbow patch on her grey issue turtleneck with the razor-edged Kuldai knife in it. "You have my attention, Mr. Walker. I assume you have a proposal."

"I am not without experience in these matters, vice marshal. I believe I can be of assistance to you, my friend Marshal Pardek, and, of course, myself and Terra."

"Get to the point, Mr. Walker."

"Your tactics just will not do," Robert Walker stated bluntly. "You see, vice marshal, if you do this your way, you will accomplish your immediate mission. You will win the battle, but not the war. The war will go on, and we may very well lose it," Walker said as calmly as possible. "No. Your plan is the way to personal and political failure. Stopping the immediate threat will merely encourage those behind the plot to redouble their efforts. We must crush the conspiracy." *But how?* Dark clouds roiled through his aura as his mind flashed through and rejected one stratagem after another.

Whatever he came up with had to include the Eagle Legion. And the Terran dead. Aidan would have to rally her own peebs, the PBM. The dead were intimately involved in the day to day doings of the Seven Worlds, and a Terran response without them would be

231

seen as seriously lacking. That alone could shake Seven World confidence in Terran progress. Playing for time, he turned, reached for a cigar from his humidor, took a moment to clip and light it.

At that moment, Colonel John Hardeman Walker, Robert's namesake, glided noiselessly into the library. The specter paused, nodded formally to the Krieg vice marshal, floated over to the chessboard, rearranged the pieces with one diaphanous hand, moving the white queen, knight and bishop to checkmate the black king. "The snake," he hissed, toppling the black king, nodded formally once more to Vice Marshal Natil, and floated out through the bookcases.

Robert Hardeman Walker saw it all in that instant. *The snake. Of course.* Walker had no doubt, but no legal proof, that his nemesis, Koscientzi, was behind this. There were too many coincidences. Koscientzi had been too well informed too many times. And Aidan had seen the word "money" in Cyrillic covering the man behind the plot. But he had no **proof!**

He blew a long cylinder of smoke toward the ceiling and met the military officer's darkening yellow-eyed gaze squarely. "What do you plan to do when Aidan reveals the plot?"

"Intervene, of course," Natil barked, "by any means necessary before they can carry out their acts."

"Ahhh, of course," Walker mused tolerantly. Tapping the ash off the long Cohiba in a crystal ashtray, he queried pliantly, "And to do this you will use the Eagle Legion?"

Natil responded with a self-controlled shrug, "I have dispatched two teams. I will use them if possible."

"But you would use the Krieg warbird, cruiser and three cutters you dispatched earlier?"

"How did you know that?" Natil demanded with an angry curl of the long black lips that bared her formidable white fangs.

"Like most people involved in inter-world politics, vice mar-

232

shal, I have my own means of obtaining information," Walker responded coolly, and punctuated his statement with a long drag on his cigar and a longer exhalation of smoke. "But I know you are pressed for time, so let us cut to the chase--another Terran expression, I'm afraid--it means *Maks Tak!*"

Natil's back straightened and she glowered at the Terran with burning impatient yellow eyes. "You are cool as an Alvarian ice snake, Mr. Walker, and undoubtedly just as cunning."

"Ah, yes, vice marshal, the snake. These men you will, I assume, kill, for they will surely not allow themselves to be taken alive, are pawns in the game of those on both sides of the veil of death who move the pieces on the chess board. And forewarned, they will be more formidable next time. We must not merely kill these men and foil this mission. To strike **this** snake dead, we must cut its head off."

Walker shook his head suggestibly from side to side searching the Krieg warrior's almond shaped eyes intently for clues: *Does she see it?* "Obviously, you will do what you choose to do, and I cannot stop you. But I believe that I can give you a way to accomplish much more." He met those mercurial warrior's eyes with the chillingly calculating eyes of a chess master, leaned in close to her fearsome fangs and whispered pianissimo into her upraised ear. "A way to vindicate yourself for exceeding your authority, indeed, to raise the name Natil to honored status among the Krieg, perhaps to elevate you to field marshal." Walker paused, drew back. Gravely took a long pull on his cigar. "It's up to you, of course."

Natil leaned forward on her haunches, slowly grinding her sharp white fangs together.

"Peter, Aidan, will you please excuse us for a private conversation?" Walker asked, gesturing toward the patio. Peter Larson had no intention of leaving his boss alone with this wolf warrior, but a look from Walker bore no argument and he and Aidan stepped outside.

Natil paced back and forth on the antique Persian carpet for several minutes as she and Robert Walker began to fence with words. Natil stiffened, recoiled, and somberly shook her head in the negative several times. But Robert persisted, moving smoothly in his expensive blue blazer, listening attentively to each of Natil's arguments, thoughtfully puffing on his cigar, refilling their glasses, almost dancing back and forth as they debated, parrying and thrusting, winning a point here, a position there, a compromise, a concession.

Finally, downing her cognac with one abrupt hand movement, Natil barked out a warrior's laugh and slapped Walker hard on the shoulder, knocking him about four inches to the left of where he had been standing.

Rubbing his shoulder, Walker walked purposefully over to the French doors, opened one about four inches, saw Aidan, gravely met her eyes with his, thought *Yes, do it, now. Call in your PBM and go with her.* A moment later he nodded, turned, and called out. "Vice marshal, Aidan is ready to leave with you."

Natil's fangs were showing in a fierce, pre-battle grin. With a low growl, Natil extended a hard, furry right hand, "It is Terran custom to seal a bargain this way, I believe, Mr. Walker."

Mindful of the razor sharp claws in that hand, Walker took it in his own. "Done and done," he said, shaking it twice.

Natil tapped her communicator twice with one claw. The Krieg war shuttle decloaked on the patio of the big house. It was time to leave Terra.

Aidan sent out a second call for assistance to her peebs. She shivered involuntarily, wrapped her long white shawl around her shoulders, and mounted the access ramp ahead of the vice marshal.

A cold chill ran down Robert Walker's spine. Either some or many would die today, he knew, beyond the shadow of a doubt. Would Aidan or Bill Peebles be among them? From the patio, Walker called out. "*Virt Inz Kuldai Zwar*! May your knives be swift."

FELS

The die is cast.
Julius Caesar

Fahd was sitting abjectly at the small pull-down desk in his bachelor's quarters, drinking expensive Scotch whiskey by the glassful. Looking at the remaining two vid games, he took a deep breath and poured himself another shot of Scotch. He had reprogrammed all the vid games so they would not trigger an explosion. *I will fail. Massoud or security forces will kill me. And then my family and my lover will be safe.*

His PCD beeped, startling him, making him jump. Incoming Terra-text. *LATEEF AHWE.* COUSIN AHMED. Cousin Ahmed was sending nice coffee. He blanched. *Code words! Discovered! Move now!* His hands trembled. A look of dismay and turmoil spread across his dark face. *Oh no! Not so soon!*

He looked thoughtfully at the ECR recording he held in his hand then deliberately wrote LUNA SECURITY: A MESSAGE FOR YOU across the cover and put it into the single, lockable drawer on the desk. *Yes. When it is over, Luna Security will go through my belongings and find this. I have given details, named names, and above all, demanded that they keep this anonymous to preserve my family against reprisals.*

In another part of Luna City, Massoud Rashid received his message, *GHALI SHAI.* COUSIN AHMED, and winced. *Cousin Ahmed was sending rare tea.* He knew that meant two things. *Move now. Expend.*

First, contact Fahd and attempt to complete the mission. Second, terminate Fahd if the man did not complete the mission and self-destroy. If necessary, kill Ahmed Khaddouri and himself. They were now all expendable. He knew that if the mission was scrubbed, the plan would go on. Others would come to complete the task. *No one must be alive to divulge the plan.*

Silently, he retrieved the thin bladed ceralloy knife he had so painstakingly shaped, sharpened and hidden away. It would pass through the detectors.

His instructions were to find Ahmed and then meet Fahd at the Luna City tube station. He tucked the blade into his trousers, said a final prayer to Allah that he honorably become *shahid*, and went out the door of his quarters.

Fahd's right hand closed around the two vid games. He thrust them into his pocket and took one last swallow of Scotch whiskey. *It is time to die. To save Quenby and my family. Perhaps she will forgive me.* A cold and terrible fury grew in his belly. He no longer wanted to die. But he must. *I have experienced ålska kön, true love. For who and what I am, not for what I can do. For the first time, unconditional love.*

He shook his head, rose and went out the door into the hallway. Waiting for the elevator, Fahd began to shake. Once you were free to contemplate what duty, honor and truth were, principles, morality, life became very difficult. His hands trembled as the elevator cab that would carry him to his death arrived. The doors opened with a *swooosh* and he blinked from the brightness of the cab lights. *Love can blind us al-Wahab said, but so can hate. Yet hate surely cannot clarify the mind. Can love?*

The doors closed and the elevator whisked rapidly downward. Fahd felt like he had entered his tomb. He took out his PCD and replayed the message he had received this morning from Quenby. The

237

one he had not responded to.

"I want you to stay with me and not go. It's up to you," she whispered in the sing-song English of the Antal.

It's up to you, Fahd repeated to himself, recalled what Petrov had told him: "Let me tell you something about the self-controlled Antal, when they say, 'it's up to you,' it means, yes, I want it desperately."

Everything in him wanted to say, "Live! Live and let live!" But it was too much to ask.

He met Massoud and Ahmed at the Luna City Station. Three men from their vid-game clique were sitting nervously on a silicate bench. Faisal Khateeb was rubbing at the skin on his dark, hairy arms, Aziz Halawani's eyes were blinking so furiously it seemed the eyelids might fly off, and Sayyid Bustani was bouncing a knee up and down. The three shot anxious glances at Fahd and Massoud. They were all about to become *shahid.*

Faisal blanched at the three long trails of dried blood on Fahd's cheek. Aware of the audiovisual monitors, and aware of Massoud's tension, Fahd greeted the three waiting men amiably. *Scared shitless. Afraid something has gone terribly wrong. You don't know how right you are. And all of this is being recorded. Well, they probably know who we are by now. And it will make the work of the Valkyrie HURT Team or whomever they send for us easier. All I have to do now is play the game to the end.* Keeping to the rehearsed plan, Fahd announced quietly "Sorry to disturb your leisure time, but you've been called to meet here because we have an **imperative task** to perform at the **mass mover.** We'll all go to the game room in the Mall later for a **vid game** session."

The code words triggered Faisal's trained response. He responded with the counter-words, "Work comes first. We have unfinished work at the mover. So let us go together," he stated aloud, then

238

he softly chanted under his breath, "*Allahu-Akhbar*," put his arms around his two co-conspirators, Aziz and Sayyid, and took the first determined step forward to march the trio off to their last task in this life.

As they trooped toward the edge of the platform, Fahd glanced over at Massoud, who had his hand in his trouser pocket, clenched so tightly around the ceralloy blade that the point of the weapon made a sharp peak four inches from the imprint of his fingers. *A knife.* Fahd met Massoud's eyes. The intent to murder was obvious in those coal dark spheres. *In case I back out before we get where we're going?* But there was something else in Massoud's assassin's eyes. *Hatred. Disgust. You can't wait to watch me die can you?*

A palm and retina scan allowed the six men to enter the next carriage that swooped silently into the station. Monitors swept the carriage for any suspicious materials, focused briefly on Fahd's cut face, but located only the two vid games Fahd had in his pocket and the ceralloy implement in Massoud's. The maintenance team of three had obvious tools in their green uniform pockets. The doors closed, the carriage began to move. *Well, they haven't locked anything down yet. I'll probably have to play this out to the bitter end.*

Fahd sat silently ruminating as the mag-lev coach whizzed along through the tubes toward the magnetic mass mover. *It was foolish of me to believe she could accept what I must do.*

They passed the Animal and Plant Husbandry Facilities and he wondered how much intoxicating beverages, forbidden foods, and lately moondust had clouded his vision. *I do what I must do.*

The coach floated silently through the Spaceport Station. *How much do they know? How soon will they be here?*

The battle bridge of the Krieg command shuttle speeding toward Luna was a large oblong single eye dimly lit in red so the swath of visi-screens over the command consoles could be easily read. Images and data in Urtok symbols glowed green, yellow and white. In front of the screens, four wolflike warriors in black battle armor, softly growling instructions to the ship and each other through neckpiece communicators sat on chairs suspended from the ceiling to facilitate walking on the slip-resistant ceralloy deck.

A globe shaped Luna City holo, separated into above and below a thin silvery ring of lunar surface, floated in iridescent miniature in the center of the battle deck.

Luna City's vital signs: every life support system, security station, elevator, cargo load, or conveyance were displayed. All along the wall of screens, colored-light streaks and winking dots flashed on and off.

A grim-faced Marshal Natil marked the location of the Eagle Legion cutter, the second group of cutters, warbird and cruiser, and the freighters currently on their way from the Luna mass catcher to the low or the high orbit station. Calculations of estimated time to intercept in yellow Urtok numbers flashed next to them.

Slightly below the silvery lunar surface of the holo, and close up on the wall of visi-screens, Natil watched a large green dot move along the lunar tubeway toward the mass mover. *There he is. Our tracers have him.* She zeroed in on it and found the astrophysicist Fahd al-Sharfa. Then she tapped Aidan Ray Good on the shoulder with one sharp claw. "Now," she snarled.

Fahd felt a wave of energy sweep through his mind, shivered as a chill breeze froze his awareness in mid-thought, then a bubble seemed to pop and he shook his head, suddenly aware of being in the moving lunar carriage. *What was that?*

EXPENDABLE

The essence of war is violence,
and moderation in war is imbecility.
Thomas Baron Macaulay

Natil observed in lupine intensity, one yellow eye flashing back and forth to the timepiece in the visi-screen, as Aidan absorbed the mental images and full emotional impacts of the man's thoughts. *Two-point-two-five Terran seconds. Good. It will pass unnoticed.*

Natil returned her attention to the visi-screen showing the high and low orbit space stations, Starfarer and Redemption as softly glowing red dots on a black field speckled with white stars. Two lunar freighters, throbbing blue points of light trailing a fading azure charge wake were closing in on the flashing yellow mass catchers of the HOS and LOS.

The low orbit station blips were in range of the warbird's missiles; the cruiser would intercept the first high orbit station blip in four hours.

Natil turned a fiercely intense face toward the pale Vita-Kor seer clutching the battle bridge railing to steady herself from the impact of what she had absorbed, and demanded, "What do you know?"

Grasping her long red hair with both hands and pulling it tight behind her head to force herself back into equilibrium, Aidan

241

answered, "Launches will be made simultaneously from the magnetic mass mover and the lunar mass catcher. Two freighters from the lunar mass catcher heading for the space stations will have armed EMP devices. Fahd will return to Luna City with Massoud and personally fire a third EMP to destroy the life support systems. Four men will remain behind on the mass mover to prevent interruption of the cycle. But there's something else. Something I must have misread. Something I find hard to believe."

Natil was not waiting. She took immediate action. "*ZyA Zakkh! Zutu Tam Luna!*" she barked, diverting the cruiser straight to Luna. It could destroy the outward bound freighters, or if need be, the MMM or the Luna mass catcher. "*ZyA Vag!*" she ordered the warbird, "*Zutu Tam LOS! Tam Luna. Tam LOS.*"

New intercept estimates flashed on the screen as the captains swung their ships toward Luna and Redemption. Designated intercept points began flashing in red on the screen where the next two freighters that left the Luna mass catcher would be destroyed. Natil decided to give the order to launch missiles.

"Wait!" Aidan cried out. "During the probe I discovered the plotters have placed one man on each mass catcher, holding a dead man signal, ready to die for the cause. If the signal remains on past impact time, they will know their plot failed."

Natil's brow knotted in open disbelief. *Had the Terran dared to invade her mind again!* She turned viciously toward Aidan, her fangs bared and her hands on the Kuldai knives. But a thought form from Aidan hit the Krieg warrior like a slap in the face: *the fact that I probed a Terran without his consent, vice marshal, does in no way suggest I would ever do this to you.*

Natil staggered backward from the force of the thought.

Aidan now spoke aloud, the ice cold anger behind her words like another slap. "Your blazing red thought forms were clear indica-

242

tion that you were about to launch missiles." She took a deep breath. "Before we left Terra, Robert Walker asked me to probe his mind," she paused, "so I could properly advise you."

"Fine, Terran," Natil barked, her eyes narrowed to blazing golden slits, and her hands on the Kuldai blades under her battle garb. "Advise me! But remain aware," she growled ominously, "that, despite Robert Walker's plan to bag the entire terrorist cabal, I will not allow the devices to destroy the Terran space stations. Short of obliterating them in close proximity to create the impression they had struck their targets, as Walker planned, what would you suggest?"

The carriage reached the mass mover station. During the usual palm and retina scan and standard sweep of the carriage, Fahd regarded his image in the ceralloy window and mused. *They have no word for honor those Antal, and this three-pronged scar upon my face says she can be violent despite her protestations that it is inexcusably evil. But her logic, that wrong cannot be right, is impeccable, despite her inability to live up to her own standards.*

The doors opened. The six men alighted and moved quickly toward the control center. Four scans later, they arrived in Fahd's office. Fahd focused on his visi-screen. All systems were in secure status.

He opened a channel to the mass catcher. "Luna to mass catcher."

Mohsen's voice echoed through the room like rolling thunder. "Mass catcher here. El-Sayed."

"LOS and HOS have requested special deliveries," Fahd announced. "How soon can you launch?"

"Fifteen Terran minutes LOS, thirty Terran minutes HOS," the voice on the other end replied.

"Have you got enough vid games to entertain you until the next launch, Mohsen?" Fahd responded with a quavering voice.

243

There was a moment's hesitation. Then Mohsen's basso response. "I have one for each hand, boss man."

"You'll need them both."

"Roger that," Mohsen answered.

Fahd slowly stroked the slashes on his cheek as if they were Quenby. "*Inshallah*, I will see you soon," he half-croaked. "*Allahu-Akhbar!*"

Fahd patched off, looked at determined Massoud and dutiful Ahmed, turned and watched a bot move along the ceralloy window, digesting moondust. He could see Luna City. He announced over the intercom, "Two bucket replacements to mass catcher, authorization al-Sharfa one," and activated the computer module.

The buzzer sounded. "Launch in five minutes." All systems went into secure status. Open doors shut. Connecting tubes were sectioned into blast-proof segments. Sensors swept every passageway with full visuals.

Six green lights lit up one after another on his screen. Everything was in order. He spoke into the mike below the screen. "All systems go. Countdown initiated. Launch one in," he checked the clock, "four minutes, fifteen seconds, launch two in nine minutes, fifteen seconds."

Everything was automated. The computers would manage the process. Nothing would go wrong. Ahmed would stay behind with the three maintenance men, lock the door after Fahd and Massoud left, and prevent anyone from belaying that order. Soon all attention would be upon the mass mover.

Yes. That was the plan. An unscheduled double launch would bring a routine security call which would go unanswered. That would trigger a security team. Ahmed and the three others would resist all efforts to enter the control room. Security would assume that the MMM launches were part of whatever was happening. It was obvious. Why draw such attention to yourself if it was not absolutely necessary? If they went a step further, they would assume that the two next shipments were the live ones, not the ones that Mohsen had simultaneously launched from the mass catcher. Even if they were successful, they would destroy the wrong targets. And the diversion would leave Fahd and Massoud free to destroy Luna City.

That was the plan. But Fahd had substituted harmless vid games for the EMP devices. *So far, so good. I will die when the security teams find us or when my EMP fails to go off and Massoud kills me. Either way, no one but myself and these would-be-martyrs will die.*

The two men quickly moved off, let the sensors scan their retinas, sense Fahd's highest priority clearance, and open the door for them. They walked quickly but not suspiciously so down the long semi-spherical hallway past two more visi-scans, placed their palms against the handprint scanner to access the tube, boarded another carriage and headed for the Luna City Mall.

Fahd had more time to think. The gashes on his cheek had begun to throb. Thoughts buzzed through his mind like angry hornets. *Right, wrong. Good, evil. Honor, truth. What was truth and what was moondust?*

As the coach hurtled toward its destination, Fahd heard a voice outside himself speaking. *The prophet said, the greater jihad is the more difficult and more important struggle: against one's ego, selfishness, greed and evil.* He glanced at Massoud, who clearly had heard nothing. He felt his previously outstanding mind control was failing him. Now he was hearing voices.

When the carriage pulled into Luna City Terminal, Fahd stiffened, frozen in awe: on the platform a slim white figure stood straight and tall, long white hair cascading across her shoulders like the torrent of doom! *Quenby! She must have used her own highest priority clearance to track us!* Streaks of silver ran from her grey eyes down her white cheeks. The tears the Antal never shed. Fahd tensed as the carriage doors hissed open, and his lover looked sorrowfully at him, the boy from Wadi Shiban. Massoud reached inside his pocket where the ceralloy blade lay ill-concealed. *I cannot let him kill her. I . . .*

He reached one hand out to restrain Massoud. "I'll handle this," he hissed at the man. "No," he said firmly to Quenby. "Let me do what I must."

"We are joined," Quenby announced in deadened tones, "where you go I go. Whether we live or die. Whether you forget this *tökmyck* or not."

No, Fahd wanted to say. You must live. But what could he say? To lie to her was impossible. To speak the truth would unleash Massoud's murderous wrath and the vengeance of Ahmar Saif on his family.

"What have you told her?" Massoud hissed.

"I will not hamper you in any way. Nor will I assist you, but I will die with you," the tearful Quenby solemnly announced.

Fahd could see the determination in her eyes. Tears welled up in his own eyes. *Why? Why had it come to this?* But he could see there was no way out. Massoud would kill her here and now if he had to. Only the cameras and the fact that they were far from their objective stopped his murderous hand. *So it must be, then,* Fahd decided despondently. Their eyes met in silent sadness.

Fahd could no longer speak.

"Then we go together," Quenby sighed. She wrapped one long white arm around Fahd, to Massoud's obvious consternation. They marched silently out of the station, across the great Luna City Mall, and down again, past the research laboratories and offices, Quenby looking only at Fahd. Fahd warily watching Massoud all the time. They reached the life support level. All were admitted.

At the next access portal, the two high-ranking scientists were given access but Massoud was denied entry, as Fahd knew he would. Massoud stood impatiently outside the doorway. Fahd looked right and left, saw no one in the large room which was abandoned until the evening shift came on. He turned as if to go back out the doorway, and when it opened to let him pass, grabbed Massoud and pulled him inside as they had planned.

Klaxons blared and red warning lights flashed in the hall. Doors hissed shut as the complex went into lockdown. "UNAU-THORIZED ENTRANT INTO THIS AREA! HALT IMMEDI-ATELY AND AWAIT SECURITY!" the speaker proclaimed authoritatively.

Fahd went to the security code box on this side of the heavy-duty hatch, pulled a small rectangular circuit fryer from his pocket, slapped it onto the palm scan, hit a second button and jumped with the shock as a small pulse of electromagnetic charge passed through to the device. Sparks flew. The box crackled, a thin wisp of smoke leaked out from under the cover and it shut down. He did the same with the retina recognition box.

"There. Now they'll have to cut their way in here," he said with finality. "No one gets in or out. With the lasers they have here, it'll take them at least fifteen minutes to cut through the door. The package to LOS launched eight minutes ago." He turned to Massoud, "I will have sufficient time to do what I need to do."

Massoud's face was a mask of rage and loathing. "So will I."

"Security breech, Luna City Life Support Center," barked the com officer on the battle shuttle. The visi-screen and holo showed Life Support and MMM Control Centers, in undulating orange, going into lockdown. Luna Security teams were white dots moving rapidly toward the locations. The green dot that was three terrorists had reached the life support center which now flashed red.

247

Even if Natil had wanted to ignore the damage to Luna City and incinerate them, the terrorists were out of range of her weapons. Then she saw the silver flashing light of the cutter that had left Terra earlier with two Eagle Legion teams, making its descent to the lunar surface. *Bajar and Peebles!*

Natil opened a link to the Eagle Legion cutter, flashed the vi-si-screen data across, and then went to voice. "Assault speed. Team A to the mass mover. Team B to Luna City Airlock One. Proceed immediately to MMM and Life Support Control Centers. Terminate threat. All means necessary." She tapped the mute voice button. "If Luna Security has not neutralized the threat within fifteen minutes, they will." Like every good officer, Natil sounded like she believed that. But she knew there was no room for error, no room for senti-ment. Bajar and Peebles had a very limited window of engagement. If they could not complete the mission within that time frame she would have to. And they would die. *Why did I allow Bajar to go on this mission? To become expendable.* She turned her attention once more to the visi-screen where the blue lights of the freighters drew ever closer to the yellow dots. *Walker's plan is flawed. And this witch has no alternative to give me.* Natil looked over at her fire control officer. She was about to give the order to fire at the freighters.

At that moment, a piercing *waaaooog* alarm sounded across the bridge and the war shuttle's computer announced, "Hull breech by incoming object, bridge sector."

A shimmering cloud of energy began to swirl on the bridge deck, gathered itself into a whirling mass of light that took first an azure, then an ocean blue, finally a deep royal blue tint, swelled in length and breadth until it was eight feet tall. A large five-part eye stared out from where the head would be.

Snuffling angrily at the unannounced intrusion, Natil curtly ordered her security chief to holster his blaster. The nimbus extended two blue waves of light and enveloped Aidan and Natil in a swirling cobalt cloud, sharing its thoughts with them.

Natil took an alarmed step backward, shot an inky look at her visitor, and then displayed her full set of fangs. "You've done what?! Modified a flawed plan? Used untested technology four thousand years old?" She snorted. "One freighter is thirteen Terran minutes from impact! And you want me to go along with this?" She glared at Vitok. He could stop her if he chose to. *But would he?* "How certain are you this will work," she barked demandingly.

"Four thousand years ago, we staked our planet on the conviction it would. It may be ancient but I believe it will suffice today," the Nord replied sedately. "We will know certainly in thirteen minutes."

Luna State Security came live on visi-screen.

The vice marshal shot a stern glance at her com officer, who nodded his head to indicate that he had sent a formal request to Luna to offer Eagle Legion assistance, as required. Natil growled, "We'll finish this discussion after I deal with Luna Security." She turned to face the visi-screen where she saw a large, grim faced man with two golden moons on his collar standing in the center of an office full of consoles and tense operators directing orders to Luna Security teams. The man turned to look through miles of space into the battle shuttle bridge with professional sharpness. The sight of Vice Marshal Natil, Aidan Good, and Vitok the Nord standing side by side made those eyes open very wide.

"Colonel Koz," Natil stated, "We have reason to believe you may need assistance to eliminate two terrorist threats. Request permission to do so." *Observe the formalities as long as you must.*

He hesitated for just a nano-second. "Eagle Legion war shuttle, we read you loud and clear. We are on our way to both sites. We, ahh, welcome your assistance."

Natil cut the channel and turned to Vitok. "Walker's plan was off beam. Yours better not be."

"Plans are useful only until the engagement begins. This is not a plan. It's a tactic. Have you ever known a Nord tactic to fail?"

"No," Natil reluctantly replied, then snarled, "but there's always a first time." She wheeled toward the visi-screens and stridently ground her teeth.

Within moments, leaving eerie footprints in the lunar regolith, like ghosts wanting to terrorize the living, thirteen Terrans in stealth suits that made them invisible, came out of what appeared to be a small lunar crater wall--the landing craft itself--flattened out until it appeared to be nothing but crater. They came at a dead run from the blind side of the MMM to precisely the point in the above-ground installation where the command office was located. A laser beam appeared seemingly out of thin air and began to cut its way through the wall.

Thirteen more hit the ground running toward Airlock One. The first invisible man to the airlock door hit the open button, and five seconds later closed the door behind the rest of the team.

Bill Peebles was the first to the inner door. He waited for the airlock to return to almost normal atmosphere and opened that door with a small oblong pass-all device woven into the ring finger of the suit. A last small puff of atmosphere dissipated into the vacuum of the lunar surface.

The team ran down the corridor to the elevator that had been raised to that level by the battle shuttle, and packed in like a nest of invisible Kuldorian vipers, rode down to the life support level, sprang out of the elevator and stopped at the access portal Fahd al-Sharfa had jammed.

The Luna Security team there nearly jumped out of their

skins as Wingmaster Bajar gave the order to clear face mask sections and fourteen faces appeared out of thin air and then became instantly invisible once more. Bajar instantly restored calm to the situation. If the Lunies raised their weapons they would be dead before they knew what hit them. The automated suits would respond at four to five times humanoid reaction speed. "Greetings gentlemen, and ladies," he rolled out in his most impeccable British accent. "Please excuse the lack of visibility, but as you can," he snorted, "or cannot see, my team has the latest Eagle Legion tactical suits on."

He tapped a button on his arm and allowed himself to become completely visible, though the suit changed to chameleon grey to match its current surroundings.

His suit had a small flat chest and hip pouch containing defensive weaponry systems. Hypervelocity kinetic laser cutters were attached to one arm, blasters were in a small pack on the back of the right and left wrists.

"Don't ask," he continued with a wave of one gloved hand. "We should not be showing you any of this. I will tell you that our Krieg partners created these for us. The suits are undetectable by any known Terran means and more intelligent than most Terran AI units. When it is over, one would hope you might forget all about them."

Natil suppressed a snicker as the sound came over the bridge mikes. She knew the word would go further and faster than a quantum intrusion. The terrifying Black Eagles would become even more so.

In the Luna Security command center, Colonel Koz stumbled in shock. He thumbed his throat mike and struggled for the right way to put the question. "Eagle Legion war shuttle. We have security breaches at Airlock One, at the Life Support Control Center, and at the north side of the Mass Mover Control Center. But we have detected no movement. We note three Terran target life signs in the

251

MMM and another three in the LSCC, but no life signs other than our own teams outside the areas. Advise."

Grinning wolfishly at the effectiveness of the Krieg equipment, Natil responded, "Our teams are equipped with stealth suits, colonel. They have reached their target locations."

"Understood, shuttle," a tight-eyed Koz responded, shaking his head in the negative, leaving unsaid, we're going to talk after this, lady. "Luna State Security forces have sealed the perimeters and are equipped with chem-bio response and explosive ordnance disposal equipment. Now your ghosts just have to get them before they do whatever they plan to do."

FAHD

*Your task is not to seek for love, but merely to seek and find all the barriers with-
in yourself that you have built against it.*

Rumi

The details of my incarnate life continue to waver in and out of my
consciousness. There are great blind spots in my recollection but I
persist in doing what Kirsan Tabiyat told me to do, to think about
the prejudices and fears I hide from myself. Painful as that is, I pierce
them one by one and with each new revelation, part the veil of forgetfulness that separates me from truth.

Death and the grave now seem but gateways. I'm pressing on,
under the guidance of Kirsan Tabiyat and the Vita-Kor Sister from
the living, Aidan Good, gaining new knowledge every day, and even
some wisdom. Aidan comes more often now, always with a sense of
urgency swirling around her like her cloud of red hair. "Kirsan and I
are pleased with your progress Fahd," she told me just a short time
ago. I cannot say just when she came for time has become even more
slippery over here.

As I drop this or that ignorance or prejudice, change, blessed
change, comes more and more quickly. I hardly recognize the being I
am becoming: he is so different from the arrogant, analytical man-
child I was before I died. Aidan and Kirsan have helped me break
down the barriers in my heart, to see the truth, to feel the love that

253

surrounds each of us like the air itself which each life breathes without being aware of it.

I find as I gain more knowledge I lose just as much in what I let go, as if only by emptying my mind can I fill my heart. It is so hard and it is so easy, just letting lower thoughts and fears fall away, seeking higher ground. I say higher and ground to use your words, but there is no up or down, and no firm footing here. Or, that is, one may find firm footing but that is imposed self-reality, an illusion. Moving on requires venturing out of the known, the familiar, into the unknown, more unfamiliar than I could possibly explain.

It requires a leap of faith over reason. The mind I was so proud of, thought was so powerful, is such a little thing, driven by such small motives. It fears the unknown, wants to hold fast to what it knows, and cries out against the leap into the nameless, unfamiliar, undiscovered beyond. It casts doubts and fear at you. "Hold fast," it cries out. "This way lies madness." Perhaps that is why so many here just relax and enjoy whatever they conceive heaven to be.

Change produces discomfort even here, and that discomfort then prods one into further change. And the greater the change, the greater the discomfort. Forgive me if I expound on what may be obvious to you, but words have become clumsy tools to me.

I am working hard to make myself worthy for the task that lies before me. I read the Kitab al-kashaf as often as I can, chanting *Alláhu, Alláhu, Alláhu, Haqq,* to understand the compatibility between reason and faith, and to find the truth. All my earth life I sought truth. My mind was my castle. Now my heart has supplanted my mind and my heart has no desire to stay where doubts arise and fears dismay. I seek truth, and truth is found in the heart not the mind.

I frequently wonder what the bittersweet opportunity to serve truth will be, and when I do that, I find myself thinking of the Antal, find myself inside a great white cloud, enveloped in a sing-song,

254

humming chant, a loving song reaching into my soul, Antal floating all about me, beckoning to me to come join with them. And I feel Quenby's spirit swirling like a cloud within my own, calling out to me, caressing me. I ache to be with her. I have tried to reach out to her on this side of the veil of death, but I cannot find her. When I speak of my attempts to reach Quenby, Kirsan and Aidan merely smile and make no reply. I wonder if this is to be my eternal punishment.

SHAHID

For what a man had rather were true he more readily believes.
Francis Bacon

Fahd worked meticulously, deliberately; he knew what he had to do. He went to the security code box on this side of the door to the main life support control room, withdrew a second small rectangular circuit fryer from his pocket, carefully placed it next to the box, pressed the activation switch and watched the sparks fly. He did the same with the retina recognition box. Then he simply swung the door open. Howling alarms went off. Luna City's life support system lay open to destruction.

Fahd stood in the doorway, pulled the apparatus off the outer retina recognition box, repeated the two-step process and fried the interior circuits. He pulled the hot, smoking device off the wall and wedged it between the door and the door frame, jamming the door to the inner sanctum open. The two sets of alarms continued to wail in eerie disharmony punctuated by "UNAUTHORIZED ENTRANT . . . HALT IMMEDIATELY . . ." Even over that cacophony Fahd heard the Luna Security team working on getting into the rooms. The acrid odor of burning metal assailed Fahd's nostrils, made his eyes tear up. *Blasters? No, the sound's too steady. They must have a high-powered laser cutter. They'll probably cut a hole in the door and inject some kind of gas to incapacitate or kill everyone.* He worked furiously on the EMP device he held. *When they punch through, Massoud will certainly kill me. Will*
256

he kill Quenby? Doubtlessly.

Quenby stood next to him, like a mournful white angel, so otherworldly, so sorrowful. He looked down, avoiding eye contact with her, rubbed one hand against the front of his uniform shirt, over his heart. Somehow he had to keep Quenby alive. But how? He looked toward the door and Massoud who had an evil smirk on his face. It was a slim chance, but better than none at all. He reached out to Quenby, took her hand, and guided her to stand by his side, with his body between her and Massoud. *My only chance of saving Quenby is to hope they don't use poison gas. Merciful Allah, let them use knockout gas and let Massoud be overcome by the gas before he can kill Quenby.*

Now he had to make it appear that he needed to complete wiring one last EMP box. His fingers danced along the surface of the vid-game wiring. He'd play for time as long as he could. At the last possible moment he'd aim it at the main control panel touch it off and shout in surprise when it failed to operate. Then turn to give Massoud a large target and shield Quenby. *I must make it appear that I was loyal to the end or my entire clan will die.* "Look, Massoud," he shouted, pointing at the far door, to distract him, "the outer door is holding. I'm almost finished. It is all in Allah's hands now."

Massoud turned his head, looked apprehensively at the smoke rising from a small diameter red-hot point on the door, then back at Fahd with eyes filled with fury and hate. "Yes. It's all in Allah's hands," he cried in a shrill, tremulous voice, "More than you know, Fahd," over the sound of the alarms and admonitions of "INTRUDER . . . HALT IMMEDIATELY!"

When Massoud saw Fahd swing open the door to the Life Support Control Room, his face had broken into a wicked leer that now was a mask of unadulterated malevolence. He bared his teeth and declared in a voice he was sure Fahd could not hear over the

257

howling sirens, "Fahd you coward! You fool! You've given me what I want. You think you're so clever, but I have outsmarted you." He clutched the blade in his pocket and began to move forward. "And now I'll slit your throats like sheep." Then the sound and smell of burning metal made him stop. Moving further away and turning his back so Fahd couldn't see what he was doing, he extracted a vidgame from his trouser pocket, popped the top and began to finish rearranging the innards as he had seen Fahd do. "It is time for me to end this charade and destroy Luna City myself! If only I had known sooner! I would have completed all the devices, and had time enough to cut the throats of this coward and his Antal houri! But *Inshallah*, I still may, and then I will die in a glorious flash of light!"

The Eagle Legion A Team's lasers cut away, creating an ever-penetrating hot red circle that dripped melting cera-metal down their side of the door, but they had not pierced more than halfway through. The walls surrounding the Life Support equipment were super-fortified alloy. Time was running out for Luna City.

Twenty five miles away, on the plains of Mare Nubium, time had run out for the terrorists in the mass mover. Eagle Legion team B had pierced a pinhole through the metalloy skin of the control room. Maintaining absolute pressure, so the whole room would not be sucked into the lunar vacuum, they switched valves and filled the area with odorless, colorless, toxic gas. Nearest the aperture, Faisal, Aziz and Sayyid crumpled to the floor before they knew what hit them. At the control desk, Ahmed suddenly turned pale, became dizzy, his breath immediately came in labored gasps, as if he suffered an abrupt blockage of his throat. His eyes rolled upwards as he tumbled to the floor.

The rest of the B Team finished cutting through the internal doorway and four troopers in gas-impervious smart suits rushed into

258

the room, tucking and rolling as they did, their smart suits detecting no live targets. They scanned the entire area for explosives and found none.

Amaka Alston paced the floor, kicking one body after another, then strode purposefully over to tap the intercom with a gloved hand and with a stone-cold voice advised Luna Security, "All dead. We're finished here. Magnetic mass mover secure," and signaled the team members outside to begin to pump the gas into the lunar vacuum where it would dissipate.

One green light flashed on the MMM visi-screen of Luna Security Command. But on another screen, two white dots flashed toward the lunar mass catcher.

Colonel Koz hit the transmit switch on his communicator. "Luna Security to Eagle shuttle. MMM Command Center reports secure. But we still have two buckets launched with authorization 'al-Sharfa one' enroute to Luna mass catcher. Request intercept."

"Acknowledged, Luna Security," Natil's com officer responded in flawless English over an open channel. He looked questioningly at his commander, who replied calmly on the open channel so anyone listening in could hear it, "At Luna Security's request, target the two buckets and destroy them at midpoint with lasers."

The gunnery officer's long black tongue ran over her fangs as she input the coordinates and pressed the fire button twice. Two bright yellow flashes lit up the blackness of space. She grinned. "Ky Rok!"

Natil calmly translated over the open channel, "Two targets destroyed." She shifted her attention to screen six which showed the green dot that was three terrorists were inside the life support center which was now flashing a second red light. She exchanged a meaningful glance with Aidan, commanded, "Do what you must at once

259

and advise me."

Aidan nodded and probed Fahd's mind again. Then she frowned and probed Massoud. "I was correct. Al-Sharfa has sabotaged the plot. He will not blow up the life support system. He's trying to delay, hoping we use non-toxic gas so the Antal female with him will be spared. But there is another EMP device, in the hands of the man Massoud. And he thinks he can finish the assembly in seven more minutes."

Natil hit her intercom button. "Bajar. Extract your teams."

"Why?"

"In six minutes I will use my weaponry on the Luna City facility."

"Six minutes?"

"In approximately seven minutes, the man Massoud will destroy the life support system."

"Massoud? You mean al-Sharfa."

"No. Forget al-Sharfa. Extract your teams."

Everyone on the battle shuttle bridge heard Bajar and Peebles poll their teams.

"We're not extracting."

Natil slashed the air with her razor sharp claws. "That was an order, wingmaster!"

"Respectfully, vice marshal, that was an order for the Eagle Legion to fail in the most important mission it's ever had. We can't allow that. We will succeed or die trying, like the warriors we are."

The battle bridge lapsed into shocked silence. All eyes turned toward Natil.

She spun toward the wall of the battle shuttle where no one could see the expression on her face, stood silently for a full three seconds, then cleared her throat with what sounded like a grief-stricken whine and responded. "Of course you will." Leaving the channel open, she signed off with the words, "*Virt Tarren Vaphut*," May the stars protect you. She tapped another button on her communicator, signaled Koz on a secure channel that she would terminate the threat with a laser guided small diameter bomb in six Terran minutes.

Koz, visible on the shuttle's visi-screen, blanched, then nodded, "Agreed, Eagle shuttle."

On the still open channel, everyone on the shuttle bridge was listening to what would be the last six minutes of Bajar, Peebles and the A Team's lives.

"Is there another way into that room?" Bajar demanded of a Luna Security officer.

"There's an air duct in the ceiling."

Seizing a flechette grenade, Bajar ordered, "Take me there."

The brawny Luna Security captain pointed at a circle about a foot and a half across in the rounded top of the passageway about four feet to his right. "We usually have bots maintain them," the captain responded crossly, as he pulled open a panel exposing a folding ladder and maintenance supplies. "It's too small for a man. A boy might be able to get through it."

"Get a ladder and some grease," Bajar shouted. Bajar stripped off his suit. The small brown man stood naked, with four invisible hands from his still undetectable team slapping grease all over him.

The Lunar Security captain muttered, "I'm dealing with madmen on both sides of the door." He said shakily, "It's about twenty feet to the main Life Support equipment room."

Peebles hit a button on his stealth suit and cleared his visor. A big, black face appeared out of nowhere. He ordered the Luna Security teams to vacate the area. "On the dead run," he told them coldly. "Things are about to go BOOM here."

They hesitated only for a few seconds. There was little they could do to assist the ghost figures. And they had no need to die to prove their bravery. The blue-uniformed captain hit the transmit button on his communicator and requested permission to withdraw. Then he and his teams ran for their lives down the walkways, firmly closing every blast door behind them.

Time to impact was now four minutes, thirty-one Terran seconds.

"The gas will rise into the air duct, Shafat," Peebles told him needlessly.

"Give me a boost, commander, and do what you must!" the small man said as he leaped from the ladder into the air duct, arms forward, one hand holding the grenade. Peebles grabbed Bajar's feet and pushed hard. Bajar squeezed and wriggled, made himself smaller, and succeeded in getting into the duct.

Peebles turned, got down on one knee and said in a loud voice, "Please Lord, let him get there before I do, but let one of us get there before Natil pulls the trigger."

Bajar crawled toward the target room ignoring the slashing cuts from pressing against raw metal ductwork.

The clock ticked down. Three minutes, three seconds.

On the bridge of the battle shuttle, Aidan heard and felt all of this and shook with grief. She looked up at Vitok, who gazed down with his five-part eye, taking in the entirety of her thought forms. His center eye widened as he understood what she intended, but he nodded acquiescence.

Aidan excused herself, strode off the bridge, took two steps and vanished.

Almost simultaneously, Val collapsed a quantum wave and appeared onto the area of the shuttle where his mother had been. Hovering in the quantum hologram the entire time, Val had been eavesdropping on all that transpired. Distressed by his mother's decision to insert herself into the gravely dangerous situation, and Natil's absolutely irrevocable resolve to immolate everyone, he decided to take action. He quickly reassessed the situation, confirmed his information, and disappeared just as he felt Vitok, who might attempt to stop him, register his presence.

Intruder alert signals sounded on the bridge of the Krieg war craft. Natil looked questioningly at Vitok. "Another quantumly intruded individual come and gone? Did it go down there?"

"*Saarp kaawta, wal fwuup a hahpa,*" the translucid blue figure replied with a nod.

Natil snarled disapproval. "The viper strikes but the eagle shall eat it? I've had more than enough of Nord prophesy and Terran witches, Vitok. Whoever is down there," she checked the visi-screen, "has two minutes, thirty-two Terran seconds to get out or be incinerated."

The large blue figure nodded again. "*Kondok, Fokhan,*" he said unequivocally in Urtok. Then he sat on the battle deck and went into the Kir trance.

Aidan reappeared in the passageway near where Peebles team was working. A horde of diaphanous figures surrounded her: PBM's, the Terran dead police force. Peebles stared open mouthed. About twenty filmy figures swooped and circled in the semi-circular access way, creating a whirlwind of gossamer energy in blazing orange and red, shot through with sharp flashes of yellow and ominous black overladings. Peebles tried to grab Aidan, but discovered that he could neither move nor speak. Aidan's PBMs had taken control of his mind

263

away from him. Shaking her long red hair violently, Aidan scolded, "I'm here. You need me. Do not interfere." She sent her PBMs through the glowing red wall and into the systems control chamber with a thrust of her pale hand.

They were not alone. Aidan alarmingly noted a quantum mass she couldn't identify lurking slightly above the PBMs who were now surrounding Fahd and Quenby. Val had rushed through with them.

Massoud completed his work on the vid game, snapped the cover shut and with a fiendish grin, turned toward Fahd. *Ha! Before I blow this place sky high I will take my revenge on the coward!* Holding the vid-game in his left, he reached his right hand into his trouser pocket, gripped the ceralloy blade, took it carefully between his thumb and forefinger and slithered closer to Fahd and Quenby. *I'll cut both their throats.*

A vortex of raging energy, guided by Aidan's unerring psychic sense, overwhelmed Massoud. Clapping his hands to his ears, he fell to the floor, opening his mouth in a soundless scream that refused to issue from his throat. His eyes rolled white in his head and his whole frame shook in terror. A dark yellow stain spread along his trousers as his body convulsed.

In the corridor, Peebles, who'd regained his ability to move, placed his large body between Aidan and the control room, though it would do nothing at all when Natil pulled the trigger. They'd all fry.

Massoud regained partial control of his mind, looked at the yellow stain and turned livid with fury. He struggled to his knees, shouted, "Fahd, you son of a dog! I found you out! I reassembled those vid games I took to the mass catcher into EMPs! They'll blow the space stations into oblivion!" He reached down and picked up the vid-game he'd dropped. "That was easy. This, constructing one from scratch, and not letting you know what I was doing, was difficult. But

264

you were too busy with your houri," he sneered, "to notice." And now I have completed the assembly of this one and I'll blow you into hell." He laughed maniacally at Fahd staring in obvious shock and disbelief. "Die you traitorous coward!" Massoud screamed. "And your houri with you!"

But taking the time to announce his revenge was Massoud's last mistake. As he staggered to the open door and aimed the device at the main computer deck, a horrific series of howls, shrieks and wails assailed his ears. His thoughts were shattered by an attacking cacophony of mental gobbledygook. The room spun, he saw flashes of swirling red light and roiling black mist, and his fingers refused to work. He could see nothing but colors, churning, eddying, red and black, pierced by a terrifying crescendo of unearthly screeching. Massoud shook, shrieking in blind terror, his unseeing eyes wide with fear of the devils that had invaded his mind.

Quenby, the least affected of the three, covered her ears and gazed forlornly straight ahead, tears cascading from her eyes.

The air duct above their heads slipped slightly downward about three inches, and a small brown hand dropped a flechette grenade into the room.

In sickening slow motion, Quenby saw it dropping, seized Fahd by the shoulders and whirled him about so that her body was between him and the grenade.

Fahd's vision cleared slightly. As if in a dream, he watched the grenade descend through the muddy red-black air, realized with an appalling jolt to the heart that Quenby was throwing herself in front of him. *Love has made her less Antal; can love make you more human?* echoed through his mind.

Though she was three times stronger, he summoned up all

the will power that had made him who he was and with every ounce of strength he had, swung her around, covering as much of her body as he could with his own. But she was a foot and a half taller: it would not save her. Still, he had to try. He was going to die. "Merciful Allah! Let me die in love, not hatred!"

With a huge BANG-HISSS, a murderous shower of needles exploded into the room.

Shafat Bajar dropped from the shaft to the floor bleeding through the grease from several nasty metal gashes and a few flechettes, knife between his teeth. The knife was unnecessary. It was over. Three bloody, pierced beings lay on the deck. He used the communicator he had taped to his left wrist to signal the shuttle. "Three targets eliminated."

Aidan folded her hands in Vita-Kor fashion, connected with Vitok in the Kir, and reappeared a second later on the battle bridge. This time, Natil reached over, clasped Aidan's hand in hers and said, "Kwet Kitr, Kulvak." She reached down, plucked the Star of Kulvar from her battle cape, and pinned it on Aidan.

A timer on the battle bridge reached zero, zero, zero. A freighter made contact with Redemption's mass catcher and set off a horrendous static lightning blast, crackle and SNAP! The sky lit up as the shock wave spread in a titanic horseshoe shaped flare around the mass catcher, toward and past the space station. All communication ceased. On the visi-screens in Luna Security, the command shuttle, the warbird and the cruiser, the lights of Redemption and its mass catcher blinked out, leaving a gaping hole in that part of space.

Vitok, Natil and Aidan looked silently at each other.

On Terra, two visi-screens showed the flash of light and the disappearance of the low orbit space station. In Alalabad the dead man signal from Redemption's mass catcher ceased abruptly.

Overjoyed, Faisal Hashim al-Wahab jumped up waving his hands in ecstasy, and bellowed, "AAAAHHH!" He had worked for twelve years to achieve this victory! Redemption was gone! "All the world is about to see this," he gloated, "the destruction of the Great Satan's Evil Work, his symbol of domination! My vengeance!"

The men in the room began to celebrate. One leaned out a window and let loose several rounds from his AK-58.

Al-Wahab shook both fists in the air disdainfully. "The fools took the bait, they pierced the plot but fell for the deception, went after the mass mover and the Luna mass catcher. *Inshallah*, Luna City will follow and in four days, Starfarer will wink out its devil's eye forever." He began to furiously pound his fist on a table, laughing fanatically, shrieking, "*Allahu-akhbar!*"

From somewhere, he heard the words, *Allâhu, Allâhu, Allâhu, Haqq* and from the same somewhere, the thought entered his mind, *With this chaos, it is safe to celebrate, to break security, just for a few seconds. They won't be able to track one call.*

He counted out one hundred and twenty seconds for the Terran communication lines to reach overload, triggered his SAT PCD. He rang up Koscientzi, and with a maniacal laugh shouted, "Vladimir! Have you not seen the flaming end of the space station? Surely, now you cannot doubt your money was well spent! We've done it! Praise Allah!"

"So it would appear, my friend," the somber Russian replied ominously, sitting tensely in his overstuffed black leather chair, a glass of chilled Vodka in his right hand. He swilled a long shot and snorted, "Tonight I shall be appropriately chagrined and sorrowful. Tomorrow I shall denounce Walker for his incompetent handling of the lunar situation, take my rightful place as Chairman of the World Com Board, and bring those Lunies to heel." Then he clicked off. A black mood spread across his face; he took a long pull straight from the vodka bottle. "The fool!" he snarled. "Breaking security, even for such an event." He took another long pull from the bottle and threw it across the room at the nineteenth century gilded mirror on the wall. "We must eliminate him now! Before he gives us all away."

"Da, comrade leader," the burly man in the tailored grey sharkskin suit replied, keying his own PCD.

TERRA

Wherefore let him that thinketh he standeth take heed
lest he fall.

1 Corinthians 10-12

At four a.m. Valkyrie Team Five burst into Koscientzi's dacha, firing as they entered. His two bodyguards dropped instantly. The security chief's phone lay buzzing in the dead man's hand, signaling the alarm that would do no good.

Koscientzi was ripped from his bed. A female trooper tore the pistol out of his hand, backhanded him sharply across the face, slipped a plastic noose around his hands and his throat and pulled them tight so quickly that he turned pale. His breath suddenly came in awkward gasps. Trying to bluff his way out, he shouted between rasping lurches for air, "What is this outrage!"

She lifted her aramid mask to reveal a dark Cossack face. "Get moving you bastard!" she said as she roughly shoved him toward the door. "I have three centuries worth of reasons to kill you. Don't give me even one more little one." Outside the door, she jerked the neck noose, making him gasp and wheeze, and unceremoniously kicked him hard in the rump until he lurched forward through the open door of the assault carrier and fell on his face. Two pairs of hands lifted him to his knees and loosened the neck noose.

269

"Well, well, Vladimir, you appear to have stumbled." Robert Walker took a spoonful of the Beluga caviar he had in a silver bowl on his lap and stuck it in Koscientzi's gaping mouth. Koscientzi spit it out in terror. "Too bad, Vladimir. That's the last caviar you'll have for quite a while. They don't serve it where you're going." Walker dipped the small silver spoon back into the bowl.

"You'll pay for this Walker!"

"No, Vladimir, you'll pay for it. We've already frozen all your assets. You can kiss them goodbye."

"And you can kiss your damn space stations goodbye!"

"No. Nothing was blown up."

"You're crazy! I saw Redemption disappear!"

"Yes. You did, didn't you? You blundering fool!" Walker began to laugh.

In Alalabad, twelve pairs of invisible feet left footprints in the sand as Team One walked right up to al-Wahab's villa in their stealth suits, sent gas canisters through the open windows of four rooms, waited for the sporadic firing and shouting to stop, burst in and rounded up sixteen terrorists.

At the same time, stealth-suited Eagle Legion Teams put sleeping gas into the oxygen supply of the Luna, Redemption and Starfarer mass catchers, took three conspirators off the installations into decloaked Krieg warships, and then revived everyone.

On Kot, Krieg justice, noted for its swiftness, was exacted in pools of cerulean blood.

And all across Terra and Kot, shrieking banshees swooped down, restraining and carrying off the dead who'd been involved in the plots, Hosney El Sawy and his servant among them. They would spend much time in the limbo world where they had sent so many good spirits. There was plenty of room there now that the good had been released.

At eight a.m., in the earth side Terran Trade Center, a large vid screen above and behind Robert Walker, Vitok, Marshal Pardek and a grinning Vice Marshal Natil flashed images of Redemption disappearing in a flash of light, then reappearing.

Robert Walker clicked on his throat mike. "In a joint operation today, Eagle Legion, PBM and Krieg forces, with the assistance of the Nord, broke up a terrorist cabal intent upon destroying the two space stations and Luna City."

A buzz stirred across the crowd of reporters. Recorders whirred, questions were shouted out.

"Communication with Luna City **and** Redemption has been restored," he announced.

Shock filled the room. Then fifty PCD's flashed on as reporters tried to get a channel to the station. Noise and chatter cascaded off the walls, the ceiling; joy, anger, relief and confusion saturated the room.

He raised his voice over the anxious shouting. "We regret the apparent disappearance of Redemption and the complete lack of communication with Redemption and Luna, but it was necessary to dupe the plotters into revealing who they were." His hand sliced downward with a vengeance. "To cut the head off this evil snake intent upon destroying twelve years of mutual progress between Terra and the Seven Worlds." He scanned the room noting the reporters recording several connected calls. "We can report the apprehension of approximately one hundred incarnate and discarnate plotters who will be tried in the Terran High Court for treason, and the Discarnate

271

Tribunal for interfering malfeasance."

Through the din, several shouts for explanation rose up. Walker turned to Vitok, to continue.

"When the EMP struck the Redemption mass catcher, its force was bent around and away from it and the space station by a device much like a cloaking system that makes an installation impervious to any known weapon by bending energy waves around it. No light, heat, radio, or other waves could enter or leave the affected areas, so they appeared to disappear."

He turned to Walker who raised one hand to still the crowd. "The devices," Walker announced, "which shall remain on the stations and Luna, were developed four thousand years ago by the Nord, disassembled a thousand years later, and thanks to Ambassador Vitok, reconstructed from the original plans yesterday. This was the first time they had been used in a real-time situation. You may verify all this at your leisure. Thank you for your attention. God bless Terra and its people, living and dead."

He, Vitok, Pardek, and Natil strode off the stage to where Aidan was sitting quietly in a large chair.

"Natil," Pardek growled, "you'll get your Marshal's stars tomorrow. Peebles will be awarded the Star of Kulzar. And your wingmaster, the Star with Swords. Like Aidan Good who is more Nord than the Nord, he seems to be more Krieg than the Krieg." He turned toward Aidan. "We owe a great debt to you and your peebs."

She smiled. *Thoughts are things,* she thought at them.

FAHD

Lovers don't finally meet somewhere.
They're in each other all along.
Rumi

It seems like it was a long time, and it seems like a fleeting second, but I am told by Kirsan Tabiyat that it was remarkably brief.

I was required to use my own powers of concentration as much as possible to pierce through to the true reality, beyond my personal reality and the reality that others sought to impose upon me.

My Imams told me that Kirsan would bring me joy and wisdom. He helped me to find truth. I am truly *shahid*, one who sees and witnesses. I died in the greater jihad, and became god's warrior for truth. Kirsan helped me to see that faith and reason's truths are not at war when both are properly understood.

On this side of the veil of death, one must come to these realizations by oneself, in the time and manner of one's own choosing.

I was aided by the sage, Kirsan, and the Vita-Kor Sister, Aidan, whom I have grown to love, because I had been given a unique opportunity, one that was locked in Terran time. Within those constricts, they were there to assist me when I needed them most, but they permitted me to flounder and folly until I could stand, as it were, on my own.

Again, I must apologize: I find using words clumsy at best,

273

but I will try to relate that event. One moment as I was chanting, *Al-láhu, Alláhu, Alláhu, Haqq. Haqq* rang out like a bell in my mind. I felt a tremendous energy welling up within me and felt a great weight falling from me like a thousand droplets of water in a rainstorm. Joy overwhelmed me. I spun, not dizzily, but ecstatically, inside the mind of Allah. There was no "I" other than the one great "I am." I cannot say for how long I remained in that state of bliss, but at some point, I knew myself as a separate being once more, and Kirsan and Aidan stood before me.

Kirsan announced that it was time for me to make the choice I had been preparing for. Aidan reached out a soothing hand to my brow and told me I had reached the point where, with a little help, I would be able to see the whole truth about my passing over. She linked her mind to mine and I felt a wave of pure white light enter me like a cleansing wind, blowing away the intellectual flotsam and jetsam that clung like a grey spider web. When the holo came, I was, at last, enhanced by Aidan's powers, enabled to see my death clearly, completely. What I saw shocked me. And I understood why Kirsan Tabiyat had not revealed everything at once to me.

Aidan Good and Kirsan Tabiyat revealed the true reality of what transpired on the lunar surface to me. I shall be forever in their debt.

It was Kirsan Tabiyat who spoke to me in the lunar carriage, reminding me that the greater, more difficult jihad is the struggle against one's own ego, selfishness and evil. And finally, at the last moment of my life, that love can make us transcend all that strives to keep us from the true reality.

It was Aidan Good who took action on the lunar surface, with her passed-beyond cohorts, to slow down the mental processes of the man who would have killed both myself and Quenby and destroyed Luna City. And she who lovingly guided me through the painful holo where I relived my last few moments in the body, filled with pain, remorse, and finally, wonder and freeing love. She took me in her care when I recoiled from what I had been and done and seen until I could recover.

Again, I cannot say how much Terran time that took.

I have often been confused by what is happening to me on this side of the veil. And though I had been forewarned that I would have to choose a path forward from honorable forks in the road, nothing could have prepared me for what Aidan let me see.

When the little brown Eagle Legion commandant dropped the grenade through the air duct, and Quenby made to place her body between my own and the grenade, I made a vain attempt to save her, abandoning my plan to appear as one of the terrorists until the very end. And I saw, in the holo, that love had finally triumphed over duty and blind obedience in my soul: I had chosen love over duty. And I knew I could not allow myself to fail now. Love gave me the strength to grasp the woman who would die to save me, whose muscle strength far overmatched mine, and somehow swing her around and interpose my own body between my love and the flying needles.

But she was too tall to be completely shielded and I saw the needles rip into her face and shoulders. I felt a terrible, slashing, burning pain from the tip of my head to my feet as the flechettes tore through my flesh and watched as we both tumbled to the deck. I heard her last, agonized whisper, "*älska kön,*" felt myself gasp, spit blood and die.

I was aghast at what I had allowed to happen, and could not bear to watch more, but a short while later, again, time is slippery over here, Kirsan came to me and said it was the moment to see the rest, and that Aidan would once again assist me.

Now, in the holo, I discerned another being soaring into the room, a boy, no more than twelve or thirteen, impervious to the hail of needles from the grenade, which passed right through its hazy spirit form. When the hail storm of needles stopped, I saw the boy morph into physical form, kneel beside Quenby and my bloodied bodies, mutter some kind of prayer aloud and run his hands slowly over the face and body of my love. Her bleeding ceased. She coughed. She began to breathe. I was overjoyed! Quenby would live!

And then the boy vanished. The door burst open and a very large man rushed through, roughly hurled my dead body off Quenby, and began to minister to her. I watched her silver-grey eyes open, to see my bloodied body lying to one side, and the tears, the tears that the Antal never shed, came forth once again and ran like rainwater down her snow-white cheeks. "*Älska kön*," she cried out tearfully.

Now, Aidan and Kirsan took me to a sickbay room on Luna. "Observe," he commanded. Aidan joined her mind with mine so I could see with her vision.

I saw Quenby, white upon white sheets. "Two lunar months have passed. She is quite nearly recovered," Kirsan told me. With Aidan's vision I saw her thought forms shining blue, tinged with silver and yellow streaks. "She knows at the last moment you chose love at the cost of your own life," Aidan murmured softly. "She will never forget you."

"And now you must make your decision. You have, on the one hand," Kirsan waved his red, seven-fingered hand to the left, "the ability to continue on the path of self-discovery, to perfect the redemption of spirit you have begun through the path of working with the passed-beyond, particularly well-suited as you, a trained scientist and true jihadist are, for the task of assisting the Terran dead to accept the changes that will bring Terra into the circle of civilized worlds."

"And the other?" I inquired.

He touched my chest with his other hand. I felt the heat penetrate and smelled sweet frangipane blossoms. He swept the air in a crimson flash of fingers, extending the hand that had stirred my remembrances of earth life, and simply paused. His dark eyes looked into my soul. "You may recross the veil of death, and walk the path of incarnate self-discovery once again, with a choice of parents and location and a deep inner knowledge of the other side of the veil."

The fragrant scent of my *ålska kön* came to me, and all at once I felt her body next to mine. *Oh, only to be near her again!*

"Do not fall into a false reality," Kirsan admonished gently. "A path once travelled cannot be trod again. The past remains forever gone. You will be a different person if you choose this way."

My pain was exquisite. To feel my great love fill my soul once again, but know that what we had could never be again. Yet I lingered, wanting only to be with her as long as I could. Tears filled my eyes. All my earthly life I had chosen duty over love, all but once, and now I wanted only to choose love, love, for love is truth.

Aidan's emerald eyes became deep lakes that drew me in, further and further, until swimming in an unfathomable green lagoon I could feel her mind piercing my innermost thoughts. "There is a further choice," rumbled through the green depths. Aidan joined her mind with mine so I could see with her vision.

Quenby was with child.

"It is Naming Day," Aidan told me. "On Alvar, pregnant females gather in the Great Stone Hall in the midst of their Aké, the ancestors who guide a spirit from the pool of dead to enter the fetus growing in each womb. The being will draw the veil of forgetfulness about its past life and begin anew, entering the womb of its mother-to-be. She will feel the soul stir within her and give it a name before the end of the day."

But we were on Luna!

277

I felt a great throng of Antal Aké swarming, buzzing, singing, reaching out to me. Then Aidan's voice, clear, resonant, like a bell. "If you choose, today you may re-enter the incarnate life as the half-human, half-Antal child."

"You may join the dance," I heard in sing-song tones.

GLOSSARY

Words, phrases, and prophesies of the Seven Worlds and Terra that might not be familiar to most Terran readers

abyt
: Coryllim language. Note: nothing is capitalized in abyt. Refer to abyt to Terran dictionary.

Aké
: Ancestors who take an active part in the Antal hive society

Al-hamdolillah
: Arabic, Thanks be to God

Allah alim
: Arabic, God knows best

Allahu-Akhbar
: Arabic, God is great!

Alláhu, Alláhu, Alláhu, Haqq
: Arabic, Traditional Sufi chant, the word for God repeated three times, followed by Truth.

All Source Intel
: Terra, Intelligence gathered from all sources, including, IMINT (Imagery Intelligence), ACINT (Acoustic Intelligence), HUMINT (Human Source), PBINT (PB Source), Van Eck monitoring

ålska kön
: Änska, Antal phrase. Union of mind, soul and body, with your true love, as differentiated from kön, biennial sexual activity

Alvar alvarn. Helmar Eskil alvarn
: Änska, Antal idiom. The planet is our defense. Helmar, the fighting fury, and Eskil the holy

	cauldron defend us.
Änska	Antal language, See Änska to Terran diction- ary. Spoken Änska has a distinctive sing-song, melodic sound. Double dots over a vowel (ex: ä) puts the spoken accent on it. A circle (ex: å) makes it stronger and longer.
assalamu alaikum	Arabic, peace be upon you
äskåarfiska	Antal delicacy: salmon, usually served cold in thin slices on thin wheat crisp bread.
Деньги	Russian, Cyrillic Alphabet, Money
Bodil,	Space city, off-planet engineering center of the Antal, one of their four cities, of which the other three are underground.
brå vak	Ancient Antal idiom, Lifeline, lifesaving, Lit: "A good hole in the ice"
CARNIVORE	English, the FBI's system to monitor email and other traffic through internet service pro- viders
dishdasha	Arabic, long flowing robe from the shoulders to the toes
ECHELON	English, Multinational global surveillance network
ECR	Energy Circuit Recording. Replaced all other Terran audiovisual recording devices by 2040. A ¼ by 2 inch oblong pane could hold 50,000 audio or 10,000 visi recordings.
egen anüt	Änska. Antal idiom, an outsider, literally "strange, other"
Eskil,	Änska, the "holy cauldron," of extreme sum- mer heat when the Antal hibernate
Eagle Legion	Terran elite tactical military unit attached to the Krieg legions

fels	Änska, "wrong"
felsmen	Änska, "wrong thinking"
Fokhan	Urtok, Military, Vice Marshal
Fjortonde	Änska: the 14.2857% who remain awake during each month of the summer and winter kön to keep the planetary infrastructure going and run the businesses
fwuup whavish	Kumlar, "Eagle of the prophesy" See "Saarp kaawta, na fwuup a hahpa
Garka	Urtok, Krieg dead who work primarily with the dead, not the living
halal	Arabic, "allowable" lawful, permissible
Helmar	Änska, the "fighting fury" of cold winter winds and snow
HRT	Hostage Rescue (HURT) Teams of the Eagle Legion, specially trained anti-terrorist units.
hjortberry	A favorite Antal breakfast drink, makes cloudy, nearly clear, slightly bitter juice.
Imam	Arabic, leader of prayer
Inshallah	Arabic, God willing
Int Kors Inen Tut Gi Ti ZyAmak!	
	Urtok, "I order you to assist me in this action."
Jintu Kor	The Nord Nine Suggestions to Rule Oneself. -Learn to distinguish the true reality from that which you desire it to be. -Separateness is illusion. Bear in mind that whatever you do, you do to yourself -No one can make anyone else think, feel or do anything. You are responsible for your

own thoughts, feelings and actions

-You cannot give others what you do not possess yourself. You must become what you wish the world to have

-Remember fear, greed and sloth are the mothers of all the negative emotions

-Accept your negativity. Only then use reason to moderate and overcome it

-Do as little harm as possible

-Master your passions

-Respect the privacy of others

Kavlak	Urtok, "Halt!"
Kavvuul	Urtok, Mild expletive, "Foolishness!"
Khut Zlot	Urtok, idiom, "Ice Heart"
Khlyvak Wokulen	Urtok, derogatory: "Barbarian Subspecies Warriors"
Kir	Kumlar, Literally: "the trance." The Nord practice of clearing of all thought from the mind, for the purpose of allowing the cosmic hologram free reign within the mind/consciousness, then with no purpose— just melding into cosmic consciousness.
Kitab-al-kashaf	the Jabar Holy book, describes the interaction of faith and reason.
Kitr Dev!	Urtok, mild expletive of approbation, "Damn good" Literally: "Long Fang!"
kön.	Änska, Period of sexual activity for the Antal, occurs twice a year, just before winter and summer hibernations.
Kondok	Urtok, "Carry on"
Konzul	Urtok, Krieg PB's working with the living.
Kul	Krieg manufacturer of military and commer-

	cial aircars, shuttles, starlifters, warbirds, cruisers and dreadnaughts
Kuldai	Urtok, flat spade-shaped knives concealed under patches in a Krieg warrior's issue-sweater.
Kulgarka	Urtok, Dead warriors, some of whom remain bellicose.
Kulzar	Urtok, Krieg God of Battle, also oath, "By Kulzar!"
Kulzar Zorx!	Urtok, Krieg oath, "By Kulzar's Topknot"
Kulden	Urtok, Krieg military camp
Kuldok,	Urtok, the Krieg way of the warrior
Kulmek	Urtok, Krieg battle droid
Kulvak	Urtok, "Comrade-in-arms"
Kumlar	The Nord language. Literally translated as "thought speak". The Nord can see the thought forms accompanying spoken words and quite often simply prefer to project thought to each other.
Kumla	A blue liquor consumed by Krieg. Enhances mental activity and produces the near-ability to read the thought patterns of others.
Kwet Kitr	Urtok, "Well done" lit: "Many teeth"
Kwu	Urtok, "How?"
Latoosh	Highly intoxicating beverage consumed by Krieg when they want to get drunk and rowdy
Lumina	During the Free-Lunar Negotiations, corporate holdings not directly related to life-safety of lunar inhabitants were not nationalized. The Lumina Corporation retained title to most of its holdings and was granted "primary

	importance" status, which it holds to this day
lüngaränga	Änska, idiom, "Tall and thin", literally "stretched long"
Må ulvor alltida ut om gömhål	
	Änska, Idiom, Traditional Antal toast for long life and good fortune ... "May the snow wolf never get in your house!" Lit: "May the snow wolf always be outside your hidey-hole"
måaksnoka,	Änska, power hibernation. The Antal method of using several small hibernations to replace the two long summer and winter hibernations
Maks Tak!	Urtok, Krieg expression of urgency. "Do it now!"
moondust brownies	Acronym for lunar-grown marijuana brownies, widely enjoyed by Lunies.
mwuk Nord, wal Nord	
	Kumlar, "More Nord than the Nord, but not Nord." Nord prophesy, guarded by the Vita-Kor sisterhood, It describes two beings who shall be at the heart of many future myths, beings who have all the Nord qualities but are not Nord.
nnn, mymor	abyt, "no, thank you"
No Ravak!	Urtok, "Not Civilized!" Placement on the dreaded NO RAVAK list meant instant boycott of goods, since Krieg warbirds would destroy any conveyance carrying them.
noka,	Änska, the Antal hibernation.
parsec	3.26 light years distance. 206,265 times the distance from the earth to the sun.
1PRD	First Terran Para Rescue Detachment,—

	called "One Perd" by the troopers—Elite medical rescue unit of the Eagle Legion
PB	Terran acronym for "passed-beyond," or deceased being who chose to reappear and actively participate in society.
PBM	Passed-Beyond Monitors: The Terran deceased police force, created to deal specifically with the dead who hampered Terran progress, or were otherwise recalcitrant.
PCD	Personal Communication Device
peeb	Terran spoken acronym for "passed-beyond" (See PB)
pil	Änska, Arrow, also the name of their starlifter

pfirus abyt pyo infito, vob saggio Terran

	abyt "Wise human, you speak our beautiful language well" Literally: "beautiful abyt [our language], well speak, you, wise human"
quantum intrusion	Becoming, then collapsing a wave function, to take form on another planet. Can produce psionic powers as side effects, but is extremely dangerous for incarnates.
Ravdok	Urtok, Mating. Love-making.
Ravik	Urtok, Mate.

Ravkul! Kulrav! Ravkut!

	Urtok, "Duty! Honor! Homeworld!" Krieg military oath
Ravkut	Urtok, "homeland".
Red Serpent	Brotherhood of deceased Terran criminals and malcontents, aligned with the dark forces beyond the grave, ready to use any means necessary to reinstate the rule of terror and

subjugation across the earth.

renhjåalt, renskjåp, rentjåal

Änska, "principles, true friendship, stimulating conversation." The three most highly valued things to the Antal

rens — Änska, "true, truth"

renskjåp — Änska, "true friend", "true friendship,"

roft — Änska, "shun"

Saarp kaawta, wal fwuup a hahpa

Kumlar, "The viper strikes, but the eagle shall eat it." Nord prophesy, guarded by the Vita-Kor sisterhood, that a great evil snake will fly into space and strike at goodness, but it shall be killed and eaten by an eagle that is Nord but not Nord.

salaam marhabat, ahlana wa salaam.

Arabic, "Hello, welcome, welcome home."

saplini — abyt, "children, offspring"

Satt Kuwar — Kumlar, "Seventh Son" Male child born to a sixth generation Vita-Kor Sister with "the Eye". This extraordinarily rare and powerful child will possess very special powers, especially healing.

skät — Antal tax, officially a voluntary tithe, but no one ever declines. That is considered highly impolite. Off-planet Antal are excused, but are not viewed kindly if they do decline, and must pay it in full if they elect to return to Alvar.

skjåp — Änska, "friend"

SDB's — Small Diameter Bombs

spinward — Dropped objects do not fall straight down in

	a space station, but are deflected spinward by a few fractions of an inch.
Spu Gi Ksum	Urtok, "spit in the ocean"
Surk	Urtok, "Immediate, immediately"
Sustainable Breakthrough Program	
	Written by Robert Walker, 2040. The document which became the guideline for Terran progress after "The Event"
svüun	Änska, "swan," also the name given to their shuttle
syrpo de seta	abyt, "silkworm"
takfir	Arabic, Disbeliever, or, one of an ultra-radical group who will adopt every single custom of the West in order to pass as a disbeliever.
taquiyah	Arabic, A short, usually rounded cap, often worn for prayer, but also worn to emulate Mohamed, whose companions were never seen without their heads being covered.
tavak	A white wolf-cat, native to the Yarr-Tik mountains of Narr, 40-50 cm in length, 30-40cm at the shoulder, 4-7 kilos weight Telepathic, solitary, long-legged, capable of great leaps, barks, howls like a wolf, has fangs both fore and mid jaw, retractable razor-sharp cat-claws on all four feet.
The Event	Reference to the time in 2040 when the Krieg War Fleet decloaked over Terra and the fate of the planet hung in the balance
tökmyck	Änska, "Insane. Very crazy"
tunnelban noka	Änska, the Antal long winter hibernation
Urtok	The Krieg language. All words are capitalized.

See Urtok to Terran dictionary. There is a military shorthand version as well, even more concise.

UT, universal translators

Devices which enable instant translation into homeworld language. Two implanted microchip versions: (1) generally available Antal technology, (2) Krieg class, restricted to military personnel

And (3) Nord genre, live nano, which also gives visual images of the thought forms behind the spoken words, extremely restricted.

Utlåanskhum,   Antal space station manufacturer

Valkyrie   1. Ancient Terran Nordic female Gods who decide who dies in battle

2. Modern day Terran Eagle Legion Group of Hostage Rescue Teams

Van Eck Monitoring

Reading what is typed, read, sent or received from the radiation the computer gives off

Va-Tor   Fraternity of passed-beyond Nord males who act as guides to the Nord and Seven World civilization

Virt Inz Kuldai Zwar   Urtok, "May your knives be swift"

Virt Tarren Vaphut   Urtok, "May the stars protect you"

Vita-Kor   Sisterhood of female incarnate Nord adepts, keepers of the prophesies and guides to Nord civilization

vita-åska   Änska, clear, powerful, intoxicating Antal liquor.

walaikum assalam   Arabic, "and peace be unto you", reply to as-

	salamu alaikum,
Wom Puk!	Urtok expletive. Lit: "Worm Excrement!"
Wosh	Urtok, "Snake"
Yarr-Tun	Sacred mountain to the Nord. Home of the Va-Tor Masters.
Za! Zakkh! Kha Pyk In Maks Tak!	Urtok, "So! Commander! What would you do now?"
Zutu Tam	Urtok, "Come Straight" Military: "Divert Course Immediately to"
Zwis Inemz Ravkul Zot	Urtok, "You are sworn to obey"
ZyAVag	Urtok, Krieg Warbird
ZyAZakkh	Urtok, Krieg Cruiser

THE SEVEN WORLDS

A preview of the sequel, <u>ALVAR'S SPEAR</u>, and more about the Seven Worlds can be found on the author's web page, <u>www.charlesfreedomlong.com</u>

ACKNOWLEDGEMENTS

This book would not have come to be without Linda's marvelous publishing assistance and the timely and often painful interventions of Linda and Shannon, who stretched me on the rack of editorial comment until I grew to fit my vision. My beta readers, David and Mark, alpha readers Vic, who has crossed through the veil called death, and Kenton, deserve great thanks for their valuable suggestions. Harrison's charitable encouragement to carry on from the roughest of beginning chapters and his inestimable contribution to the back cover blurb, and the instigators, Abraham and Tammy who made me ask the "what if" question that began this entire Seven Worlds series.

Any errors that remain in the manuscript are the responsibility of the author alone.

ABOUT THE AUTHOR

Charles Freedom Long talks with deceased people all the time. After years of seeing the dead portrayed in countless fatuous ways, Charles decided it was time for someone to show them in a manner some might consider more truthful. That is, life continues beyond the change we call death, the personality survives passing beyond the earthly life and moves on into other dimensions. So, with the help of some friends on both sides of the veil called death, he began writing science fiction, fiction to be sure, but with a spiritualist point of view.